THE CHARLATAN'S CROWN

TALLENT & LOWERY: BOOK FOUR

BY AMY LIGNOR

SUSPENSE PUBLISHING

The Charlatan's Crown
Tallent & Lowery Book Four

By
Amy Lignor

PAPERBACK EDITION

* * * * *

PUBLISHED BY:
Suspense Publishing

The Charlatan's Crown: Tallent & Lowery Book Four
Copyright 2014 Amy Lignor

Cover Design: Shannon Raab
Cover Photographer: istockphoto.com/DavidMSchrader
Cover Photographer: istockphoto.com/kwasny221
Cover Photographer: istockphoto.com/da-kuk

ISBN-13: 978-0692217771 (Suspense Publishing)
ISBN-10: 0692217770

To Kathy:
This one's for you!

ACKNOWLEDGEMENTS

The *Tallent & Lowery* adventures have been such an amazing process for me, and there are literally many who stand behind me and beside me in order to create these adventures for everyone to enjoy…including me.

Leah and Gareth have become family, leading me through this labyrinth of history, action, drama, suspense, and all the other emotions that make up the spectrum of life. But this couple could not have graced anyone else's life but mine if it was not for John and Shannon Raab. This couple, much like *Tallent & Lowery*, are incredibly kind and amazingly creative and supportive when it comes to this series, as well as general 'life' itself. I want to thank them with everything I've got for the friendship, belief, faith and humor they have with me…especially knowing I'm seven bubbles off plumb. (Right, Shannon?) I'm grateful to be a part of their lives and extremely privileged to have Leah and Gareth's home at Suspense Publishing.

To the cache of friends, reviewers and writers, you have no idea how much easier you make life. Mark Adduci, Joy Pickering, Sophie Pickering, M.J. Rose, Jon Land, Joy Feldman, Diane Lunsford, Ellen Feld, Michelle Horst, Emma Michaels, Amy Ferris and so many more…your encouraging pats on the shoulder for a rough day, and your cheering and smiles for a good one, make all this even more fun!

Mom, Uncle Ron (welcome to the sunshine!), Kathy, Keith, Maia, Ryan…most supportive family on the map, you rock. And a special thank you to my dog, Reuben; I couldn't have a better sounding board.

To the fans out there across the globe who have shared your excitement about *Tallent & Lowery*, I thank you so much and I will work hard to make sure you enjoy their adventures to the very end.

And, always and forever, Shelby…you are my North Star, guiding light, best friend, and my heart. You and I remain THE 'team' I love most, and I am so thrilled to see you take on your own adventure. I love you.

Until Next Time, Everybody,
Amy

PRAISE FOR "THE CHARLATAN'S CROWN"

"Amy Lignor's stellar *Tallent & Lowery* series gets an adrenaline-charged boost with "The Charlatan's Crown." Her latest ups the ante in this continuing battle of good versus evil, adding a creepy Stephen King-like feel to the desperate quest of these two supremely appealing heroes who are all that stand between us and conquest by unimaginably dark forces. The latest and greatest in the best horror series being written today, as scary as it is scintillating."
—Jon Land, bestselling author of "The Tenth Circle"

"Amy Lignor's *Tallent & Lowery* team is RIVETING!"
—International bestseller, M.J. Rose

"Get ready for another fantastic roller coaster ride of fun and adventure from the series that just keeps getting better and better!"
—The Feathered Quill

"Lignor offers up a deliciously evil character; one all readers will hope appears again and again!"
—Night Owl Reviews

"If you're looking for a fantastic read, one that will swallow you up and force you to read late into the night, check out, *"The Charlatan's Crown"!"*
—Ellen Feld, bestselling author

"When evil is at its worst, *Tallent and Lowery* are at their best. "The Charlatan's Crown" is no imposter and Amy Lignor is the coronated queen of suspense!"
—J.M. LeDuc, Author of "Sin"

THE CHARLATAN'S CROWN

TALLENT & LOWERY: BOOK FOUR

AMY LIGNOR

PROLOGUE

The eerie music seeping through the cracks in the prison walls sounded like a nest of snakes hissing their announcement that she was about to die. Her skin crawled; it felt as if the invisible creatures were entering her chamber of hell with only one mission in mind: suffocate, bite and destroy. The notes went on and on…rising and falling; the empty cavern distorted the echo, but when the end came the crescendo was ear-splitting, threatening to turn Neith's brain into oatmeal.

Attempting with all her strength to block it out, she tried to concentrate on something complex in order to keep her mind from abandoning her altogether. She had to hold on to her sanity. There was no way Neith was going to allow herself to become yet another skeleton lost in this decrepit place that'd once played host to a dead Reich's dirty little secrets.

The runes flashed before her eyes. She'd been able to read them for years now. Time had, at least, given her that one gift of sight. Locked away for decades she'd been able to learn the intricacies of the ancient language. Turning the small wooden blocks in her hand, Neith began to shake them like lucky Vegas dice, eager to cast them across the cold stone floor and unveil what would be the final outcome to her weary eyes.

She aimed her gaze at the ground. Only one symbol landed face up – < – just one; the symbol that announced the imminent arrival of a person who held the fire of life in their soul.

Suddenly, the cell door smashed against the unyielding stone. Daniel Bauer, her captor, walked across the threshold with her evening meal held tightly in his hands. His pleasant smile was wide and insincere. Strutting forward, he set the tray down on the stone ledge that jutted out from the mildew-covered wall.

One manicured brow climbed up his forehead as he stared down at the small tile on the floor. "I would think, considering how long you've been here, that you would've stopped believing in magic as a means to see the future." He ran a hand through his light brown hair. "If you want to see what's coming, Neith, my guards will be glad to escort you to a window. There you will see the banners flying high once again, trumpeting our inevitable return."

The drops of water that fell on her straight, black hair from the damp ceiling of the old dungeon felt like ice. Neith shivered. But not from the cold; not even from the handsome young man with the evil power beaming in his hungry brown eyes. No. The fear came from seeing the well-known tattoo carved into his skin.

She attempted a smile. "If you don't believe I have the gift of sight why do *you* still keep me here? You must be tired of having me around after all these years." She grimaced. "Your father spent his time and money watching out for me, feeding me…beating me in order to find out where the emerald was. It seems ridiculous for his son, who thinks nothing of me or my talents, to continue his useless mission."

"Especially when I already know where the emerald is," he nodded, before staring at the wall, recalling the face he longed to see again. "Not to mention, what a lovely owner it has now. The stone of the most powerful being rests on the soft, tanned skin of a beautiful lady every single day. I so look forward to the pleasure I'm going to get in retrieving it."

Neith's stomach lurched. "You'll be as big a failure as the rest of your pitiful ancestors were."

Daniel's gaze returned to Neith and he smiled wide. "I'm adopted, remember?"

"Do you?" She pointed at what was left of his swastika marking. "Seems to me that you're already making the same mistakes they did."

Shaking his head, Daniel's eyes lit with determination. "That's where you're wrong, my lady. I have no desire to continue their silly plans. They were nothing but charlatans attempting to rule a kingdom that never even existed. I have other, more powerful things in mind. And, unlike them, I'm smart enough to bring *my* dreams to fruition."

He absentmindedly rubbed his slightly blackened hand. "I remember the pain of your daughter's fingernails when she tore the skin from my bones. But it doesn't matter; she massacred nothing more than a symbol. The need, will and power to create a true kingdom is locked in my soul."

"Careful," Neith said quietly. "Your own idiotic ego is showing. To most people that symbol stands for the worst, most disgusting men ever created."

Slowly taking the pistol from his belt, Daniel held the cold steel comfortably in his hand. "You know? You're absolutely right. It is a waste of time to keep you around. You're a real bummer, Mrs. Tallent."

Neith squirmed at the married title, knowing that her husband had been granted a divorce long ago upon her strange and unfortunate disappearance.

Daniel continued, "You're still very beautiful. I have to give it to my old man. He certainly knew a good thing when he saw it. For me, however, you're just an older, broken version of what I want for myself—minus the hair, of course."

Lips set in a frown, Daniel squinted. "In fact, you've been with us so long that I can't find one similarity between you and the auburn-haired woman of my nightmares." Tilting his head to the side, he raised the pistol level with her forehead. "Your black eyes have grown dull and lifeless under the weight of your mistakes; nothing like the stunning sapphires set in the child you created so long ago."

He scratched the scruff on his chin and remained in deep concentration; the pistol never wavered from its victim. "Maybe my father was wrong. Perhaps you don't know anything about the gem or its remarkable setting. It could be that you were just simply in the right place at the right time when the old man stumbled across the information."

Neith could feel the happiness build inside her as she stared down the barrel of his weapon. There was a part of her that yearned for her life-long sentence to come to an end. But he was right. The weight of her mistakes was crippling, and Neith knew they had to be corrected before she could even think of leaving this horrible world behind.

Daniel suddenly let out a loud laugh that echoed in the chamber and momentarily stopped the ghostly snakes from calling her to hell. "Then again," he said, putting the gun back in his belt. "I *should* hedge my bets…just in case. You may just end up to be the bargaining chip I'll need to convince your daughter to help me find the crown."

It was her turn to laugh. "You said yourself that my daughter despises both me *and* her father now. She won't bargain for my life. Until a few months ago she didn't even know I existed." Neith hung her head. The shame was overwhelming. "I did what I had to do, but that does not excuse my lies. I hid away from her all her life. Why should she care now after all these years of deceit?"

"Maybe she won't." Daniel shrugged. "But I watched Leah; I watched her carefully. Her belief in others will always be her downfall. She doesn't understand the evil she's dealing with."

Lifting the silver dome off the tray, Neith looked up from the succulent steak that'd been prepared for her. "Really? You think that's true?" She laughed and rolled her eyes, as if making fun of a child's wish. "Leah's met that evil head-on many times. From people who wanted power, to—" Neith grinned. "What was your word? Oh, yes, to charlatans like yourself. She's faced them many times and has beaten every last one of them."

Daniel's eyes darkened into thunder clouds filled with rage. Neith cut a piece of the flavorful meat and began to chew, enjoying the anger she'd sparked. "How many is it that she's hidden from you now? The entrance to the Almighty; the Sapphire Staff; the Ark… Leah has made it impossible for you to ever lay your hands on the artifacts you and your ancestors would kill for."

"How can you know that?" His eyes flashed with rage and

confusion.

Neith bit her tongue, knowing that she couldn't reveal the Athenian friend who'd been secretly feeding her the data she needed.

Daniel Bauer's breath came in gasps and his hands balled into fists by his sides. "It doesn't matter, anyway. It's too late. No matter who—," he glanced down at the mystical tile on the floor, "or, *what* you've used to get information about your daughter, it's over. The past no longer matters. I have Athena's sword and shield. Leah didn't win that one."

"You won nothing." Neith tried to hide the trembling in her limbs. "They are nothing but golden trash."

Grabbing the tray off the ledge, he threw it across the room, causing the rusted chains that'd once held the wrists of the condemned to rattle in the cell. Strange screeches and high-pitched noises appeared, as if his anger had awakened the traumatized, tortured souls, allowing them a chance to vent at their murderers. "They're the most powerful weapons of the most powerful warrior who ever lived!"

"They won't work for you, Daniel," Neith said, struggling to keep her voice calm and even. "You must've figured that out by now. I'm sure you've already held that spear in your hands and felt nothing."

The rune stared up at him from the floor. "Tell me what you know."

Neith snorted. "The answer doesn't exist on a piece of wood. Athena, Odin…many of the gods and goddesses were helpers of the oppressed; common people who were pushed down by political regimes that didn't care about them. You should be well educated on that subject." She spat the words in his face, as she stood on shaking legs. "The weapons of Athena won't help you. There's no one strong enough to silence the masses. Many have tried. You're not virtuous enough to make Athena's weapons work. They will only do so for the one who doesn't wish to rule."

Grabbing her by the shoulders, Daniel shook her in his grip. "There *is* one. And when I put his crown on my head, Athena's weapons will work. All the so-called virtuous people will fall at my feet…*including your daughter!*"

Neith could feel a mother's love well-up in her soul, and her back straightened with the shot of courage that raced up her spine. "Make no mistake. My daughter will destroy you."

His grip tightened. "I took a bite from the apple and received the gift of the Divine. I have supreme knowledge now, so I would be careful who you place your faith in, Mrs. Tallent." His spit rained down on her face, bathing her in bitterness. "You forget your place."

The blood was suffocated in her veins by the strength of his hands. Neith could feel the power inside the young man; a power that he was determined to use in order to don the one artifact that could destroy millions.

Neith wanted to scream. She knew that the power of the Garden had been twisted in his perverted mind, and was already turning his soul black. "No, Daniel," she began, trying not to stutter with the panic that was rising in her soul. "It's you who has forgotten… one very important thing, in fact. Leah faced the *real* serpent, and destroyed him."

"Lowery destroyed him," he immediately corrected.

"Because of his love for *my* daughter," she shot back.

Releasing his hold, Daniel slammed Neith back against the wall. "Yes, well, I won't suffer from that affliction. Leah will join me or be killed, taking you *and* Mr. Lowery to the grave with her. Maybe poor little Anippe will have to join the party, too."

Neith's voice tightened in her throat. "Leave her out of this."

Daniel clucked his tongue inside his cheek; his eyes lit with the recognition that he'd finally touched upon the woman's deepest fear. "In fact, I think Anippe will have to join us. It'll be a nice reunion for you. After all, you've been separated from your girls for so many years that it would be a real shame to keep you three apart any longer. Aye?"

As he exited the dank tomb, Daniel made a point to slam his boot down on top of the now soiled dinner, mashing it into the rock. The blood from the rare piece of meat crept into the crevices of the cracked floor; the scarlet puddle merged with the stains of the witches' blood that'd collected in the stone long ago.

The metal door slammed shut. Daniel glanced one last time at the small wooden tile on the floor. Seeing that the arrow had turned, the tile had now transformed into a V – for victory. He swallowed hard.

"You have doubts," Neith remarked, her smile returning. "For a split second you found yourself wondering who the real victor will be."

Daniel glared at her; blatant hatred beamed from his eyes.

Neith laughed. "She comes quickly."

Putting his arms through the bars, Daniel Bauer leaned against the metal. He seemed to struggle with his vast array of emotions, as he tried to hold on tight to a powerful dream. "You're an ungrateful woman, you know that? I deliver you from the depths of that disgusting cave where you were surrounded by death. I bring you into my home…my castle; yet, you're still so rude and ill-mannered."

"I do wonder how you accomplished that feat." Neith stared at him. "How can you keep a woman chained inside a tourist trap that serves thousands without anyone knowing about it?"

Daniel offered an easy, carefree wink. "It was quite easy, actually. You see, the government took back this land when the War was over. They wanted to make it a point to show the pure horror that'd once happened here. So they rebuilt the shattered pieces in order to honor the memory of the miserable curs my family had supposedly no right to torture."

"But what they didn't realize was, in 1934, a lease was paid in full for this land. And the lease was for one hundred years." Daniel offered the brilliant smile of one who knew far more than the common man. "Hence, the tourist trap is no more. I still have, oh… about twenty years left on this property, and I intend to use it well. In fact, with the help of a few trusted acquaintances, I'm acquiring a great many properties that once fell to the Allies."

Neith took in a weary breath, knowing now that there was no one close enough to hear her screams. She hung her head. The intense aura of pleasure that surrounded her captor was more than she could take. She knew he'd thought long and hard about what his next moves would be and how to execute them perfectly. Perhaps he wasn't as crazy as his father, *or* the infamous man who'd adopted him into his family so many years ago.

Prayers erupted in her heart and her head. Neith begged God

to help her own brilliant child learn what the evil gemstone was before it was too late, and destroy it before it fell into Daniel Bauer's greedy hands. A warm glow suddenly filled her soul as she caught sight of the small tile. Leah *was* brilliant—beyond brilliant now that she, too, held the answers to life's biggest questions inside her soul.

Raising her head, Neith stared into the amused eyes on the other side of the bars. "There's one more thing you forgot, Daniel."

"What's that?" He laughed.

"Leah also took a bite from the apple."

Daniel clenched his hands around the rusted bars until the old flecks of iron sliced into his palms.

Neith smiled wider. "You're not the only one with Divine knowledge."

CHAPTER 1

"Divine knowledge, my ass," Leah shouted at the narrator, as the old black-and-white documentary played on the ancient television in the basement of the New York Public Library. "The guy was a scummy little idiot. Case closed!"

The narrator continued, undaunted by the miffed librarian, as the screen suddenly filled with a horrific picture. People were lined up side by side, carrying their meager belongings in their arms and holding tight to the hands of their loved ones. The faces were a mixture of anxiety and fear. Some, however, were actually smiling, as if they had no idea that they were about to lose their lives in the most gruesome of ways.

"*They were marched, two by two, into the showers of death.*"

Leah's stomach turned over at the narrator's announcement. Hitting the fast forward button, she tried to skip over the terrifying images of the very real past. "There must be *something* about an emerald in here," she muttered.

The old VCR chugged along until Leah hit the button and a new scene filled the screen. There he was…the ultimate slime. Hitler was standing on an elevated podium that'd been decorated with the dark purple carpeting reserved only for royalty. He looked down on the cheering crowd from high atop his throne, and Leah was amazed. There had to have been hundreds of thousands of people waving and smiling—paying homage to their esteemed leader.

Shaking her head, Leah stared at the big orange cat lying on top of a pile of books. "I don't get these people. The guy wanted to create a race of tall, blond, fantastic looking people, right?"

The cat's eyes widened as if he was wondering how best to respond to the visibly angry human.

"But he was a short, pudgy maniac with a rooster's neck, brown eyes, and greasy black hair. *Hello?* Makes no sense. Could these people not see how ridiculous the guy was?"

The cat stretched his large paw up in the air and set it on her arm, as if consoling her the best way he knew how.

Leah couldn't stop the confusion inside her brain. The lack of intelligence in any situation was the one button that could make her temper kick into high gear in seconds. "Think about it! The guy wanted to inbreed a bunch of Nordic glamour-dolls. It's like he wanted to live in *Deliverance*, for crissakes. Genetically created morons." She rolled her eyes and sighed. "Yeah, because that's just what this world is lacking...*more* idiots."

The cat sucked in his large stomach and opened his mouth, sending a small squeak into the air as if agreeing with her wholeheartedly.

She glanced away from him and stared at the large, round emerald lying on the worn coffee table in front of her. Leah sighed, as her mind once again replayed the completely psychotic events of her once normal life.

A haunted house, a serial killer's path, myths that shouldn't have existed, had all led her to the actual gates of a realm Leah had never believed in before. Then...saving a young man who was now her own true love's brother-in-law had brought about a new journey that'd been even worse. A hidden chamber with a staff that held power beyond all imagining. Next stop had been a monastery with secrets galore, and a famous mode of travel locked within a volcano. She'd read the words of the person who had once been nothing but a myth to her. She'd found a sister she never even knew she had, and then...Daniel Bauer had entered her life and stolen the artifacts that she'd tried desperately to protect.

The last puzzle was all about saving her own beloved father, but after leaving Jericho far behind, Leah hadn't spoken with him since. He had returned with her and Gareth to the States, promising to explain to his current wife that his old wife was still very much alive and, even worse, tell her how much he still loved the woman from his past.

Leah felt the bile rise in her throat. She hadn't allowed her father to apologize to her before he'd boarded another plane and rushed back across the Atlantic to find her real mother. She'd chosen to stay away from him entirely. Leah wasn't ready to accept the story of some stranger who'd given birth to her. She had no desire to hear why, so many years before, the woman had chosen to disappear and play dead.

Shaking her head, Leah again struggled to file the information away in the card catalogue of her brain; she just wasn't ready to deal with a family that'd changed so dramatically in just a seven-day period.

Seven days… It was still unbelievable to her that it'd only taken that much time to abduct her father and send her and Gareth on a mission to save his life. That was the time allotted by the mystery man for them to discover ancient clues to a location found only in books. Following the words of Plato, she, Gareth and Anippe had flown to Athens and found the sword and shield of Athena, the warrior goddess. From there, Leah's eyes had been truly opened at the Garden of Gethsemane by a once mystical friend. Then, they'd risked their lives in a horrifying tunnel of Queen Cleopatra's making to meet their enemy in Herodium—a palace built for yet another man who believed he was the end all and be all of human existence.

On and on they had run—to Temptation and back—until Leah had finally solved the ancient puzzle that would save her father's life. The last leg of the journey had brought them to the middle of ancient Jericho, where she'd planted the seeds—one of the Son, one of the warrior, and one of a monster—into the sacred earth. With her own two disbelieving eyes, Leah had watched the olive tree burst from the ground and allow her admittance into a world she still had difficulty accepting. But it was certainly hard to remain a cynic now that she'd seen the stone markers of the First Family with her own eyes.

Leah felt the tears in her throat screaming to get out. Family.

One minute she'd had one and the next, everything she'd ever known to be true had been reduced to a figment of her imagination. Her father, the man she swore would never lie to her, had been exposed as just that…a true liar. Her mother, at least the woman Leah called Mother every single day of her life, had turned into a victim. And a young Egyptian woman, who'd been a thorn in Leah's side from the moment they'd met, was now her sister.

Leah felt the weight on her shoulders and let out a huge sigh. All she could count on while she tried to figure out a way to locate Daniel Bauer, retrieve Athena's weapons, and somehow stop this enemy from embarking on a plan to destroy innocent lives, was the familiar, comfortable space that surrounded her. "At least this doesn't change," she whispered to the cat.

It warmed her heart, this paradise. Far above her was the Rose Main Reading Room, and level after level, rising above her head, were the words of literary icons. Leah knew beyond a shadow of a doubt that without her library to come home to this last adventure would've killed her stone dead.

The ancient coffee pot gurgled away in the corner, sending the aromatic fumes wafting through the basement. The old pipes, as always, clanged inside the walls. The building sounded like a belligerent child throwing a temper tantrum, upset at the fact that it had to once again heat up on a Sunday, its one day off, all because of Leah's crazy life.

The cat let out a loud meow, pulling Leah's focus back to the couch. She gazed down at the wide, manic eyes set in the fluffy face. Staring up at the ceiling, the cat's head moved back and forth in short, quick movements. Standing on his hind legs, he batted the air with his front paws. Leah laughed. He reminded her of a small, determined velociraptor competing in a tennis match.

"What is it?" She stared up at the ceiling, searching for the spider, roach, or other creepy-crawly that'd grabbed the cat's attention. But except for a few abandoned webs, the ceiling was bare.

The cat let out a husky growl.

"Sorry, man. I don't see anything."

A heartbreaking yowl was uttered as he continued to glare at the ceiling. He was *so* intense, in fact, that Leah suddenly wondered if some alien ship was going to fall through the roof of the New York Public Library and land in her lap. It certainly wouldn't be a shock, not considering the crazy stuff she'd seen in the past few years.

"Killer cobweb?" Leah smiled and rested her head on the back of the couch. She joined her orange friend and took a good look at the air above. Maybe the answers to life's mysteries awaited her on that bare white ceiling, and all she had to do was take the time to look.

"Hello!"

The basement door suddenly flew open and Leah jumped, sending the already anxiety-ridden cat racing across her lap with his razor-sharp claws extended. Knocking over a pile of books, he sent her coffee mug careening over the edge of the glass table, smashing it into a million pieces on the old green carpet.

Leah jumped from her seat when she felt the sharp claws gouge her flesh. "Dammit!"

Gareth stopped at the threshold and smiled at the scene. "Aww. When did you get a cat?"

Leah rolled her eyes. "You could have knocked first. Give us some warning that you were about to barge in and scare us to death."

Dropping his knapsack on the basement floor, Gareth Lowery offered her the most beautiful smile ever created. He stepped forward and took her into a huge hug, planting a passionate kiss on her lips.

Leah shivered from the familiar, mind-blowing intensity that the pair had built between them over the few strange years they'd spent together. His kiss deepened, and the scruff of his cheeks—cold from the wintry weather outside—rubbed against her warm skin.

Gareth finally drew back. The emerald eyes that held Leah's future were filled with a hunger that made every nerve-ending in her body scream for more. She tried to calm the beating in her ears as the sexy growl filtered through his lips. "So, what's the cat's name?"

Taking a deep breath, Leah stepped back. "I just told you. Dammit."

"You named a poor little cat a curse word?"

"When did you become Miss Manners?"

Gareth put his hands on his hips and offered her an annoyed

glare.

"It was the only name he'd answer to." She shrugged, flopping back down on the couch.

"Besides, it was easier. I was constantly saying, 'Dammit, will you get down? Dammit, get off those books!' Name just kind of stuck."

Gareth's laughter broke through his attempt at discipline. "You never cease to amaze me, Madame Librarian."

"I hope I never do," Leah remarked. "We wouldn't have anything left to talk about if I got boring."

"Who needs to talk?" Gareth winked, leaning in to steal another kiss.

Leah cupped his chin in her hands and nodded at the cat. The disgruntled animal had returned and was sitting on the armrest of the couch, staring wide-eyed at the large presence of Gareth Lowery. "Not in front of the kid."

"Speaking of…" he began, his brows moving up and down on his forehead.

"Don't start." Leah pushed him away. "Let's try the cat first and see how it goes. We'll call it a dry run."

"Killjoy." Reaching into his pocket, Gareth pulled out a letter. "This came for you."

Leah looked down at the elegant handwriting and smiled. Young Mary, the girl she'd once saved from certain death, had written to her. Ever since that horrible day in France when the awful William Knight and his sidekick, Robert Dorsey, had tried to take Leah's loved ones away from her, she and Mary had been constant pen pals.

Gareth took a sip of coffee and grimaced at the taste. "I don't see why you get all crazy about kids still. You *like* Mary."

"She's not a kid," Leah replied.

"She's thirteen. She's not exactly heading for a nursing home anytime soon."

Leah turned her focus back to the letter in order to avoid the creepy conversation regarding motherhood. Staring down at the picture that Mary sent, Leah couldn't help but smile. The young girl with the long brown hair had certainly grown taller, but the bright white stuffed lamb was still clutched tightly under her arm—her comfort in a world that'd already shown her some very frightening things. "Mary isn't just a kid…she's my prodigy."

"Your prodigy?" Gareth's voice held a laugh.

"Yeah." Leah passed him the photo. "Just look at this." She shared information from the letter, "The girl is on her way to study for a month in Germany before heading to Crete with her school. I mean, she's got it goin' on. In fact, she's like half-me, half-Sigmund Freud. One of a kind. Not like those little soul-sucking vermin who come into my library and—"

"*Touch stuff*," Gareth ended her familiar speech with a grin.

"Exactly."

Staring down at the perfect script, Gareth pointed at the small < drawn by Mary's educated hand. "What's that?"

Leah offered a proud smile. "She's been studying runes. I sent her a book to get her started, and because of her constant vigilance when it comes to education, Mary has discovered that the left arrow is my symbol."

"What's it mean?"

Leah looked back down at the letter. "It is the Kenaz symbol, and it stands for a beacon or torch. I am the owner of the vital fire of life, and friend to the power of the light."

"Okay. You sound a little pompous, though. Maybe I should rethink breeding with you."

Leah punched him in a well-muscled arm. "I'm telling you the kid's a genius. I don't think I could've described myself any better."

Gareth stared down at the paper; his brows furrowed on his forehead. "Oh, wait. That makes sense now. You didn't say that the torch was also the beacon of a mean woman who tested my patience every five seconds."

"How'd you like a torch up your—"

"Now…now. Watch your language." Standing, Gareth pet the cuddly cat. "No cursing in front of the child."

The orange and white Creamsicle closed his eyes and rubbed against Gareth's hand in visible pleasure, offering a loud, contented purr.

Leah sighed. "Traitor."

CHAPTER 2

Taking a seat across from Leah, Gareth stared at the emerald disc on the table. He couldn't believe it was the same one he'd bought in Whitechapel so long ago. When he'd first found the gemstone for sale in the location that'd once played host to the worst killer in history, it'd been nothing more than a lovely piece of jewelry to offer to a woman he was truly falling in love with.

The luminescent green teardrop was extraordinary then, but now here it sat; large, flat and round with no sparkle to be seen. All the magical luster was gone; their nightmare had hardened it into jade, which was actually perfect for a cold, heartless man like Daniel Bauer.

Reaching across the table Gareth touched it with his fingertips. It was still freezing cold against his skin. It had been since their return from Jericho, where Bauer had attempted to wrench it from Leah's neck. The eruption of anger once again consumed Gareth's soul. Every single time he thought of that vile little weasel all he could hear were the last words Daniel had said to Leah: "*We're not through.*"

Gareth felt the muscles of his body tighten under his clothing. He wanted to find the scum and bury him so deep in the ground that it would take thousands of years for any archaeologist to unearth a single bone from his wretched skeleton. Gareth even clung to the false hope that biting the apple from the Tree of Knowledge had only worked for Leah, and Bauer hadn't been able to use its power to escape. God willing, he was still stuck in there, still searching for a way out that simply didn't exist.

Glancing at Leah, Gareth heard the familiar, frightening voice flow out of the television behind him. "*I believe today that my conduct is in accordance with the will of the Almighty Creator.*"

Turning, Gareth stared at the picture of the Führer prattling on and on about what a wonderful guy he was and what an absolute supreme world he was going to create. He looked back at Leah's weary face. "This is what you've been doing all night?"

The gorgeous woman offered an imperceptible nod, as if the deep well of strength he knew she possessed had run dry. "I've tried everything I can think of," she rubbed her tired eyes.

"After my dad—" Gareth watched her cringe at the now foreign-sounding title. "After what *he* told us about the Nazi's having something to do with that emerald, I've been trying to uncover anything that would tell me what the stone originally was meant for, where it came from, or what it could possibly have to do with Hitler."

Gareth sighed deeply; his heart hurt for the woman he loved. The pain that'd come from all the family secrets recently unveiled had tarnished her once perfect relationship with her father. But no matter how much Gareth wanted to take her in his arms and comfort Leah, he knew that sympathy was not what she required. He'd known her long enough to understand that it was best to allow her brilliant mind to keep running until she chose to let it rest. "And?" he asked.

Opening her eyes, she offered him a smile. "And... After all the books, videos, magazines, articles and research reports, I came up with only one concrete fact about old Adolf."

He cocked an amused eyebrow. "Which was?"

"He was short."

His laughter bubbled up again, as Gareth thanked the heavens for creating the woman sitting across from him. "That it?"

"Isn't that enough?" Her eyes grew wide. "History has shown that short people have very serious ego issues."

"Yet another reason to dislike children, I suppose?"

She snorted, "Do I really need another one?"

"You were short once," he reminded her.

Leah grinned. "I grew out of it."

Gareth shook his head and took a deep breath. He knew the answer. There was one man who knew more about this subject than anyone else. Unfortunately, it was the same man who sat at the top of Leah's shit list. His smile disappeared. "Why not just ask your father, Leah?"

Anger immediately flared up in her sapphire eyes; rays of light shot from the sockets making it look as if a nest of mythical snakes had been hidden there just waiting to strike.

"Because my beloved, lying, pathetic father turned tail and ran!"

Gareth tried to keep his voice calm, not wanting to add to the pain. "When did he leave?"

"48-hours ago."

"New Years Day."

"Yeah." Leah nodded fiercely. "Starting off with a clean slate this year, I suppose. Wanted to get back across the ocean and find the woman who makes his heart go pitty-pat. Course, it didn't matter that he broke the heart of the woman he's been with for the past thirty-odd years. Not to mention the fact that he didn't shed a single tear leaving his three other children in the dust without a second thought."

"God," Gareth grimaced. "How are the girls taking it?"

Leah shook her head; her breathing calmed down as exhaustion overtook her. "I called Mom…Mary—no, Mom—yesterday. They're still in shock."

"Maybe we should go see her."

"I told her I'd go to the salon with her soon. That cheered her up a little, I think."

"You hate the salon."

She shrugged. "I figured I could take one for the team."

"I love you." Gareth said, leaning forward and touching her knee. "You're a good kid."

"It's not her fault. I mean, we never had a close relationship, but at least now I know why. I wasn't hers. She had to live every day being constantly reminded of the woman my father secretly pined for. Must've sucked for her."

Kneeling, Gareth took her lips with his. The love he felt for Leah was like oxygen. Without her, he knew it would be mere seconds before Death came to greet him. "Hey! I'll go to the salon with you. Hell, I'll *buy* it for your mom. I can probably even set up her own salon franchise if she wants."

Leah's smile was tight as she reached up and touched his rugged cheek. "You won't need to do that. The old man signed over everything to her before he left. The house; his partnership; the bank accounts—everything. Mom is now officially a billionaire divorcée."

Hitler's voice suddenly burst through the room. "*Great liars are also great magicians.*"

Leah snorted. "Ain't that the stinkin' truth."

Gareth settled back in the chair and kicked the ugly stone to the floor. "Do you know where your father went exactly?"

She shook her head. "He left a message on my answering machine. Said he was going to try and retrace the steps you and I took to save him. That could mean he's anywhere from Athens to Qumran by now."

"I wonder what he thinks he'll find."

"Who knows? He knows something about that stone, though. But *we're* going to figure it out first. We always do."

Gareth tried to keep his mouth shut but the need was too great to ignore. "Obviously Bauer knows something about it, too. Considering the swastika tattooed on his hand, he probably knows even more than your father does."

"I'd love to beat the information out of Bauer."

"You're not going anywhere near Bauer!" Gareth's voice came out loud and angry. He could feel the twinge of fear inside him every time he thought of Leah being in Bauer's presence. There'd been something about him—an evil charisma that Leah simply couldn't see. Gareth knew she'd felt a faint attraction to the man before he'd turned into a raving lunatic before her eyes. The fear of straying, however, didn't bother Gareth. He knew that loyalty was the first and foremost piece of Leah's character. But he wouldn't put it past Bauer to somehow get the librarian under his strange spell when she wasn't looking.

Leah just stared at him. Her sapphire eyes bore into his soul, and he suddenly felt like he was sitting under the gaze of an expert lie detector, like she was judging his silent thoughts and nervous twitches. Her perfect eyes had always captured him with their power and beauty, but ever since they'd left Jericho, they seemed to hold a power that was almost fearsome to behold.

She asked quietly. "I'm not scared of Daniel Bauer, Gareth. In fact, he should be scared of me."

Gareth attempted to lighten his tone, "*I* certainly am."

Rolling her eyes, Leah took a paperback from the pile in front of her and tossed it at his head.

Reaching behind him, Gareth pressed the mute button on the television set, banishing the dead maniac's voice from the room.

Hesitating, he stared down into his mug of lukewarm coffee and listened to the slight rattle of the basement windows as sleet bounced off the panes. There was so much to say. He wanted to just forget all about the next step of this nightmare, but he knew she'd never let it go. As far as Gareth was concerned, he'd call Daniel Bauer right now if he knew where the bastard was and ship the now ugly emerald to any address he gave him. Who cared? The Nazi's were certainly over, Hitler was certainly dead, and Bauer's threats were nothing but useless words spoken by a pain in the ass who apparently wanted to be a part of history. Gareth had to convince her to drop it. "Leah…"

Immediately she raised her hand in the air. "Please don't. I keep remembering Robert's words in the Garden of Gethsemane."

"Robert?"

"You remember him." She nodded. "He's the caretaker who watches over the tomb. He said that, 'with gold and silver and an army behind him, one man can be unstoppable.' "

She hung her head. "I'm the one who supplied Bauer with that gold and silver when I led him into Jericho. I found that stupid Silver Scroll and he won the treasure of a lifetime. Because of my dumb decisions, he also has Athena's sword and shield to protect him now." A tear released and ran down her cheek. "*I* did that! *I* gave her to him. And now *I* have to stop the army he's apparently building."

Gareth reached across the table and took her hand. "*We. We are going to stop him.*"

CHAPTER 3

"But, first things first," Gareth added. "We need to call Trish in Whitechapel and see if she can tell us the name of the store in Athens where she bought the emerald in the first place."

Leah felt a smile bubble up through her tears, remembering the unique, hysterical shopkeeper from their first adventure who definitely ran the tightest ship in England. "You know? I really miss her."

"Well, you two have a lot in common."

Leah raised an inquisitive brow at the strange statement. "Like what?"

The gorgeous grin returned. "You're both highly intelligent, organized, and you both scare the living crap out of me when you get that determined look in your eyes. I'm telling you, if you two paired up you could conquer the world. Entire realms would fall at your feet."

"Huh. Something to think about." Leah laughed.

Gareth glanced at the pendant that he'd cast to the floor. "She may also be the one who got us into this mess in the first place."

"What do you mean?"

"Well…what if Trish stole that emerald from somewhere?"

"C'mon! The helpful, dutiful, gotta' make a sale English shopkeeper is secretly a thief? She wouldn't steal. She would've just bargained her ass off to get the stone for half its value. Or, she talked the poor owner to death until he gave it to her for free just to get rid of her. But *steal?* I can't see that happening."

"You're probably right." He nodded, after listening to the truthful description of the woman who'd sold him the stone. "But why would a Nazi artifact have been stashed in a swap shop in Greece?"

Leah sneered. "Maybe it was Eva Braun's engagement ring, or something. Trish said that some swarthy guy with eyes black as a shark's was standing in the shop glaring at her the whole day, remember? Maybe he was some private guard of Hitler's."

"The SS? A man whose career was over decided to protect the stone since 1945 *after* Adolf had committed suicide and been branded a fool? Why?"

Leah offered a smirk. "A *really* loyal employee who wanted to try and keep his health insurance?"

Rolling his eyes, Gareth punched the numbers into his cell phone. A huge sigh escaped his lips as the answering machine came to life across the ocean. "Trish." His voice was filled to the brim with impatience. "It's Gareth Lowery...*again*. I'm sure you remember me."

Leah snorted. "Boy, we certainly think highly of ourselves, don't we?"

"And I'm sure you remember that woman?" He winked at her. "The real pain in the butt that I bought that emerald for when I was over there?"

"Sweet." Leah giggled.

"I need you to call me back as soon as you possibly can, day or night. I have some questions I *really* need answered about that particular pendant." He read off his phone number and slammed the cover down on the expensive device. "She's still not there. *Dammit!*"

The large cat let out a thundering meow from behind Gareth's chair, and pole-vaulted onto his lap.

"See?" Leah laughed. "He likes that name."

The cell phone rang out and the cat, looking highly disgusted, padded across the coffee table and took his place on top of the books. Leah couldn't help but laugh when the small beast threw his large butt down on a picture of Hitler. "That's a good boy. Might as well cover up one ass with another," she said, petting the purring animal on his head.

Noticing that Gareth had gone completely silent, Leah stared over at him and felt a jolt of fear race down her spine. His emerald eyes were dark as pitch as he held out the phone to her.

"It's for you," he whispered.

"Who is it?"

"Just take the phone. I swear it's not your father."

She grabbed the phone and brought it to her ear, never taking her eyes off the strange look Gareth wore. "Yeah?"

"Leah…it's me."

She exhaled quickly. "Anippe." Although still a bit uneasy when she spoke to the sister she never even knew about, Leah had learned to like Anippe…well, sort of. When she wasn't being a royal pain, she was tolerable. But Leah wasn't quite sure how to talk to someone who had gone from stranger to sibling in one minute flat. "Um… what's up?"

Anippe issued a small giggle at Leah's slightly awkward tone. "Don't worry. I didn't call to bond or anything."

"Sorry," Leah took a deep breath, "I didn't mean—"

"It's okay. Believe me. I'm not really sure what to say to you either. But the last time we spoke you told me I could call you and Gareth if I needed anything."

Leah chastised herself for making the poor woman jump through hoops. "Of course. What do you need? Are you okay?"

"I'm back at Herod's palace."

Leah hesitated, "Why? That place is pure evil, Anippe. You shouldn't be there by yourself. What if Bauer decides to go back there?"

Anippe cleared her throat. "There's not much chance of that."

A small panicked heartbeat began in the base of Leah's throat. "What do you know?"

"Nothing…personally, I promise. But, Leah, there was an article in the newspaper here a couple of days ago. Some guy had given a talk in a beer hall in Berlin. It was a very complimentary piece about how this new 'up and comer' was reaching out to the German people and saying all the right things."

"Right things?"

"You know, how to make more money, live a better life—things like that."

"That doesn't sound so bad." Leah reached for Gareth's now cold coffee and took a swallow. "Why would that bother you?"

Anippe began to stammer. "There was a picture…Leah. The picture looked a lot like…Daniel. At least…it may have been him. The photo was kind of fuzzy."

Leah slammed the mug down on the table. "I wish *someone* would explain to me how a treasure hunter geek fits into all this? I know he had a tattoo but a lot of creepy hopefuls still get that to show power, join a group of racists…whatever. And Bauer's background is Australian, not German. He got away with billions in gold and silver, so why Berlin? If he got out of where we left him then he should be in Palm Beach laughing his ass off right now."

"Leah." Anippe's deep breath was audible. "The tattoo isn't the only link. Our father…I mean, your…oh…forget it! Mr. Tallent mentioned the Nazi's. What if this guy is actually one of them?"

"Anippe, the Nazi's fell apart. They were wiped out way before we, or Bauer, were born. Only wannabes are still around—idiots who think it's right to bring back the beliefs of that disgusting group. Trust me, in 1945 their party was officially over."

"The same year they found everything in Nag Hammadi," she mumbled.

Leah sat up straighter. "What do ancient biblical documents found in jars during that dig have to do with the Nazi's?"

Anippe sighed heavily. "I don't know. The timing is just an odd coincidence, that's all. And Dad…I mean, David, told me yesterday—"

"Whoa! Wait a minute." Leah could feel her anger mix with sudden jealousy. "Back up. My father's with you?"

Nothing but silence came from the other end of the line. "Anippe? Anippe, answer me!"

Her voice suddenly sped up like an out of control train about to slide off its tracks, "He came back over here to follow the steps we took. He wanted to see where we went and why. He showed up at the Coptic Museum and asked for my help. He *really* wanted to come back to Qumran and walk through Cleopatra's mines."

Leah stood up from the couch so fast that Gareth jumped from his seat. "Are you crazy?" Leah yelled into the phone. "Those mines had scorpions, wolves and God only knows what else, buried in there. What the hell is wrong with him? Is he trying to get you both killed?"

Anippe's voice was barely a whisper when she responded; she seemed to be debating on whether or not to argue with her brand new sister, or defend a father she'd just met. "It's not like that, Leah. Retracing our steps is necessary to find out why Bauer is doing what he's doing and…where Mom might be." When she continued, Leah's heart sank, "When we were at Herod's palace…we found the bodies under the pool."

Leah's stomach immediately revolted as she remembered that horrific scene; the mass of skeletons stuck beneath a floor for all eternity. The coffee began to climb back up her throat.

"Jesus! What the hell does Dad want from there?"

"The diadem…the broken crown that was on Herod's head. Dad was really excited to find it. He thinks it can help us solve all this and find…Mom. And now that we have it, he wants you to bring the emerald to us at—"

"Enough!" Leah could feel her flesh turn fire-engine red; her skin felt like it was melting off her face. "Put *our* father on the phone. Now!"

Gareth spoke softly, "Don't say anything you'll regret, Leah."

Regret? As far as Leah was concerned regrets wouldn't be an issue considering how unbelievably mad she was at the man who should be the one sitting in a cave right now being tortured by Satan, himself, for the pain he'd put his family through. If any Tallent should have regrets, it was her father. Leah wanted nothing more than to climb through the mouthpiece and beat him to death, as she suddenly heard the faint whisperings coming through the line.

"Leah?"

"What do you think you're doing, Dad?" she screamed. "You can't go into those mines, and you *certainly* can't take Anippe in there. You'll both be killed! And even though you getting what you deserve wouldn't be the worst thing in the world, you are not going to hurt that girl any more than you already have!"

"I have no intention of hurting your sister," her father replied calmly.

Leah felt herself cringe at the still strange truth.

"But I need to get in there."

"Why?"

He answered quickly, "I just need to make a quick check. I think you have it, but I need to know if the emerald you're wearing is definitely the right one."

Leah could feel the panic begin to outweigh the anger. "The right one?"

"The one I think it is. Those mines are full of emeralds; I just want to be sure."

Her sarcasm immediately took over. "Need cash, Dad? Is that what this is all about? You signed over everything to Mom to clear your conscience, and now you're going to risk the life of another daughter in order to get more?"

"Don't you dare talk to me that way! I'm your father!"

"Not anymore," she screamed back. "Put Anippe on the phone!"

She could almost hear the stunned silence; a reaction from her harsh announcement as his breathing stopped.

Anippe's voice was the next she heard as the tentative tone reappeared, "Leah…if Dad's right, that emerald you have comes from a very famous crown; a crown that could hurt a lot of people depending on who's wearing it."

"Herod's crown was broken when I found it in the pool," Leah stated.

"I know. But I think if the emerald was set into it the crown might…mend itself."

Anger threatened to overwhelm her. "Mend itself? What are you *talking* about? Aliens landed in Herod's palace thousands of years ago and left a mystical crown before heading on to Roswell?"

"No," she continued, ignoring the sarcasm, "Dad thinks it might be…biblical. And well beyond King Herod. We don't believe Herod was the original owner."

Leah glanced down at the sapphire eye etched into the back of her hand. She remembered the pain and agony she and Gareth had gone through that'd resulted in that picture being fused to her skin, and the information they'd learned that alerted Leah to the fact that she was a protector of artifacts she hadn't even known existed. Leah knew Anippe bore the same marking, although in the emerald color that the rest of the guardians shared. She shook her head. It was still too much to accept. She didn't want to be a protector of anything. That was Gareth's job.

"That's it." Leah spoke slowly into the receiver, "I've had enough of Dad, these adventures, and all the twisted thinking. Let me remind you that I have to find Daniel Bauer and get back Athena's weapons because it's my fault he has them. Those are the only artifacts I'm looking for. I am not about to get embroiled in some new ridiculous religious quest that'll end up killing people I love."

"We'll be fine," her father's voice reappeared.

"I'm not talking about *you!*" Leah glared over the table at Gareth who was now signaling her to disconnect. "I won't be drawn into another one of your lies, Dad. You betrayed me almost since the day I was born, and you abandoned Anippe without a second thought."

"That's not true! Your mother—"

"*My* mother is in Connecticut recovering from the concussion you gave her when you hit her upside the head with a shovel."

He sighed. "She knew I'd been married before, Leah. She knew it all."

"Apparently she thought the first wife was a dead deal."

"I thought so, too. Maybe she is." Leah heard him choke on his words. "But I have to at least try to figure this out. Daniel Bauer told me she's still alive. If he's not lying, I have to find her. Someone knew about that emerald's power a long time ago. All we knew is that it had Divine power, and if set into a very special crown there would be massive repercussions. They kidnapped your mother in order to get me to give up that stone."

"*You* give up the stone? You're telling me you had this creepy thing in your possession?"

"No. I saw it a long time ago, Leah, that's all. When we were in Qumran studying the Coptic jars that were found buried in the sand, we found out about the emerald and went looking for it. But your mother and I barely got out of Cleopatra's mines alive."

"Me too, Pop!" Sarcasm threatened to take her over the edge.

"Jesus, were you ever honest about anything? Or, was everything that came out of your mouth one gigantic lie?" Leah took a deep breath, remembering how scared she'd been when she was told her father would die if she didn't decode clues that solved the last puzzle she'd been given. "So the reason those freaks who worked for Daniel Bauer kidnapped you and your brother, Aaron, was because they wanted the stone and thought you had it."

She tried to harness her rage, but the wounds he'd inflicted were all too fresh. "Trust me," she seethed. "Once Bauer got free of Jericho, I'm sure he went and killed your first wife. He knew the stone was around my neck by then and there was no reason to keep her alive."

"Please don't say that." Her father's terrified voice made Leah's blood run cold.

She cleared her throat. "If you loved her so much, why didn't you just give the damn stone to them a long time ago?"

"I never took it out of that cave. I swear."

"Well…somebody took it out, Dad, because it ended up in a swap shop in Athens," she reminded him.

His voice grew loud, "I swear to you, I never touched the thing. When we got out of the mines safely, the emerald was still in there. All we knew was the myth about its power. We wanted to find the second half of the puzzle which was the crown, and bury it. That way nobody would ever put them together, figure the puzzle out, and have the ability to alter the world. Not to mention, have the power to kill millions of people. We were trying to save lives, Leah. Please understand."

She shook her head, as the tears rolled down her cheeks. "No. I don't understand. I don't want to hear anything more about the stupid stone. I'm finding Bauer and I'm going to get back Athena's weapons. I'll *give* him the damn stone if he wants it so bad, just as long as I can return Athena's things to their proper place and people."

The voice, filled with fear, quivered through the phone line, "Don't even joke about that. The emerald in Bauer's hands would destroy all of us—including you, Leah."

She snorted. "He couldn't do anything worse to me than you

have…Dad."

CHAPTER 4

"Put. Anippe. On. The. Phone," she demanded. Leah shut out the voice of a man who'd once stood so tall in her eyes.

A worried Anippe spoke softly through the line, "I know this sounds crazy but if Dad's right that emerald is the one from—"

"I don't *care*. Listen to me, Anippe. Do *not* go into those mines. This is a man who treated you horribly. Don't take his word for anything!"

"Leah," Gareth whispered. "Come on."

Slamming the cover down on the phone, Leah cut off Anippe's voice as she begged her to listen. She threw the phone into Gareth's lap and fell back against the cushions of the couch. "Don't say it."

Gareth leaned forward. "Just one thing? It won't be about your father, I promise. As always, it's all about me."

Leah finally nodded at the pleading emerald eyes.

"I loved my parents more than life. When I was just eighteen, I lost them both. That car accident changed my life forever. I was suddenly on my own, raising my little sister, when I was still basically just a kid myself."

"That's right." Leah sighed, remembering his tragic past. "You lost the parents you love all because they went out one night to meet with some guy they didn't even know to tell him where the 'Truth' was buried. And for what, Gareth? The world hasn't changed. There are still creeps like Daniel Bauer walking around. Knowledge doesn't help when the world just keeps getting worse."

"They died for something they believed in," he reminded her.

"They died because an idiot decided to get drunk that night and slam into their car!" Leah shook her head. "Don't make this something it isn't, Gareth. They were taken from your world by a jerk that had one too many, not by some biblical prophecy or predetermined fate."

Gareth shook his head slowly. "My father was a brilliant astronomer and scientist; Mom, a brilliant astrologer. She saw their death in the stars, Leah. Maybe they both did."

Standing up quickly, Leah knocked against the table and scattered the books on the floor. "If that's true then they, no offense, should've stayed home."

Gareth's voice remained passive. "They went out that night to fulfill their dreams. They wanted the truth revealed so that others could get back their faith. They were proving there really is something else to go to once this is all over, which makes people happy, Leah. People want to be content…at peace."

"I don't buy it."

Gareth sat back and stared up at her rigid frame. Their gazes locked. Any observer would be awestruck; the sapphire and emerald eyes staring at each other held the strongest bond one human being could possibly feel for another.

"You *saw* it, Leah," he said, completely confused. "You saw the gate…you saw all of it. You even read the words of the Son. You know how deep faith runs inside peoples' souls. You know the stories are true. Some people—like you and me—fight for what they believe in. I protected the Father's home and you chose to protect His Son. My parents simply wanted to prove they existed in the first place. That was their passion. And, I think if I could talk to them today, they'd say they don't regret a thing."

"They sound like the best people in the world, Gareth. Really." Leah smiled. "Doesn't surprise me though, considering the son they created."

Gareth reached out for her. "I want to hold you, lady."

Stepping over the mess she'd made, Leah sank into his arms.

His voice was like a vessel of strength and protection in her chaotic world. "You've been hurt by the man who'd never lied to you. Your dad was your whole world. But all you really found out about him is that he's human, Leah. He must love your mother very much. Her disappearance obviously came from something truly sinister, and it must've made him want to curl up and die." He gripped her tighter against his body. "If he loved her half as much as I love you, I can understand why he's over there searching. Considering who *their* daughter is, I would say they must be pretty great people, too."

Leah calmed down under his soothing, beautiful words. "Anippe said she thinks Bauer's in Berlin."

"Makes sense," Gareth whispered, "considering the Nazi reference made by your father."

Leah's brows crinkled on her tired forehead. "I suppose. But really...what would an Australian archaeologist have to do with the Third Reich? He wasn't even born when it went down."

"I don't know." Gareth shrugged, smoothing the long auburn hair with his fingers. "Supremacists still exist, Leah. People who think this world would be better if it was an Aryan nation are still around. Maybe Trish will be able to help us when she calls back. Maybe when we find out where she found that emerald, things will be more clear."

"Then we go back to Athens?"

He nodded. "We'll have to. Talk to the owner of the shop and see if there's anything they can tell us...if they even remember it. Maybe the emerald has something to do with Athena after all, and it'll make some kind of sense."

"My dad thinks he may know what it is." She swallowed hard. "He says it has something to do with Herod's crown."

"Hmmm. Can't see the connection there. Herod was a really pompous guy. I would think if he had an emerald that size, he would've worn it in his crown, not hidden it away in the mines where no one would ever see it."

* * *

Gareth looked down at the round, flat stone that looked like a small Frisbee. It made no sense. If the stone had some sort of Divine power, which it must have considering how badly Bauer wanted it, how would it have gotten from deep inside a mine protected by dangerous creatures to the middle of an Athenian marketplace for any common person to purchase it? And, in this case, transport it back to the very location where Jack the Ripper tore apart his final victim? He was completely missing the thread that had to connect this puzzle together.

Moving his gaze back to the table, Gareth let out a sigh and rested his chin on top of Leah's head, breathing in her delicious lavender scent.

"What?" she whispered.

"This is where it all started, beautiful. That metal book that Carnegie hid in the cornerstone of this building. Right here is where the truth started to unfold and the secrets started to be revealed. The gate, the staff, the ark…I wonder what else is out there."

"Peace and quiet would be nice," Leah snorted. "But if the next gigantic secret to be revealed is that you and I are related, I'm gonna kill myself."

"That would be something, wouldn't it?" He laughed. "We certainly wouldn't get into heaven after breaking *that* Commandment."

"Eww."

"Maybe we were Adam and Eve in another life?"

Leah let out a laugh. "Nah. I hate snakes, remember? I'd never trust one enough to take its advice."

"And it would be difficult to find a fig leaf to cover me," Gareth added, letting out a roar of laughter at Leah's rolling eyes. Kissing her, he lifted the librarian off his lap and pressed her against him. "Let's clean this up and go home. We deserve a leisurely Sunday afternoon in bed."

"Amen to that." She smiled. "Wait. Are you going to make me watch action movies again?"

"Not the action I was hoping for."

CHAPTER 5

The basement door burst open on its hinges, causing Leah to let out a scream.

Gareth jumped back, practically pushing Leah to the ground, as a figure covered in a mass of fur ran into the room. What looked like a snow-covered animal rapidly began removing layers of protective scarves and gloves.

Leah laughed out loud when the familiar librarian's wet mane of hair finally emerged from the winter clothing. "Skylar, what are you doing here?"

The woman who worked under Leah as an assistant librarian ignored her boss completely, choosing instead to stare at Gareth. "Well…what a nice surprise." Skylar attempted to bat her eyelashes at the handsome man, but the wet, icy mascara stuck to her cheeks.

Leah shook he head at the silliness, as Skylar looked down at the scattered books. She issued a small gasp as the horrific symbols stared back at her from the pages. "My God. Is this what you do down here? You're starting your own Nazi party?"

"You found me out." Leah shrugged. "Of course, I don't mind other races and religions. My only quest is to cleanse the world of flirty, obnoxious librarians."

"Wouldn't that include you?" Skylar muttered.

Leah rolled her eyes. "You don't even get here on time on the days you're supposed to work, so what possibly brings you here on a Sunday?"

Turning on her very high heel, Skylar walked to Gareth. "Look! I rushed right over to show Leah." The large diamond caught the overhead light and immediately illuminated every dark corner of the basement.

Gareth smiled wide. "Good for you! When's the big day?"

"Six months." She giggled, clapping her hands in front of her. "Can you believe it?"

"What are you two yapping about?" Leah asked, picking the last book off the floor and setting it on top of the pile. "What big day?"

Skylar remained where she was and continued to gaze up at Gareth. "I'm marrying a count," she purred.

"On account of what?" Leah snickered. "Are you pregnant?"

Skylar twisted her neck around so quickly, she slapped Gareth in the face with her long wet hair. "*A Count.*"

"Oh," Leah remarked. "Well…good for you. Will you be moving to Transylvania, then?" She bit her lip. "Oh, wait, you said *a* Count, not *the* Count, forget it."

Dismissing her completely, Skylar turned back to Gareth as if he was the sun and she was a beach bunny longing for a tan. "He has a home on the island of Crete. Can you believe it? He came to the benefit last week," she continued; her voice dreamy. "That's where we met."

Gareth placed his arm around the young woman's shoulders. "That's sweet. Leah and I met at one of those."

"You've only known the guy a week and you're getting married?" Leah interrupted. "Gareth and I have known each other for years."

The rugged man immediately stuck out his lower lip at her words. "Sad, isn't it? She still won't make an honest man out of me."

"Shut up or I'll throw the cat at you," Leah sneered.

Skylar smiled up at him. "I would've walked you down the aisle a week after we met."

"Yeah," Leah muttered. "Kicking and screaming…dead or alive."

Skylar shot her a glare. "I stopped by to let you know that I'll be leaving in a month to join him on our island." She giggled with delight at the thought. "So you'll have to hire someone to take my place."

"But how can I possibly do that?" Leah gasped. "Where else am I going to find another librarian who spends all her time standing in front of the mirrors in the ladies room admiring herself?"

"Careful, *Miss* Tallent, your jealousy is showing." Throwing on her white fur coat, Skylar winced at the ugly brown slush stains of a New York City winter that'd colored the once perfect mink. "I'm registered at Tiffany's by the way. Just so you know."

"I'll be sure to get right over there and pick something up." Leah smiled.

Skylar started up the stairs, waving her hand above her head like the Queen dismissing her faithful subjects

"The Countess Skylar?" Gareth laughed as the basement door settled back into place. "She should fit right in." Reaching out, he grabbed Leah's worn-out leather coat hanging from the rack. "Wanna' have a double-wedding with her and the Count?"

"Only if I can register at Tiffany's."

"I'll buy you Tiffany's."

She sent him a smirk. "Do they have letter openers? I've always wanted a fancy crystal letter opener."

Helping her with her jacket, Gareth turned her around and kissed her hard on the lips. "Lady, you'd be dangerous with a letter opener. They're really sharp, you know."

Offering a dramatic eye roll, Leah snorted, "I carried the Staff of Moses; I think I can be trusted with a letter opener."

Taking her hand, Gareth pulled her to the door. "Let's go home and start on those action movies."

Leah jumped when the phone in Gareth's pocket began to squeal.

Hanging his head in disgust, Gareth opened the cover and stared at Leah. "I just want to get you into bed!"

A startled voice shot through the phone line. "*Pardon me?*"

Bringing the cell to his ear, Leah began to laugh.

"Is this Mr. Lowery?" The words were so loud Gareth had to hold the phone away from his ear in order to hear her clearly.

Leah listened to the rather strained voice now bellowing through the room.

"This is he," Gareth replied.

The bellow turned into a scream, "I think we have a bad connection. I can barely hear you. I'm calling from Whitechapel. You know…in England?"

Gareth's eyes immediately lit up. "Trish? Thank God. I've been leaving messages for days."

"This isn't Trish. This is her sister."

"Oh…excuse me," he responded. "Is Trish there?"

A long pause came from across the ocean, leaving Gareth to wonder if the call had disconnected.

But the voice finally came back with an audible hiccup. "The store has been closed for a few days. I just received your messages. Is there anything I can help you with?"

Gareth sighed. "Actually, I really need to talk to Trish."

What sounded like a sob broke through. "I'm sorry, Mr. Lowery. That won't be possible."

"Why?"

"My sister was murdered."

CHAPTER 6

Gareth's pulse slowed to a desperate thump, as he fell back into the chair behind him. Leah rushed to his side and knelt down, listening to the devastated woman.

"Murdered?" Gareth whispered.

"Yes," her voice broke. "You've obviously been here? In Whitechapel?"

"Yes."

"Then you know what…happened here a long time ago?"

"Jack the Ripper."

"Yes." The tears began to overwhelm her voice. "Five days ago I came to get my sister for lunch and she was…in the back room. Someone had…sliced her throat and hung her from the ceiling."

"My God!" Leah exclaimed.

"I'm so sorry, ma'am," Gareth breathed into the phone. "Did they find the person responsible?"

"No." The woman's pain and confusion echoed in the basement. "A neighbor said he saw a tall man go into the store around nine in the morning and leave at around noon…right before I showed up."

"Is there a description?" Leah shouted into the phone; her heart pounded inside her chest.

The poor woman was barely holding it together. "No. Marshall. He's the shopkeeper next door…said he was shoveling off his front stoop when the man passed by. He had on one of those ski masks—

the kind you wear in winter. All Marshall could say was that the man had frightening eyes. Black, he said. Like—"

Leah's throat went dry. "A shark."

* * *

Tallent and Lowery made their way home through a wretched storm of sleet and snow, as if they were in a fog. They didn't even notice the brutal winds that accosted them from every side. Remaining silent, they rode the elevator to the top floor. They'd removed their cold, soaked wardrobes and stepped under the blissfully hot water of the shower. There, they held each other.

Questions buzzed in their minds like a hive of angry bumble bees had invaded their thoughts. Trish's sister had looked up the sales records for them on the shop's computer, offering the name of the store in Athens where the emerald had been purchased by Trish. The same store where a man with eyes as black as a shark's had watched Trish purchase the glittering pendant and return home.

"He must have followed her," Gareth whispered into Leah's hair, as he held her against him.

"Why wait?" she said. "Why not follow her back to England, steal the stone and…take care of her then? Or, better yet, just follow her through Athens, wait for his chance, and snatch the stone away before it ever left Greece?"

"I'm not sure about the Greece theory, but maybe if he had waited until she was back in England, we ended up arriving before he could steal it. Maybe I bought it so quickly he didn't have time."

"Then why not follow us back to the hotel and take it then? Why wait three years, then go back to Whitechapel and kill the woman who hasn't even had the stone in…forever?"

"I don't know. Maybe it was Bauer."

"Bauer has brown eyes, not black," Leah whispered, as the face of her enemy floated in her mind. "Besides, he knows I have the stone."

"Maybe he wanted to eliminate anyone who'd ever seen it, like covering some Divine trail, or something."

"Tie up loose ends." Leah nodded against his large, warm chest. "But what loose ends? Trish had no idea the pendant was anything but a regular old necklace."

"I just don't know, sweetheart. But we'll figure it out." Gareth leaned back against the shower wall and stared at the most beautiful woman he'd ever seen. "Did your father say anything else about the stone? Anything other than the possible ownership by King Herod?"

She shivered. "He said it might be far more biblical than just Herod. A far worse history, in fact."

"Of course. Isn't everything lately?" Gareth sighed. "Is there anything biblical even left that we haven't already found?"

"Nothing I can think of, but you're the one who was raised on this stuff, not me."

Reaching for a towel, Gareth dried her skin and wrapped her in his arms. "We'll figure it out," he repeated. "We always do."

Leah buried her head in his neck. "That poor woman."

"Look, you haven't slept in a long time, sweetheart. I want you to rest."

"I'll rest on the plane to Athens."

* * *

Famous last words, thought Leah.

Her mind was not about to let her sleep. Her eyes were as wide open as Gareth's. Not even the surly flight attendants who seemed to horde the coffee away from her like it was the nectar of the gods, could upset her now. She was too far gone to worry about the little annoyances that were a part of everyday life.

Gareth held her hand tight. They remained silent as the mammoth piece of metal flew them across the ocean—taking them back to the beginning of their last terrifying adventure.

After a long, quiet flight where only fear and confusion seemed to be their co-pilots, the landing bell finally dinged in the cabin and the safety lights flicked off. Gareth took the lead, as Leah followed him out, through the terminal, and into the warmth of the bright Athenian sun. The freezing cold northeast temperatures were gone, yet Leah still felt like her body was encased in a block of ice.

As they stood in line waiting for a taxi, a long black car appeared out of nowhere, speeding down the tunnel. The limousine squealed to a stop in front of their surprised faces.

Gareth grabbed Leah's hand, ready to run at the slightest sign of danger.

The car door swung open and a woman appeared from the dark interior. She smiled wide and flung her arms around Gareth. "Hey there, bro. How you been?"

Gareth dropped Leah's hand and picked the small woman up in his arms. "Kathryn?" Giving his little sister a big kiss, he set her down.

Kathryn ran to Leah.

"Oof," Leah gasped, as the Little General hugged the stuffing out of her. "Jeez, you've got some power in your little self."

Kathryn laughed.

"What are you doing here?" Leah asked.

"I had to talk to you two."

"How did you know we'd be in Athens? I'm not about to go with lucky guess." Gareth said.

Kathryn smiled wide. "I'm psychic. All this religious stuff has made me get the 'gift.'"

"Give me a break."

A deep laugh came from the interior of the limo, as Emmanuel, Kathryn's husband, exited the vehicle. "Actually, it was I who tracked you down."

Gareth turned at the voice. Surprised, he held out his hand to his brother-in-law and friend. "You psychic, too?"

Leah hugged Emmanuel and stared at the married couple. It was the first time in a long time she'd felt any kind of relief. "It's so good to see you guys. We haven't been together since the wedding. How was your honeymoon?"

Gareth grunted. "Definitely *not* what I want to hear about."

Kathryn punched him in the shoulder. "We're married, bro. Gotta' get over it. There has to be some lovin for a marriage to work."

Emmanuel's face went white, as Gareth turned on him. The young man raised his hands in the air. "Please don't hurt me."

"Stop being ridiculous." Leah pushed Gareth aside. "Your sister's certainly old enough for some lovin."

Gareth covered his ears. "Seriously…I think I'm gonna puke."

"Hi!"

Leah jumped back, as a tiny person stepped out from behind Emmanuel's back. "*Mary*? What are *you* doing here?"

The young girl held tight to her bright, white lamb. Leah tried to contain her grin when she noticed that the little animal was aging quicker than his owner. The small pink nose had been sewn on more than once, and one glass eye was missing. She nodded at the toy. "He's lookin' a little weary, kid."

Mary smiled. Her straight white teeth gleamed in the sunshine and her long brown hair bounced around her shoulders. She took a step forward.

Leah eyed her strangely. "You're not gonna hug me, are you?"

"No." Mary giggled. "You've gotten better over the years, though. I can see it in your letters. But I don't think you're quite up to hugging just yet. I still have to prove I'm not carrying around any teenage cooties."

Leah patted her and the lamb on their heads. "Nice girl."

Gareth could no longer ignore the angry horns blasting all around them from travelers who were sick to death of their little family reunion intruding on their day. "I think we should continue this elsewhere."

Climbing in, Gareth closed the door and the enormous car rocketed away from the curb.

* * *

Leah couldn't keep from staring at Mary.

"What?"

She shrugged. "You grew up pretty fast. Last time I saw you, you were one of those…"

"*Soul-sucking vermin who touched your stuff*?" Mary grinned.

Kathryn laughed out loud. "God, she's got you *down*!"

Gareth wiped the tears from his eyes, and stared at Mary. "What are you doing here, kiddo?"

"I was in Germany with my school." She looked over at Leah. "I wrote you that in my letter."

Leah nodded. "I just got it yesterday."

"Wow…the mail *is* slow. I thought my dad just liked to yell about stupid stuff."

Leah grinned.

"Anyway, our school took us to the UNESCO building at the University of Paderborn and I saw Emmanuel there!"

Emmanuel nodded. "Kathryn and I have been there for a few months working on some sites in the city. They also have an excellent computer science center there."

Mary chimed in, "Not to mention the largest computer museum in the whole world."

Emmanuel leaned forward; his gaze perfectly matched the young girl's excitement. "Did you know that it was named after the founder of Nixdorf Computers? The company became the fourth largest computer company in Europe."

Kathryn shook her head, and looked at Leah across from her. She pointed at her husband and the girl. "They're like two geeks separated at birth."

Emmanuel slapped her on the knee. "It's good to know things."

"He's right," Leah agreed. "And if he ever gets picked to be on *Jeopardy*, you'll be a bloody billionaire's wife."

"So, how exactly did you track us down?" Gareth asked. Leah could hear the note of confusion and anxiety buried in the familiar growl.

Emmanuel's words came out in a rush, "I reconfigured the satellite optimal relay and then—"

Gareth raised his hand in the air. "English."

"I basically tracked your cell phone." He grinned.

"See how easy that was?" Gareth laughed.

Leah turned back to Mary. "Isn't your school worried about you?"

She shook her head. "Nope. I called my dad and he said I could tag along with Emmanuel and Kathryn since they were coming to see you. I'll meet up with my class at the next stop."

"Where's that?"

"Knossos. We're going to study the Minoan palace. There's a whole bunch of teams there right now excavating."

Gareth whistled. "Wow. The island of Crete. Cool!"

Kathryn spoke up, "Actually, Emmanuel and I are on our way to Crete, too. That's the next place that UNESCO's sending us, so we'll be able to drop Mary off."

"Seems like Crete's the hot spot right now." Leah grinned. "If you happen to run into a strange woman who bats her eyelashes a lot and wants you to call her Countess, don't worry about it. She's not a freak, just a librarian."

Turning to Emmanuel, Leah continued, "So why the rush to find us?" A flicker of terror raced through her soul as she noticed the sudden flush of Kathryn's cheeks. "There's nothing wrong with you, is there?"

"Well, *you* would probably say so." She offered a sheepish grin.

Gareth shot forward. "Dear God, what is it? Are you sick?"

"No." His small sister stifled what sounded a lot like a giggle. "I'm pregnant."

"*What*?" From the corner of her eye, Leah watched the skin tighten on Gareth's face, transforming it into a mask of death. "How the hell can you be pregnant?"

She tried to hide her laughter, but it burst from her throat like a tornado when she witnessed the truly distressed look on her true love's face. "The normal way, I would assume."

Gareth glared at Emmanuel, his face was red as a beet. "You got my sister pregnant? How could you do that?"

Kathryn tried to speak, but her words were barely intelligible through her laughter. "He's my *husband*, bro."

Leah slapped Gareth on the arm. "Quit it. Repeat after me: *Congratulations my dear sister and longtime friend. I'm so happy for both of you.*"

Gareth turned and looked out the window, repeating Leah's words in a disgusted grumble.

"See that?" Leah leaned over and kissed his cheek. "Now, was that so hard? Besides, you're going to be an uncle. You should be delighted!"

"And," Kathryn said. "We want *you* to be the godmother."

Leah felt the blood immediately drain from her face. "That doesn't mean I'd have to be in the delivery room, does it?"

Kathryn started laughing again. "God, you're just like him. You're so perfect for each other, it's sick."

Leah swallowed hard.

"No. You only have to go to church on the day of the baptism."

The breath that Leah exhaled felt amazing, knowing she would definitely not have to be in charge of screwing up a poor kid's life. "Now, *that* I'll do."

"And you have to care for our baby if anything happens to us."

It was Leah's turn to glare at Emmanuel. "Don't you dare let anything happen to the two of you. If you do, I'll take your body to the first witch I meet, bring you back to life, and kick the crap out of you!"

CHAPTER 7

Just a short hop from Syntagma Square, Athens' busiest shopping district, the limo pulled over and dropped the five happy people off in Kolonaki.

Leah stared at the fashionable women walking in and out of the chic shops in herds. She stared down at her weathered blue jeans, broken-in jacket, and mud-stained leather boots.

Gareth rubbed her back. "Want something? I can give you my card."

"Oooo, take it," Kathryn whispered. "We could find some really awesome stuff for the baby while we're here."

Leah looked over her shoulder into Gareth's smiling eyes. "The Little General has become a walking pile of goo."

Kathryn kicked her leg. "Hey! If I want to act like a silly first-time mom, I will." She added, with a smile, "But don't think I can't still kick your ass."

Mary burst into laughter, as Gareth reached for his wallet and handed Leah one card out of what seemed like a hundred. "Spend anything you want." He turned to Emmanuel. "I've heard that they're dangerous when they're hormonal."

Emmanuel rolled his eyes. "This isn't hormones, man. This is the real her. When the hormones hit...*Jesus*. Let's just say I'm not looking her directly in the eye after that until the baby comes."

Gareth added, "I would also suggest not talking, snoring...

breathing."

Kathryn shouted back over her shoulder, as she grabbed Leah's arm and started walking, "I can hear you!"

* * *

Gareth slid two bistro-style tables together in front of the small café, and they sat down in the lovely warmth of the Grecian sun.

Leah's feelings were in turmoil. Her heart was still full of pain for the loss that Trish's sister had just gone through, not to mention thinking of the oncoming battle with Daniel Bauer to retrieve Athena's weapons; but sitting on the cozy street, watching the happy faces of the people passing by, surrounded by the ones she loved most in the world, made her heart burst with happiness.

Gareth took the menus from the waiter and waved him away before turning to Emmanuel. "Why'd you go through so much trouble to track us down instead of just calling with the happy news?"

Gareth noted the quick glance between Emmanuel and his bride.

Kathryn nodded.

"Gareth." He took a deep breath. "We've been in Paderborn for a little while. Kathryn and I stumbled across something when we were searching a site there. It's in a tunnel under a monument. We think you and Leah need to see it."

"Why?" Leah's happiness turned slowly cold.

"After you left Jericho and called Kathryn—told her about that Bauer guy—the emerald, the swastika…everything…"

Leah stared out the corner of her eye and sent Emmanuel a knowing look. She wanted to make sure that they didn't say too much in front of the young girl who'd been exposed to the hideous pain and agony of one of their adventures already.

"Anyway," Emmanuel cleared his throat. "This site that we found is located at the Externsteine rock formation, just outside of Paderborn, in the Teutoburger Wald. We found a tunnel by mistake and we…saw some things in there. Things that seem to have something to do with what you both went through. I think maybe it could help solve all this and, hopefully…maybe, find your real mom."

Mary's ears perked up. "Your mom's missing?"

Leah shook her head and offered a small smile. "No. My mom's back home. But there's another lady who I've never met who may need my help."

Mary's eyes grew wide. "You're lucky. Two moms. I miss mine so much sometimes, it hurts."

Leah swallowed hard. A shot of guilt passed through her heart as she realized how tough Mary's life had been. Reaching out, she took the girl's hand. Her mind was silent. She just didn't know what to say to ease a child's heartbreak.

Kathryn smiled at Mary. "I lost my mom, too. I still miss her so much that I cry…a lot."

Leah exhaled when Mary smiled back, comforted. Leah continued quickly, trying to change the subject, "I think I might be able to find this lady if I can just figure out the puzzle I'm working on."

"I'm really good at puzzles. Did you see the runes that I'm studying? Pretty soon I'll learn the whole language."

Leah grinned. "I bet you will. But I think this puzzle is something I have to figure out on my own."

"I can't help?" Mary's eyes grew sad, making her look as forlorn as the barely-held-together lamb under her arm.

"Maybe. Let's wait and see." Leah winked.

Kathryn picked up the menu. "Hey! They have Exohiko here."

"What's that?" Leah and Mary spoke in unison.

"Lamb."

Gasping, Mary clutched her friend tighter and covered his ears with her hands.

Leah stuck out her tongue. "I'm with you, kid. There's no way I'm eating one of those cute, fluffy little things with pink noses. It's like kicking the Easter Bunny in the butt."

Mary laughed.

"Okay," Kathryn sighed. "How do you feel about large animals with no personalities that were born to be chalk outlines? Oh… wait," Kathryn giggled. "I would assume you're partial to them too considering you're dating my brother."

"Hey," Gareth yelled. "I have a personality."

"Yeah, right."

Leah tried not to laugh at the sibling scrap.

"Bifteki?" Kathryn said.

"Watch yourself."

Emmanuel grinned at Gareth. "It's beef, man. Plain old burgers."

Mary jumped happily in her seat. "That's way better."

Leah looked over at Kathryn. "It had *better* be beef."

"You're so paranoid."

"Gareth, there's something else," Emmanuel continued when the waiter walked away, "There's a castle that overlooks the town of Paderborn called Wewelsburg."

An alarm bell immediately rang in Leah's mind, as the ever-dependable card catalogue opened inside her head. "That's the castle that Heinrich Himmler owned."

"Who's that?" Mary asked.

"A pretty bad guy back in World War II. He worked for Hitler."

Mary took a sip of tea and looked around at the lovely scenery, completely uninterested in the boring adult story that would not involve the exciting technology of her generation.

Leah leaned away from Mary and lowered her voice. "What about it?"

"He didn't exactly own the castle, Leah," Emmanuel corrected. "Himmler leased it. Then, when it was all over, the town took it back. They rebuilt it and made it into a museum. They wanted to preserve it; show the kind of sleaze these men were, and honor the poor people who died at the concentration camp."

"There was a concentration camp inside a castle?" Gareth asked

Leah answered, "It was a small one, outside the castle. They brought people from other places like Belen or Auschwitz and put them to work building Himmler's ridiculous dream home. Some worked themselves to death, were starved, or basically killed outright."

Gareth shook his head and sighed. "What the hell are we getting ourselves into *now*?"

"Don't tell me they started up the concentration camp again? I would think the town would be against something like that," Leah said.

Emmanuel shook his head. "I don't think anyone would allow that party and their ways to reappear."

"You'd be surprised," Leah mumbled, recalling the determined look in Bauer's evil eyes. "So, what's the problem with the castle?"

Reaching for a napkin, Emmanuel took out his pen and proceeded to draw on the thin paper, passing it to Leah when he was done.

She stared down at the strange symbol. ⊕ "So? What is it?"

Mary leaned over her shoulder. "That's the Solar Cross."

Leah stared at the girl and felt another spurt of pride when she looked into her soft, innocent eyes. "What's a solar cross?"

Mary tried to keep her sudden happiness of being able to help her heroine in check, but it didn't work. She clapped her hands in glee. "I know something you don't?" she giggled.

Leah shrugged. The kid absolutely did know something she didn't, and she found herself very humbled by the look of utter respect that shone in Mary's gaze. "Go ahead. Let's see how smart you are."

Mary began, "It's said to be one of the oldest religious symbols in the world. People used it in Europe, Asia, America…everywhere. It was even found carved into Indian art dating back thousands of years ago."

"What's it stand for? God?"

"No." Mary shook her head quickly. "See inside? That's an equal-armed cross inside a circle, which stands for the sun. It represents the solar calendar. You know…the movements of the sun through the four solstices."

"Summer, Spring…"

"Winter, Fall," Mary ended with a laugh. "Sometimes they add the equinoxes, too, and then it looks like an eight-armed wheel."

"Anything else, Miss Know-it-All?" Leah smiled at the detailed presentation.

"The one you're looking at was referred to as Odin's Cross in Northern Europe. He was the big guy in Norse mythology, like

Zeus was to the Greeks."

"Odin, huh?"

"Yup. Everyone always wondered who was stronger between the two. My friends talk about it all the time online."

Leah groaned.

"What's wrong?" Mary's face formed a mask of confusion.

Gareth laughed. "She's a librarian, honey. She likes books. Leah sees computers as the enemy that's taking over the land."

"You wonder why?" Leah pointed at Emmanuel. "The man tracked your location from thousands of miles away with one of those…things. I'm telling you, it's like Big Brother is everywhere."

Gareth nodded at Mary. "Go on, honey. I know you love, Leah, but don't listen to her rantings. She should have been born in the 1920's."

Kathryn let out a snort. "Yeah, that way you two would be the same age."

Mary giggled as Gareth reached out and slapped his sister's arm.

Kathryn returned a solid blow. "Hey! Watch out for the baby!"

"If you're carrying it in your arm, you have serious problems." Gareth grunted, rubbing his sore shoulder. "Go on, Mary."

She smiled wide. "Well, history says that Hercules beat Thor who was *way* stronger than Odin. And, Zeus could beat Hercules. So, that would mean Zeus was way stronger than Odin…right?"

"Kid's got a point," Gareth said.

Leah saw the waiter walk through the door with their food. "Go wash your hands," she said to Mary.

The girl raised her eyebrows, but left the table quietly at the command.

Kathryn let out her breath. "Man, that kid's smart."

"There's only one small thing she left out," Leah said, directing her speech at Gareth.

"What?"

"The swastika is a form of the Solar Cross."

Emmanuel nodded, and Leah caught his gaze. "What does this have to do with the castle?"

"The museum was suddenly closed a few months back. The rumor around UNESCO is that, in 1934, Himmler leased the castle from the town for one hundred years. He paid in full up front. One of his descendants, supposedly, showed up and claimed that the castle was rightfully his for at least another twenty years. They took it to the judge but the court had to uphold the original lease. It was made as a binding contact, and it stood. The museum had to close up shop and leave."

"There hasn't been a lot of activity up there; a few cars and trucks go up now and then, but mostly it's just really loud music that comes off the mountain. Last week, however, a huge delivery truck went up and, not a day later, banners were flying from every turret."

"Banners?"

"Huge solar crosses in bright blue on a yellow background."

Leah sighed. "Maybe they're followers of Odin."

Kathryn's lips pursed into a frown. "Or maybe the old Nazi's have returned. They're just using nicer colors this time around."

"Lovely," Gareth muttered, taking a huge bite out of the perfect burger.

Leah banged her fork on the table. "Shit! Guess we are going to Germany after all."

Gareth nodded back at her. "Get a look at the inside of that castle."

"How?" Leah sat back in her chair and studied the man who she trusted more than life. "Walk up, knock, and say; 'Hi. Is there a freak by the name of Daniel Bauer living here? We need to steal back some ancient weapons belonging to a powerful goddess. Don't mind us, though. Carry on with the building of your new Reich.' " She rolled her eyes and offered him a smile. "Got another plan?"

She watched in wonder as the emerald eyes suddenly lit from within. It looked as if a light bulb had gone on deep inside his soul, and his unique gaze radiated with new knowledge. "What?"

"All we need is to be invisible." Gareth smiled. Grabbing Emmanuel's arm, he lifted him out of his seat. As the duo hurried down the crowded street, Gareth shouted back over his shoulder, "We'll meet you at the store!"

Mary returned to the table. "What's the matter with them?"

Kathryn shrugged. "They're guys. This is how they act. Probably saw some old, famous football player who ran seven hundred yards and scored fifty-six touchdowns twenty years ago. Not to worry."

Mary giggled. "You're funny."

"Laugh now, kid," she said. "Eventually you'll find one you love more than life and then, *boy*, are you gonna have a permanent headache."

"There is *one* thing that's good about men, though. One that I find truly helpful," Leah added.

"What's that?" Mary looked at her.

"They're very forgetful."

Kathryn sighed. "What's helpful about that?"

Picking up Gareth's glossy black credit card, she waved it in the air, and the three females enjoyed a laugh in the Land of the Gods.

CHAPTER 8

Leah knew she should hurry, but the day as so warm and the company so comforting, that she found herself moving at a turtle's pace from shop to shop. Idling in front of large windows packed with beautiful trinkets, Leah let the peaceful hours go by. She wanted nothing to spoil the rare happy time she had with her friends.

The shopping bags were full of toys and clothes for Kathryn's future scion. Leah even bought Mary a new lamb. She thanked Leah profusely and carried her new purchase in the shiny bag by her side. But the well-worn friend remained under her arm. Leah understood. She smiled to herself as she rubbed her palm against the worn-out leather coat. You never gave up your safety blanket in a world that was getting crazier by the minute.

"Hey, kid," Leah began. "Sorry about sending you away from the table back at the café. I didn't really care if you washed your hands."

Mary nodded. "I know. My dad does that when he wants to say something he doesn't want me to hear. Or, wants to do something he doesn't want me to see."

Leah laughed. "Good. Then you know."

As the three ladies strolled among the booths of the open-air market of Monastiraki, far away from the slick boutiques and trendy coffee shops, Leah spotted the small blue entrance of the tiny store. There was no sign to announce the shop's ownership; only an X was mounted above the doorway. "Always marks the spot," Leah whispered, as a strange feeling crawled over her flesh.

Kathryn crinkled up her nose. "The shop's name is ten?"

"No," Mary chimed in. "That's a rune. It means gifts. It's like a balance between all things. So the shop must sell…"

"All things?" Leah attempted a grin.

"Exactly." Mary laughed.

The moment she stepped over the bright blue threshold, a wave of claustrophobia overtook Leah. Everything imaginable was for sale within the tiny space: Jewelry, statues, tapestries, dishes—hundreds of items stacked upon hundreds of items littered the numerous shelves that circled above Leah's head.

"Wow," Kathryn breathed. "Man. You could furnish three palaces with this stuff."

Mary took off around the corner of one of the shelves and was instantly swallowed by the wealth of colors and scents.

Leah followed quickly, picking items up that'd fallen victim to the girl's lightening quick advance. "Hey! Be careful!" She shouted at the fast little body, as a statue of the familiar Hero's Companion fell into her hand.

Leah winced when she stared down at the idol. Athena's eyes were made of marble; hollow, cold and unforgiving. It looked as if she was well aware that the woman holding her in the palm of her hand was the one who'd come to her resting place—like a thief in the night—and made off with her most valuable possessions.

Very carefully, Leah placed the goddess back on her shelf and whispered, "Don't worry. I'll get them back."

"Leah…over here!"

Following the loud voice, Leah turned yet another corner. Bumping into Mary, she could see that the child was delighted with what she'd uncovered; her face was absolutely glowing.

"Look at all this jewelry," Mary said in a voice filled with awe.

Leah scanned shelf upon shelf of truly immaculate pieces. There were no glass or velvet boxes holding the precious stones prisoner. Nor did any alarms beep or blink around the works of art that most likely were worth huge sums. They just lay there, in piles, waiting for someone to come along and snatch them up.

Kathryn walked up behind Leah and reached out for a beautiful onyx hanging from a sterling silver chain. "Wow. This is gorgeous." She reached for another; a rope of pearls that seemed to stretch from Leah's head to the heel of her boot, and proceeded to bite down on the slightly dusty strand. "Not only beautiful." Kathryn smiled. "But also very real."

Leah scanned the room, looking for anyone whose job it was to make sure that strangers wouldn't load up their pockets and race out the door. "Hello?" she called out. "Anybody here?"

Not even a cobweb stirred at her request.

Mary placed a pair of golden earrings into her lobes and watched them dangle in an intricately designed, dust-covered mirror. "I look like Cleopatra. I wish I was her," she said, dreamily.

Leah flicked the heavy metal with her finger. "Trust me, kid, you wouldn't like it. The asps were real, you know."

Mary shivered at the thought and set the earrings back down on the shelf.

"Can I help you?"

Leah let out a squeal of surprise, as she turned around to meet a tall man who'd suddenly appeared out of nowhere with a big, black Doberman by his side.

The animal locked his eyes on Leah and issued a low, guttural growl.

"Jesus," Kathryn whispered, inching away from the sharp, white teeth.

The man just offered a smile and pointed at the door. The dog looked up at his master and marched to the threshold without a single bark. "Good Poochy," he said.

Leah tried to calm her rapid heartbeat as she watched the sleek, well-muscled canine lumber to the doorway and lay down. "Poochy?"

The man grinned. "What would you have me call him?"

She shrugged, keeping a wary eye on the animal that could rip her face off with one wink from his master. "Oh, I don't know… Killer? Devil's Spawn?"

"Sam?" Kathryn mumbled.

Leah looked at her in confusion.

"You know," she whispered, "as in, 'Son of.'"

The man disregarded the rude American with a well-practiced and often-used roll of his eyes. "Are you ladies looking for something in particular?"

"Actually, I'm partial to emeralds," Leah remarked.

"Emeralds?" He tilted his head to the side, as if sizing her up. "A good choice with your auburn hair. I happen to have this lovely bracelet and earring set. It's said to have been once owned by the wealthy mistress of a Grecian god."

Leah looked down at the brilliant gems resting in the palm of his hand. "I'll bet."

Kathryn mumbled, "I would've held out for a Corvette."

Mary giggled.

"Well…he was a *god*, after all."

Leah cleared her throat, as the man's gaze became increasingly annoyed. She definitely didn't want him to turn to his companion and order the Doberman to feed on their insolent hides. "They're very lovely, sir. But I was actually looking for a pendant—an emerald teardrop that you may have had here a while back?"

The man gave a slight nod, and stared into Leah's eyes. His hazel gaze was accented with golden flecks that seemed to race around his pupils, like twenty-four carat planets dancing around the sun. "I did have something like that here once. A very long time ago. I'm afraid it was sold."

"To an English lady?"

He broke the contact between them and pointed to one of the upper shelves. "It was there."

Leah moved her eyes to scan the empty spot. Without a word, the man turned away and marched out the front door. The dog sat up quickly; his ears stood straight up on the top of his head and his back legs twitched. But instead of following his master, the Doberman stared at the women and didn't move an inch.

Kathryn whispered, "Great. How do we get past that thing to get out of here?"

"Look at this!"

Leah turned around to witness Mary balancing on a broken stool. The young girl reached up to the shelf and grabbed for something that was lying there. She stepped down carefully and placed them in Leah's hand.

Staring at the strange wooden tiles, Leah glanced at Mary. "Runes?"

She nodded. "See? That one's you. The one I told you about in my letter." Leah stared down at the familiar < as Mary continued, "You're the beacon…the torch."

Kathryn stuck her head around Leah's body and stared at the small tile. "Excuse me?"

Mary looked at her and smiled. "Leah's the owner of the vital fire of life."

Kathryn shrugged. "I'll buy that."

"This is part of the Elder Futhark."

Kathryn stepped back; her face was a mask of shock. "Hey, young lady! You watch your mouth! You're too young to swear."

Leah laughed out loud, and turned to Kathryn. "The Elder Futhark is the name of the tiles; twenty-four runes which make up an ancient Germanic/Norse alphabet that people used for writing, divination…even magick."

"Oh," Kathryn said. "Whatever."

Mary beamed with pride. "That's right! Runes are an oracle people once used to seek advice and see what was coming in their future."

"So…it's like fortunetelling," Kathryn remarked.

Mary sighed loudly, causing Leah to giggle at the frustrated teen who now sounded just like her. "No. Runes are just a way to analyze the path in life that you're walking, and try to see your destiny. But the future isn't fixed by the runes. Everything you do, every choice you make, can change your path—which then changes your destiny. That way, if you don't like what the runes tell you, you can just make a decision to change something in your path to hopefully get a better future."

Leah smiled wide. "Did you also know that when people made runes they took a branch from a fruit-bearing tree and cut it into small pieces? Then they either marked them with blood, or carved symbols into the tiles and scattered them on top of a white cloth. That's why they call it casting. Then—"

Mary broke in quickly, "Then they'd invoke the gods, raise their eyes to the heavens and pick up three runes."

Leah pat her on the back. "*You've done well, young Skywalker.*"

Kathryn shook her head in disgust. "This is the first time I've been the dumbest one in the room."

"Don't feel bad," Mary reached out and took her hand. "It's really difficult to learn how to read runes. They say that the god, Odin, hung from the World Tree for nine days and nights to be able to achieve the knowledge of the runes. And the whole time he was impaled on his own sword."

"Yuck." Kathryn stuck out her tongue. "So what did Zeus do?"

Mary laughed. "I don't think Zeus cared much about runes. I never heard a story about him when it came to these."

"Well, he was the top dog. He probably just read the newspaper or something to keep up," Kathryn said, with a wink.

Leah nodded. "CNN."

Mary rolled her eyes and looked back down at the tiles. "Your rune isn't the only one here, Leah. This one," she said, holding up a tile marked ᚱ, "means travel—taking a journey."

Leah rolled her eyes. "I really want to stay home more."

"And this one," Mary continued, holding up another strange symbol ᛟ, "is Othala. It stands for an ancestral property…some kind of house."

"Well, there it is then," Kathryn said. "You, the beacon, are going to travel to an ancestral house." She nodded. "I'd say they were right on the money."

"But there's more," Mary said, quietly.

Leah looked down at the two tiles still sitting in the young girl's hand. "I thought the reading was only made up of three tiles?"

Mary nodded slowly. "It should be, but these other ones were up there too. This one is Algiz ᛉ. It's usually a shield—some form of protection." The young girl's voice came out like a whisper from the mouth of a dead soul. "Maybe you'll need it to get by this man."

"What man?" Leah stared at the strange tiles and felt the fear rise in her throat.

Mary held up the last one with a slightly quivering hand. "This is Mannaz. It's usually okay. It stands for the Self, or the whole of humanity and where the world is heading. But on the shelf it was upside down."

"So?"

"So…" Her eyes grew wide. "When it's upside down humanity, or the Self, is headed for depression, despair…they will face their own mortality. It can mean one man or mankind. But I think it's a man, Leah. Just one man. He'll be cunning and manipulative, and you'll have no help…no protection against him."

"Except the shield," Leah reminded her of the other tile as she thought of Athena's mighty weapon. She stared at the ominous looking tile as if searching for Daniel Bauer's face inside the…ᛗ.

Mary shook her head. "I don't think so." Tears began to gather in her wide, frightened eyes. "It was next to *him*, Leah. He'll have the shield. You won't have a chance."

CHAPTER 9

Kathryn let out a scream and Leah grabbed for Mary, as the Doberman suddenly produced a stream of fierce, angry barks.

"Jesus!"

Leah focused on Gareth and Emmanuel standing just outside. Gareth was holding his green knapsack out in front of him, barring Satan's minion from getting any closer to his flesh.

"Gareth?"

"Leah…have the owner call off this damn dog! Tell him I'll buy anything he wants."

"The owner left," she shouted back.

"Wonderful."

Emmanuel's soft, soothing voice filled the room. Leah watched him step from behind Gareth and walk toward the irate beast. Her eyes nearly popped out of her skull when she witnessed Poochy become silent and bow his head to the handsome young man with the calm tone.

Kathryn looked up at Leah; pride beamed in her eyes. "Ain't he great? He's going to be an excellent father."

"Do me a favor?"

"What's that?"

"Don't name your kid Poochy."

Emmanuel began to spoil the suddenly loving, docile dog. The Doberman threw himself on the floor with so much power that the statues rattled on the shelves. Rolling over, the once vicious canine allowed Emmanuel to stroke his belly.

Leah, Kathryn and Mary tiptoed around the placated beast and ran out into the safety of the sunshine.

Gareth winced. "What exactly is Cujo guarding in there? The entire wealth of ancient Greece?"

"Lots and lots o' jewelry."

"The Hope Diamond?" He grasped the bulky knapsack and brought it to his chest. "Was anyone in there who could help? Did anyone know about the emerald?"

Leah shook her head. "No. But someone left runes in its spot."

"Runes?"

She nodded. "The kid read my future, and it looks like our next step is definitely going to be Germany."

"But Leah—" Mary's voice held extreme worry for the death of her friend at the hands of a conniving, manipulative man who loomed in her path.

Leah stared into her big, brown eyes. "I don't believe in any of that crap."

The child's gaze darkened. "Yes, you do."

"Okay," Leah whispered, "then don't upset Gareth. His day's already been shot to hell."

"Why?"

"He can't stand dogs. They scare him to death."

* * *

"*Leah*? Is that you?"

The flesh on Leah's back began to crawl up and down her spine, as the familiar face materialized from around the corner of the tiny shop.

"It's me. Khait. Remember me?"

Leah stole the small wooden tiles from Mary's hand and dropped them into the deep pocket of her long, leather duster. "Oh, yeah. You showed us around the Acropolis a few months ago."

"And Plato's Garden." The woman nodded.

Leah smiled. She'd never forget the strange meeting that'd

occurred with the older woman that day. Khait had issued a warning to her at the time to not take the weapons of Athena beyond the city walls. Leah wondered what Khait would say if she knew that they were now in the hands of a wannabe Nazi. "Yeah…the garden. I forgot about that. How have you been?"

"Good. Good. Lots of traveling."

"Not a tour guide anymore?"

She shrugged. "No. I've had a million things to do. Been sitting up with an old, sick friend lately and I've barely been in Athens at all."

"Sorry about your friend." Leah could tell that the woman had hardly slept. Dark circles enhanced the baggage under her eyes, and her pale, translucent skin mirrored that of a vampire who'd gone too long without a hearty vein to feed upon.

Khait offered a thin, worn-out smile. "Life goes on, I suppose. But we have to help the ones who need us the most. No matter what, their happiness comes first."

Leah remained silent.

Khait took a deep breath. "So…what are you two doing back in Athens?" Her gaze moved quickly between Leah and Gareth. He stayed quiet, clinging to his backpack and eyeing Emmanuel who was now sitting on the stoop with his new best friend.

"How was your journey after you left us? Did you find what you were looking for?" Khait's polite gaze turned into an oddly angry glare that caused Leah's soul to freeze.

"Turned out well. Thank you for asking," Leah replied. "We just came back to do a little sight-seeing. Gareth and I enjoyed this place so much that we decided to bring some of our loved ones back with us." Attempting to keep the jovial tone in her voice, Leah could hear the alarm bells pealing in the recesses of her brain. She didn't believe in coincidences. They were just too easy.

Khait's smile leveled out into a firm, straight line. Leah took note that the woman kept her gaze directed at the base of her throat. "That's nice," she mumbled, glancing at Mary. "Is this your daughter?"

Leah shook her head. "Friend of the family. Say hello, Mary." She squeezed Mary's shoulder and then pulled her hand away quickly, staring down at it with a smile. "Wow, pal, you're covered in dust from that old shop."

Mary placed her beloved lamb in the glossy bag with its newly purchased twin, and stared down at her clean palms in quiet confusion.

Leah smiled. "We need to wash our hands."

Mary nodded.

"I can't shake." Leah put her hands in the air. "Wouldn't want to get you dirty. It was really nice seeing you again, though. My best to your sick friend." Leah side-stepped the haggard woman and followed behind Mary, pushing her gently down the street toward the busy café.

* * *

When they exited the small bistro and walked back around the corner, Leah watched Gareth offer the woman a bow. He was still clinging to his knapsack like a drowning man to a life preserver. White knuckled, he clutched the bag, using it as a shield against the now ridiculously lovable puppy.

Leah looked down at Mary and winked. "All clean," Leah announced. She came to stand beside Gareth and locked her arm in his. "I'm sorry we can't spend more time with you, Khait, but we have to catch a plane."

"Really? Where are you going now?"

"Gareth and I aren't going anywhere. But my sister-in-law is taking this young lady to the palace in Knossos."

Khait offered a somewhat confused smile. "Well, that's wonderful. I've been there. You'll love it." She nodded at Kathryn. "I can't tell you how many surprises there are in those ancient walls."

"Yeah," Kathryn snorted. "History's great, ain't it? Bones, blood, monsters, sacrifices…it's just got it all."

Khait offered a small, uncomfortable laugh and waved goodbye to the group.

Watching her depart, Gareth leaned in close to Leah's ear, "Did you see the guys in the black suits with the shiny silver buttons?"

Leah nodded. "The minute she appeared."

CHAPTER 10

The twin engines powered up for their next trip.

Leah grabbed Mary and hugged her as hard as she could. "Got your lamb?"

The girl nodded; a coating of tears covered her big, brown eyes. "He makes me feel better."

"He'll keep you safe." Leah's voice grew louder, "Enjoy Crete. Say hi'ya to the Minotaur for me. Kathryn will take care of you until you can catch up with your school group."

Mary straightened her back as she glanced around Leah. "Okay."

Leah felt the small object Mary pressed in her hand. "I forgot to give this to you," she whispered.

Looking down at the tile, Leah stared at the lightning bolt ⚡ . "What is it?"

"It means victory. It was on the shelf, too."

Leah's pulse quickened. "Was it next to my tile or his?"

"His," her voice cracked.

"Well." Leah increased her smile. "I guess it's a good thing that we changed the direction of my path then, huh?"

Mary nodded, as Kathryn kissed Emmanuel and took the child's hand in her own. Emmanuel hugged his wife. "I just want to help out Gareth and Leah in Paderborn and then I'll be right behind you."

Kathryn grinned. "Just be careful."

As Leah and Gareth stood back and watched Emmanuel walk his love to the plane, Gareth's comforting arms appeared around her waist and he pulled Leah's body against his own. Looking over her shoulder, he stared down at the lightning bolt carved into the small tile. "What is it?"

"It means victory."

"That's a good thing, isn't it?"

Leah turned. Just in case their new well-dressed stalkers could read lips, she hid her face in Gareth's chest. Raising her chin, she stared into his worried emerald eyes. "Two of these exact same runes, side by side, were the symbol for Hitler's SS men...his elite bodyguards. Himmler was their commander. Up until 1930, every SS man had to take a special course in runic magic because Himmler was such a believer in it.

"Unlike the gypsies—who Hitler didn't believe had the power to see the future—he had the SS lock up members of the Magi in concentration camps. But *they* weren't killed. They were kept alive to be part of a research institution called the Ahnenerbe."

Gareth remained silent, letting the knowledge sink in.

Leah continued quietly, "The institution studied magical runes, among other things, and it was Hitler who chose the runic symbol of the sun to be the official insignia of his Third Reich. The Magi who survived their imprisonment testified that Hitler was actually doomed from the very beginning because he bent his symbol at right angles in a counterclockwise direction, which is the exact opposite of the real symbol. They said since he 'twisted history,' Hitler would never be allowed to find what he was after or achieve success."

"Because history can't be re-written."

Leah nodded. "Exactly. Maybe Bauer, if he is a follower, is getting it all wrong too. He's already twisting everything to fit what he wants the world to be. Take Athena's spear, for instance. It has a power that came from history...from a goddess who helped the poor and downtrodden being persecuted by others. If Bauer's trying to use it for personal gain, then he might fail the same way Hitler did."

Gareth spoke softly, "But he got the emerald right. He figured out that the stone has some kind of power. And, unfortunately, we still don't know what that has to do with Bauer's plans, Hitler, or anyone else from history. Whatever we do, Leah, we *can't* let him get his hands on that stone."

"Don't worry." She spoke against his chest, "I think I may have done something that'll change our outcome."

Gareth's voice was low and distant, "Me too."

Squeezing the rune of victory in her hand, Leah closed her eyes and said a prayer to her favorite Friend.

CHAPTER 11

They stood in the Domplatz—the center of the old town of Paderborn. It was a lovely place; even though the brisk winter winds raced through the valley and caused goosebumps to appear on their flesh, the actual town was as close to picturesque as a person could possibly hope for.

The trees were covered in a thin blanket of snow. The sidewalks were bustling with happy folk who wore smiles planted firmly on their faces as they traveled door to door, work to school, shop to shop. The residents didn't even seem to notice the long building with the high tower that threw huge shadows across their town.

Leah stared into the open door of the Paderborn Cathedral. Down the aisle, located in the cloister, she observed a strange window depicting three hares running around in a circle. The rabbits looked normal, yet the artists had constructed it to look like they only had three ears between them. "What's that?"

Emmanuel answered, "No one really knows. There's actually a project going on called 'The Three Hares Project' right now. Various archaeologists have found this symbol located in France, Germany, China, Afghanistan…everywhere. The emblem appears on the Buddhist cave temples in China; Islamic items of worship; it's even been linked to the Virgin Mary. But no one knows exactly what it is or what it means."

"Are you telling me there's something *you* don't know?" Gareth slapped him on the back. "I'm shocked."

Emmanuel laughed and pointed north. "Over there is where the foundation of Charlemagne's palace was discovered."

"Charlemagne?"

"He launched his first major attack against the Saxons here in 776," Emmanuel said. "That's when he destroyed the Irminsul, which is near the entrance to the cave I told you about."

Gareth nodded, taking it all in.

"Charlemagne built a very powerful home here in Paderborn. It was like his base of operations for destroying the Saxons and installing Christianity. When he finally defeated the Saxon army and their leader, Widukind, surrendered, Charlemagne met with the Pope, and the Bishopric of Paderborn was born."

"Thus, the Roman Catholic Church arrived." Leah smiled.

Emmanuel laughed. "You got it. The Pope even transferred the relics of St. Liborius of Le Mans here and made him the patron saint of the city. And Charlemagne was made the first ruler of the Holy Roman Empire."

Leah pulled her leather coat tight around her slightly shivering body.

"We should go inside," Gareth remarked.

She shook her head and stared at Emmanuel. "Let's see it first."

As they joined the bustling crowd, Leah noticed that Emmanuel became talkative, tossing a historical snippet her way every few minutes, interrupting her anxious thoughts with trivia that would help calm the agitated librarian down. "There's a huge UK presence here. Almost five thousand British troops are in the local army camps."

She was confused. "Banners are flying from a castle that, once upon a time, stood for the absolute worst of humanity, and there are troops here doing nothing about it?"

Emmanuel sighed. "If it is Daniel Bauer, Leah, he hasn't broken any laws. Whoever took back the castle from the district of Paderborn does have a valid claim to the hundred year lease that Himmler made, which means they have every right to decorate it any way they want."

"This is too weird." Leah stared at Gareth. "I really don't mean to harp on this point, but how would an Australian be a relation to a German military man?"

"Maybe it's not Bauer." He shrugged. "Maybe it's some other wingnut."

Leah could feel the shadow of Wewelsburg Castle bearing down on her long before she ever set eyes on the monstrosity looming over the Alma Valley. She raised her head and gasped. The seventeenth-century castle seemed so out of place in the picture-postcard scenery. Although the structure was made from yellow stone and the towers were topped with lovely, bell-shaped domes, there was still a sinister energy radiating off the monument to evil. She stared at the bright blue and yellow banners hanging from the turrets; brilliant colors that stood out in the snow white world. "Looks like Cinderella's castle, not a Nazi Mecca."

Emmanuel nodded. "Actually, it was many things before Himmler showed up. Originally, it was a Saxon stronghold. The foundations that were excavated turned up a burial pit that had hundreds of strange things inside; human remains, Neanderthal skulls, Bronze Age jewelry, carved utensils—all kinds of stuff. It was also used as a second residence by the Prince Bishop of Paderborn."

Leah gazed up at the large fortified tower on the north side of the castle; no banner hung from that one. It looked dark and foreboding, like a sleeping beast that'd been left unadorned and alone for a reason. "So after the Bishop died…that's when Himmler showed up?"

Emmanuel shook his head. "Not quite. In the seventeenth century they used this castle for witchcraft trials that spread across Europe like the plague."

"Witchcraft?" Gareth interrupted. "Like Salem?"

"It was far worse here than in America. The territories that were ruled by the Catholic Prince Bishops bordered on ferocious when it came to persecuting the women in question. The locals were actually kept inside the dungeons of Wewelsburg and tortured until they confessed in a courtroom that was buried deep within the castle. There were over a hundred thousand supposedly killed inside its walls."

"And since that wasn't enough brutality, bring on the

concentration camps," Gareth mumbled.

Emmanuel tilted his head in thought. "Maybe the victims of the camps who died as soon as they arrived were the lucky ones. At least they avoided being starved or experimented on. Himmler was truly insane. He used this castle as his headquarters for the SS. After a while, Himmler came to believe that the SS were a Knightly Order; a racially elite force, like the ancient Aryan warriors who were higher up on the ladder than even the Knights Templar."

"Were they Christians?" Gareth asked.

Emmanuel shook his head. "In Himmler's mind, the SS and Hitler had taken over Christianity as *the* religion. But he idealized the prehistoric German culture which was based on the purity of men. I've heard tons of strange stories about the SS officers and their so-called pagan meetings," he sighed. "But…I can't imagine that they're true."

Gareth snorted. "Their people were among the sickest in human history, pal. I'm sure they're all true."

"I'm sorry," Leah interrupted. "I just can't wrap my head around something here. In World War I, didn't the Jewish people…like… lay down their lives for Germany…for the Fatherland?"

"They did," Emmanuel answered. "You would think that kind of loyalty would be recognized, but the gift to them—their reward— was annihilation. Himmler's supposed knights wanted a world of chivalry, as it was in the medieval times. And they believed that they couldn't have that without cleansing themselves of Jewish values."

"But medieval chivalry was based on the principles of mercy and defending the weakest of mankind, like women and children. It wasn't based on what god or religion you believed in," Leah argued. Her mind was spinning at the ridiculous logic behind the Nazi ideals.

Emmanuel offered a sympathetic smile. "Himmler's knights ignored all that."

"Apparently."

"Himmler was intent on creating a new world order. And that," he continued, pointing up at the monstrous castle, "was supposed to be the center of that clean, fresh world."

The group shook violently when a blast of cold air, like the combined screams of the victims who had died here, hit them head on. The mighty trees of the forest bent under the power of the stiff gust, and the snaps and cracks of limbs sounded almost like the demons from long ago were laughing at them—daring them to walk underneath their branches and enter the castle that was literally from hell.

CHAPTER 12

"I need a drink," Gareth shouted above the wind.

Emmanuel nodded. "Let's go back to the University. We have a beer hall close by."

Leah laughed, "Beer at a college. How very American."

The group huddled close together as they retraced their steps through the now dwindling crowds, and past the Cathedral of St. Mary, St. Liborius and St. Kilian. They could see the huge grounds of the University of Paderborn in the distance. A little farther down the street Emmanuel ran up to a polished oak door and threw it open, ushering his friends into the cozy, warm hall.

Leah turned and walked over the threshold, stopping herself from taking two more steps down the sidewalk and running into the shop next door. She could feel the drool gather in her mouth as she breathed in the most sensuous smell she'd ever come in contact with wafting from the bakery's door.

But instead of succumbing to the urge, Leah stepped into the pleasant hall. All around her was pure rustic décor. The tables and chairs were hand-carved and polished to within an inch of their lives. Sheaves of barley and lavender hung from old wooden beams above their heads, and at the center of the comforting area sat antique brewing equipment. The two big vats were made of polished copper and really brought home the true essence of German ingenuity.

Leah stepped up to the huge sign that took up the entire east end of the friendly pub. Strange names littered the wall, offering dozens of choices. "Wow, these people are definitely beer people."

"God bless 'em," Gareth laughed.

Emmanuel snickered. "There are so many shades, colors and kinds to choose from, you could stay here and drink for an entire month and still not sample the whole list."

"It sure would be fun to try," Gareth stated in a wistful voice that sounded like a man who wanted nothing more than to relax into normalcy.

Emmanuel slapped him on the back. "You have blonde lagers to black lagers. There are some called easy-drinking beers, and others like the Eisbock, which should be sipped…slowly." He smiled wide. "They can really hurt a guy if he's not careful."

Leah looked him up and down. "Apparently we have a real connoisseur in our midst."

"Well…I *am* going to be a father. I need to have this information handy so I can teach my son later in life."

"And, if he's a she?"

Emmanuel's eyes grew wide. "She's not allowed anywhere near these places!"

"Amen to that," the future uncle agreed. "University boys drunk on beer…nothing good can come of it."

Leah burst into laughter. "You two are so full of it. I bet even *I* could drink you under the table."

Gareth raised an eyebrow.

"But I won't."

A young waiter appeared out of nowhere and hustled them to an empty table in a darkened corner of the bar. As Leah watched the winter sun begin to disappear from view, people began racing through the door, ready to begin their long-awaited Happy Hour.

Gareth looked up at the smiling waiter. "The lady wants a blond Kölsch."

"I already have a blond New Mexican."

"Funny." Gareth continued, "We'll have an edel; you can pick which one."

The waiter moved away from their table.

"What's an edel?" Leah asked.

"It's a designation. It means 'noble.'"

"You're so girlie."

Emmanuel laughed out loud, as a couple of men began to set up stools on the small stage. "Must be having a show tonight."

Leah took a drink of the cold brew placed in front of her and immediately felt her insides warm up. She closed her eyes and enjoyed the fresh taste. "Okay. I like this."

Gareth raised his glass. "Good. Maybe when this is all over I'll bring you back, get you all liquored up, and take advantage of you."

"I love your hopeless romantic side."

Gareth's smile didn't quite reach his eyes, and Leah knew he was deep in thought about what the next few days would bring. Even their comforting banter couldn't dissuade either of them from listening to the alarms ringing in their brains, waiting for the next shoe to drop.

Leah scanned the dimly-lit pub. She suddenly wondered if Bauer would have the nerve to appear from behind the bar and come over to greet them. Remembering his look of pure evil back in Jericho, she shivered at the thought. God knows what he'd taken out of Paradise to aid him in his plans. Leah cringed, wondering if she could stop whatever those plans might be.

"I have to ask you something." Emmanuel began, "I haven't seen the emerald since the wedding. Did you guys hide it somewhere?"

Leah leaned forward and kept her voice low, suddenly feeling as if Bauer had planted everything from cameras to microphones in the small building. "That stone's safe. What I need to know, Emmanuel, is what we might be up against. I mean, say Bauer *is* part of some Nazi cult who wants to relive the glory days those heartless scumbags tried to have. Will the sword and shield of Athena help him do that? *Can* he possibly resurrect the Reich with the power of the Hero's Companion in his hands?"

Emmanuel set down his glass, and offered her a serious stare. "I've been thinking about that since I first got your call."

Leah remembered the horrible evening when she and Gareth had made it back to the hotel. She'd just found out about her father's lies, and Daniel Bauer had been left inside Paradise with a wealth of treasure and knowledge and Athena's irreplaceable weapons at his disposal. She shook the horrible memory from her mind, filled with guilt for the goddess she'd let down.

"Leah," Emmanuel began. "Considering the history behind Athena, I don't think that spear of hers is going to give any power to this guy whatsoever. I wouldn't worry about that part. Something tells me he probably just shows them off like museum pieces rather than actually trying to use them."

He continued, "I think the more important issue is the way you said he looked when he grabbed for the emerald around your neck. That's obviously his true goal. He needs that for whatever he's thinking of doing. Kathryn and I searched every section of the internet," Emmanuel stopped, smiling at Leah's disgusted expression. "As well as the *books* in the University library." He winked. "But we couldn't find any mention of a sacred emerald that had anything to do with Hitler, Himmler…no one. We even cross-referenced it with Athena, Jack the Ripper—because Trish bought it and brought it back to her store; we even looked into Aleister Crowley and every other person and place that your paths have led you to. But…nothing. Every single search was a dead end."

"What about the Bible?" Gareth interjected. "Leah's dad mentioned there might be something extremely 'biblical' about it."

Emmanuel thought for a moment and finally shook his head. "I'll have to research that one, but even in all my study I can't think of a biblical emerald. Maybe something to do with the Grail?"

Leah shook her head. "No. We know that's sitting in Glastonbury, and an emerald isn't part of it."

"I'll get on the internet when we get back and see what I can find out."

Leah took another long sip of the fantastic brew and watched Gareth drain his mug. His eyes constantly scanned the bar as the crowd grew larger with each passing minute. Leah had a hunch he was looking for the strange men they hadn't seen since leaving Athens behind.

"Okay," Gareth spoke. "So I want to answer Leah's question, because I agree that Himmler could not possibly be related to this Australian dweeb. What do we know about Himmler on a personal level?"

"I only know the basics." Emmanuel shrugged.

Gareth looked over at Leah. She shook her head in response. "I did most of my studying on Hitler. Mean and short."

Emmanuel grinned. "A good summation."

"But I never read anywhere that Hitler hung out near, in, or around this castle."

"You wouldn't," Emmanuel confirmed. "Hitler never came here."

"He never visited his second in command who was building the home base of the new, clean, fresh world?" she was completely confused.

"Who knows what old Adolf thought of Himmler's plan? Maybe the Führer secretly thought the guy was an idiot. But nowhere does it state that Hitler ever stayed or even visited Wewelsburg Castle. Like I said, Leah, I only know the basics."

She waited, as Gareth signaled the waiter for another round and then joined her in silence, staring at Emmanuel.

Taking a deep breath, Emmanuel began sharing everything he knew, "Himmler was the organizer of the concentration camps; so, in essence, he was the mastermind of the Holocaust. He was the founder and officer-in-charge of the Einsatzgruppen death squads. But he sure didn't start out very interesting.

"Born in Munich to Bavarian parents, Himmler was basic middle class all the way." Emmanuel shook his head at the irony that a seemingly boring child would end up becoming one of the most frightening monsters in history. "However, Prince Heinrich of Wittelsbach was his godparent."

"That may be why he thought so highly of status," Gareth spoke.

"Probably." Emmanuel nodded. "He was a devout Catholic; that fact was written in his diaries which he kept from the age of ten well into his twenties. The University has access to some of them. He also really loved World War I. He had an obsession with it; begged his father to use his connections to sign him up. Trouble was, he wasn't much good at military training. And once the Versailles Treaty was signed, they discharged him without ever letting him be a part of even one battle."

"What about women?" Leah interrupted. "They always come

into play somewhere in a crazy man's background."

Emmanuel shrugged. "Not much on that score either. People said that he was anxious and nervous around females. But he finally did get married to a nice blonde-haired, blue-eyed lady."

"Shocker," Gareth grunted.

Emmanuel smirked, "She was seven years older than him, and her name was Margarete. They had one daughter who Himmler doted on."

"No sons?"

Emmanuel shook his head. "I remember reading somewhere that they'd adopted a son, but Himmler wasn't really interested in the boy. Probably because the kid wasn't his. Eventually he left his wife and took up with his secretary."

Leah laughed. "One thing that will never change."

"Well, you can't knock his work ethic." Emmanuel bristled at his own statement. "The guy went from being nobody to the German Chief of Police. When he became the Commander of the SS, there were only about three hundred of them total. He brought their numbers up to almost a million soldiers fighting for the cause. Himmler went on to become Germany's Interior Minister before he decided to seek peace with Britain and the U.S. in 1945."

"Why did he do that?" Leah said, leaning back in her chair.

"Saw the ship going down, I suppose. When Hitler found out about it he declared Himmler a traitor and stripped him of all the titles and ranks he'd accumulated."

"Was he arrested?" Gareth asked.

"Yeah. They got him. Unfortunately, he bit down on a cyanide capsule before he could pay for the horrors he'd done, and they ended up throwing his corpse in some forest somewhere."

"Couldn't happen to a nicer guy," Leah remarked. She hoped beyond all hope that there was just such an unmarked grave waiting for Daniel Bauer.

CHAPTER 13

Leah turned her head to search for what had made the crowd break into sudden applause. Wolf-whistles came from the slightly intoxicated guests, as they stared at a man weaving his way through the room like an overgrown snake.

He moved with the strength and agility of youth, but possessed a head of long white hair that hung down his back in a sleek ponytail. His face was covered with bright red greasepaint, and he glided through the audience, making his way to the stool that'd placed on the stage. The man stopped dead center in the middle of the spotlight and smiled wide. "Welcome, my children, to the Palace of the Occult."

Leah snorted.

Emmanuel leaned over the table, and whispered, "This guy must be mimicking Erik Jan Hanussen."

"Who's that?" Leah whispered back.

"They called him Hitler's Rasputin. He was a clairvoyant, mind reader, occultist—basically a whack job that made predictions for our pal Adolf. Adolf's second in command, Himmler, had his own Rasputin. Went by the name of Wiligut, if I remember correctly."

Leah snickered, wondering why all the bad guys throughout history seemed too long for the one man who had briefly taken over Russia by selling the idea that he was a magical healer to Nicholas II and his anxiety-ridden wife, Alexandra. "Rasputin," she mumbled. "Too bad it's not him we have to deal with. The dude was nothing more than a powerless charlatan who only knew how to scare everyone to death."

Lifting her head, she turned back to the subject at hand, "You're telling me that the scariest dictator in the world was listening to a clairvoyant and basing his war decisions on a two-dollar act? Now, that's funny."

"Wanna' hear something even funnier?"

Leah nodded at Emmanuel's smiling face.

"He was Jewish. Hitler had him assassinated."

The voice from the stage shouted at the audience, "Will the boy whose mother passed away recently walk to the stage and greet me?"

Leah watched the eyes of the supposed mythic turn to slits. Staring at the faces around the bar, she noticed that four people at different tables began to stand, and her gaze immediately flitted back to the strange man center stage. His eyelids were closed; his lashes firmly planted on top of his cheekbones. He held up his hand. "I will only need the one in blue."

Leah watched as a young boy with big eyes looked down at his clothing and walked slowly toward the stage. She laughed. "The guy cheated. He looked to see who moved and then just picked one."

Gareth shrugged. "What did you expect?"

The mystic opened his eyes. He now wore yellow contacts, and the contrast with his red face was almost frightening.

"You may rest easy, son. She has gone to Valhalla."

The boy's face immediately relaxed.

"However, you should know that your father cheating on her was the cause for her early demise."

Leah gasped with the rest of the crowd. The young man's face turned bright red—a perfect match with the accuser's painted mask. Suddenly, the boy turned on his heel, marched back through the tables, grabbed his coat off the bar, and slammed the large oak door behind him.

The mystic opened his cat's eyes once again and scanned the crowd. Leah could tell from the faces around her that the patrons were frightened of being the next one called out by the creepy magician. A wide grin spread across the man's face. "Perhaps I should warn his father not to open his door on this wintry night. I do so *abhor* bloodshed."

Gareth gave a disgusted sigh. "I've seen enough." Rising from his seat, Gareth wrapped Leah's coat around her shoulders, and the trio headed for the door.

Leah felt icy cold fingers stroke the sapphire eye on the back of her hand. She turned quickly, coming face to face with the sinister looking clown. "You will see Valhalla *very* soon," he said.

Gareth grabbed the man's arm and ripped him away from Leah. "If you don't get your hands off her *you'll* be seeing it in about five seconds."

The man's lips parted to reveal his bright white teeth. The subtle move made the red makeup on his skin crack and peel, and Leah shuddered. It looked as if the man's face was melting right before her eyes.

She felt Gareth's protective body behind her, as he pushed her to the door and out into the cold night air.

Emmanuel looked at Leah, as the heavy door slammed shut behind them. "What's Valhalla, again?"

Leah swallowed her fear. "Heaven. Valhalla's another word for Heaven."

CHAPTER 14

Dawn broke through the small window of the dorm room, allowing the sun's rays to creep slowly across Leah and Gareth's sleeping figures.

Leah pressed her body into the man she loved. She wanted to stay here for the rest of her life. She wanted to feel warm and safe—the way she only felt when Gareth Lowery was by her side. She stroked her hero's chest, as a deep sigh emanated from his lips. His emerald eyes opened slowly and stared at her. He could hide no emotion; the love, passion, commitment and worry were shining from the depths of his soul.

Leah bent down and took possession of his warm lips. Her hands ran the length of his body, and her heart skipped more than a beat when his strong fingers brushed against her flesh. After years together, sharing the dreams and nightmares that seemed to wait around every corner for them, she still yearned for him, as if they'd just met yesterday.

For too brief a moment, Leah tossed her concerns, anger and fear out of her mind. She locked all the questions inside the card catalogue in her brain and focused all her concentration on the sensual man whose spell she was constantly under. Who needed to see Valhalla when Gareth Lowery offered Heaven on Earth?

An hour later there came a timid tap on the door, and Emmanuel's voice broke through their passion and peace.

"The storm didn't do any damage last night. We shouldn't have any problem making it to the cave this morning."

Gareth groaned against Leah's lips, "Go away."

Leah laughed. "We'll be down in a minute, Emmanuel."

Putting a hand on the back of Leah's neck, Gareth pulled her back down on top of him to meet his hungry mouth.

Another knock sounded on the door.

Picking up the alarm clock beside him, Gareth threw it at the offender. "That was not a minute! Go away!"

"Uh…sorry. I'm…um…looking for a Ms. Tallent?"

"Mrs. Lowery," Gareth whispered in her ear. "Doesn't that sound better?"

Lifting her head, Leah swallowed hard, staring at the man's honest expression. She knew he was the one—there was no question in her mind. But the woman inside who'd been walled-up a long time ago, making a decision to stay alone through life with her books and her peace, still could not take that next step.

Offering a smile, she moved down the length of him and stood up. Tying the robe around her waist, she walked to the door.

There stood a young boy, red in the face, holding out a box to her. He peeked through the narrow opening of the door and saw the large man sitting up in bed, aiming emerald arrows of fire directly at him. "Have a nice day," he mumbled.

"Don't you want me to sign something?"

He was halfway down the stairs in seconds. "No need, ma'am."

Closing the door, she stared at her mate. "You scared him, you big tree."

"I thought I was girlie?"

"Not to him, apparently." She stared down at the address on the box.

"Who's it from?"

"Mary." Leah tore open the small cardboard box happily and lifted out the bright, white lamb. A note hung around the furry animal's neck. *You should have this one. That way we'll both be safe.*

Leah felt her heart fill with love at the girl's concern...not to mention her listening skills. Smiling, she sighed with relief.

"See?" Gareth winked. "Deep down you like kids."

Her grin faded fast. "No. I like *that* kid."

"Because she's just like you. And I can pretty much guarantee that if you had your own...*our* own...they'd be just like you, too—considering the power of DNA."

"What if she's like you?"

"Well...I *am* girlie." He shrugged. "So I can teach her stuff. Like where the hottest clothes are, or how to put on eyeliner. You know...the things that are simply way over your head."

Leah threw the empty box at him. "I thought all men wanted sons."

"Can't stand them." Gareth snorted. "We're all a bunch of jerks. Why would I want to bring another one into the world?"

Leah shivered as the cold room. "I need a shower. This conversation is making me ill."

"Good," Gareth snickered. "Before, it always made you want to kill yourself, now you just want to vomit. We're making progress!"

* * *

The morning grew unnaturally warm. Last night's bitter cold winds had exited the valley and already the heat of the sun was beginning to melt the thin layer of snow that remained.

Leah reached into the pocket of her jacket and rubbed her palm against the soft, furry lamb inside. Mary was right. It did give her comfort in the strange, crazy world they were now walking through.

Gareth bumped her with his hip. "Whatcha thinking about?"

"I want to buy a dog."

His face immediately grew stark white. "What?"

Leah laughed at the panic in his eyes and the thin line of sweat appearing on his upper lip.

"Do you want to kill me?" he stuttered. "Do you not remember that thing in Athens?"

Leah sent a grin to Emmanuel walking beside her now terrified partner. "I didn't mean that one. I don't want the Anti-Christ for a dog. I mean a smaller, fluffy thing."

"What's wrong with Dammit back at the library? It's fluffy."

"A dog provides security, Gareth."

"That's because they can rip a man's arms and legs off in seconds."

Emmanuel jumped in, "Kathryn and I are going to get a dog."

Gareth's eyes grew wide. "Are you *nuts?* It'll eat the baby."

Leah laughed.

"Not a wild, rabid wolf, Gareth," Emmanuel replied, rolling his eyes. "All children should have a dog to grow up with. The dog will protect them and love them…it's *good* for a child. I had two German Shepherds when I was a kid."

Gareth groaned, as they walked up the wet hillside. "You people are sick. German Shepherds are like…three hundred pounds."

The laughter bubbled up inside of Leah, as she stared at the man in wonder. He looked like Adonis and fought like Hercules, yet Gareth was scared to death by the very mundane thought of a tame animal living in his presence. She decided to throw out an ultimatum. "If I have to think about kids, you have to think about getting a dog."

His eyes grew wide. "That's blackmail!"

Leah shrugged, and Gareth stuck out his tongue, threw back his shoulders and marched faster up the hill. "Let's go!"

* * *

When he reached the top, Gareth turned the corner and found himself staring at a strange wall of rock. There were five tall stones in all, standing side by side on the slightly frozen ground. He stepped toward them and rubbed his hand against the sandstone, staring at the relief that someone had carved into the rock over a million years ago.

The etching was of a large cross sitting atop an old, bent tree. The tree was sagging under the weight of the mighty symbol that seemed to be pushing the tree into the ground.

Emmanuel came up behind him. "They call that the 'Descent from the Cross'. People believe that it represents the humiliation of the Irminsul when Christianity triumphed."

Leah joined them and stared at the strange symbol. "It's almost evil. It's like the cross is…killing the tree."

Emmanuel cleared his throat. "You're not wrong. It's kind of the general consensus around here that this formation was used in the religious activities of the Teutonic people and their ancestors. The Saxons held this area in high esteem. There are writings that suggest the Irminsul—a pillar that was said to connect the heavens with the earth—once sat in this very spot. This relief represents the tree that Odin hung from for days and nights trying to gain the knowledge he needed to move on up the pillar and enter Paradise."

"Valhalla," Leah whispered.

Gareth's brain felt like it was going to explode, as he turned to the beautiful sapphire eyes. "You think that's what the crazy man meant last night?"

Leah nodded. "I don't believe in coincidences. I think somebody around here is leading us directly where he wants us to go."

Anger filled Gareth's soul. "I don't want to be played, Leah, and certainly not by Bauer. Let's get the hell out of here."

He physically shivered, when Leah's eyes grew wide. He could see the familiar card catalogue spring open inside the librarian's mind. "What?"

"There was a pillar here that reached from the earth into the heavens," she began. "What, if nothing else, have we learned from our travels together, Gareth?"

The images of the zodiac burst into his mind. He sighed. "In order to get to Heaven—"

"We have to go through Hell."

CHAPTER 15

Leah turned quickly on her heel and stared at Emmanuel. "What else happened here? I mean, Nazi-wise?"

He thought for a moment. "Well...a guy by the name of Wilhelm Teudt strongly suggested that the Irminsul had actually sat right here until Charlemagne came and destroyed it."

"Effectively bringing in the power of the Roman Catholic Church," Gareth added.

Emmanuel nodded. "Teudt joined up with the Nazi party in 1933 and wanted to turn the Externsteine into a scared ceremonial site. Himmler agreed with him and created the Externsteine Foundation. Together they brought back the Armanen-Orden which was, put simply, a religion based on Celtic and Germanic ideas."

Leah nodded. "The myths of the gods."

"Odin." Emmanuel nodded.

"What did they do here?" Gareth asked.

"There are just rumors now." Emmanuel suddenly slapped his forehead with his hand. "God, I'm so stupid!"

"What?" Leah stepped forward.

Emmanuel sighed. "When Kathryn and I found this cave and saw what we saw, I was just thinking about Himmler and the SS. I didn't even *think* about the ritual aspects of it all."

Leah waited as patiently as possible for him to continue.

"The rumors are that the Odinic, or Armanic order, would

celebrate seasonal festivities here. They would go into a room where a table was covered with a black cloth, and place a spear or a sword in the middle of the table and then summon Odin's spirit—or any other dead souls who happened to be floating around."

Leah whispered, "Athena." She stamped her foot on the ground. "That's what the little creep is probably using the spear for! Some ancient voodoo crap!"

Gareth nodded. "Use a goddess to call a god. Makes sense."

"But Athena wasn't even in the same myths and stories as Odin, she was the daughter of Zeus," Leah mumbled. Her brain was running at top speed, attempting to reach the answer that seemed to be buried just beyond her grasp.

Emmanuel continued, oblivious to their conversation, "There were bowls and candles on the table. The worshipers, men dressed in black," he whispered, "wore patches on their sleeves that read **AO**. They'd light the 'spirit flame' and call for Odin. They read Odin's runic poem, the 'Edda', and then the…blood sacrifices would start. It was always supposed to be animal blood. But the rumor surrounding Himmler was that he used real live people."

Leah's stomach lurched.

"They'd bang a gong inside the meeting place and begin to chant. They'd cast their runes and wait. The sacrifices would only stop once the spirit flame was extinguished. That meant Odin had arrived and accepted their offerings."

Gareth groaned, "Nothing like taking an ancient spiritual rite and turning it into a bloodbath. Himmler was one sick son-of-a—"

"Runes?" Leah mumbled.

Emmanuel turned to her. "The 'Edda' is a collection of Norse writings about Odin—some are heroic, others are mystical. Some are based on the runes. Those tiles are actually the foundation of ancient Nordic mythology. I think the originals used are kept in the University of Iceland. Himmler had his teams comb through them, as well as this site we're standing on, in order to prove that the Germanic people were the one and only Aryan race."

Leah felt sick to her stomach. "Show us where you found the cave."

Gareth took her arm, as she began to follow Emmanuel behind

the formations. "Please tell me you have that emerald with you."

Leah turned to him. "Why?"

"Remember what happened the last time we walked into a cave?"

Leah could still feel the stingers of the scorpions puncturing her flesh, and the face of the evil wolf that knocked her to the ground, ready to devour her inside Cleopatra's mines. The minions of Satan had been around as they'd ventured from Qumran into the heart of the desert. But the emerald around her neck had kept Leah and her friends from suffering a fate worse than death.

She stared up into his handsome face. "Kathryn and Emmanuel have already been in there. I'm sure there isn't anything that can hurt us."

Gareth shook his head. "Yeah, because so far our adventures together have been all hearts and flowers."

Leah tried to offer him a smile as they followed behind Emmanuel and stared down into the black hole that was located off to the side of the ancient monument. If someone hadn't been looking for it they wouldn't find it, she thought. The small, round hole was hidden carefully between two stone pillars, and was barely large enough to allow a human to fall through.

Emmanuel began to remove the stones and ferns that he'd placed over the entrance in order to camouflage it even further from a tourist's eye, or worse, any followers of the spiritual practices who still wished to use bloodletting to contact a god. "Kathryn and I left some torches inside, so we'll be able to see when we get down there."

Leah stared into the eerie blackness. "Just…drop?"

Emmanuel grinned. "The floor is actually only six-feet down. Someone wanted to make it easy to get in."

"Yeah. You wouldn't want your sacrificial victim to get all bruised and battered before it was time to get their throat slit."

Gareth put a hand on Leah's arm, as she stepped forward. "I'll go first." He smiled.

Leah kissed him hard. She wanted to communicate the intensity of her emotions; she needed him to know with all her heart that he was the one person who made her want to live forever, as long as every day was spent by his side.

CHAPTER 16

Emmanuel was right. As soon as they hit the ground inside the cave and took a few steps forward, a dim light began to shine from around the corner.

Leah followed behind Gareth as they moved into the next hallway. It was quiet, too quiet. There were no demonic animals. There were no symbols—Nazi, or otherwise—carved into the earthen walls. It was also, Leah noticed, strangely clean. It looked as if the dirt under their feet had been swept, leaving the floor with a vaguely glossy sheen, as if a million feet had walked this path since the beginning of time and pounded the crude sediment into fine grains of sand.

Gareth walked slowly down the corridor. His head turned right and left, scanning for any sign of danger.

Leah's stomach clenched when he suddenly stopped, ripped a torch from the wall, and stepped back. "What the hell is that?"

She peered over his shoulder, and gasped. The light from the torch flickered and illuminated the tiny little faces of the tiny skulls implanted in the wall directly in front of them.

"Shrunken heads?" Leah mumbled.

She jumped a foot in the air when Emmanuel burst out in laughter behind her. Easing his body past the team of Tallent and Lowery, he walked to the wall. "They're rings."

Ramming his fingers into the dirt, he extracted one of the small silver artifacts from the wall.

Gareth whispered over his shoulder, "The Nazi's followed *The Hobbit*?"

Leah hugged him from behind. "Really. I don't mind the movie obsession you have, but maybe you should turn on The History Channel once in a while."

"History's boring," he grunted.

"This is from a man who spent thirty years of his life searching for the gates of Heaven."

Shrugging his shoulders, Gareth peered down at the ring in Emmanuel's hand. "These are the Ehrenrings," he said.

Leah came from behind Gareth. "The SS rings?"

Emmanuel nodded.

Turning to her confused hero, Leah let him in on the background, "These were called the Honour Rings."

"Officially," Emmanuel added. "Unofficially, they were called the Death's Head rings."

They stared at the thick silver band decorated with a skull sitting atop a pair of crossed bones reminiscent of the famous symbol that belonged to the pirates of the high seas. The skull was the traditional symbol of Himmler's SS men, Leah knew. It was the same symbol that many other military units had used in the past. It was meant to remind the soldier who wore it that he must be prepared at any time to give up his life for the cause.

Scattered around the band were the carvings of ancient runes. Leah took note of the two lightning bolts side by side, twins of the same one that Mary had found inside the small Athenian shop. Beside them was the Hagal rune, which stood for the faith that these sinister men had in their leaders and the ideals of their organization.

Gareth turned the ring between his fingers and stared at the back.

Leah spoke up, "What are those?"

Emmanuel looked down at the arrow symbols. "That's not a rune. The designer of the ring, Karl Wiligut, added that. It's supposed to be the symbols of salvation—the camaraderie of the brotherhood."

He pointed at the inside of the band where a small name had

been etched into the metal. "The ring was a personal gift from Himmler to his men. They would have to display extraordinary valor in battle, and also have a completely blemish-free record, in order to get one. If they stepped out of line and had to be disciplined, they'd have to give the ring back."

Gareth's lips twitched into a slight smile as he stared over at Leah. "Men wearing rings…kinda' girlie."

"I was gonna say," she replied. "So…what the heck are these things doing in here?"

Emmanuel explained, "When the soldiers died the rings were returned to Himmler, and he stored them inside the castle, like a little memorial to the fallen. Over fifteen thousand of them had been returned to him by the end of the War. He certainly didn't want the Allies getting their hands on his most sacred possessions, so when he knew the ultimate battle was lost he told one of his men—Heinz Macher, I think it was—to use explosives to blow up the castle and bury anything that was inside so that it wouldn't fall into the hands of the enemy. I suppose this cavern is the final resting place for all those things."

Leah interrupted, "The castle was blown up?"

"Only parts of it. The original castle was built in the early 1600's, but during Himmler's self-appointed reign of terror, he was really only obsessed with the North Tower…which is odd why that wasn't the first to be blown up."

"Why is that?"

"The North Tower was supposedly where Himmler held all the secret meetings with his so-called knights. I guess some really sick stuff happened in there. It was on March 31st, 1945, when Macher began his work, but only the southeast tower, the least important as far as Reich artifacts was concerned, was blown up; the rest of the complex remained pretty much unharmed. Some locals think that the Devil dwelled in the North Tower and saved it from destruction. Others think either Macher ran out of explosives, or was just too pompous to think that the Allies would actually win, so he scrapped the order."

"Demonic possession or a lazy employee? Chances are the simplest answer is the right on," Leah remarked.

Emmanuel's smile grew wide. "These rings aren't the only thing they blast-sealed inside this cave."

Gareth slipped the Death's Head jewel into his pocket, as they followed behind the now quick-moving man. As they turned the corner, Leah had to shield her eyes. The torchlight became blistering as it illuminated the vast piles of gold and silver—a cache worth millions—that was scattered across the floor.

"Wow," she gasped.

"Yeah." Emmanuel nodded. "They had a stronghold, a kind of medieval treasure chamber to keep for their Order's use. Apparently, Himmler wanted to make darn sure that the Allies didn't get their hands on any of his wealth."

"Maybe he thought he'd survive and come back to claim it," Gareth said.

Fear rose in Leah's throat. "Are you sure these aren't the items that the Silver Scroll I found talked about? Maybe this is Daniel Bauer's loot that he stole from underneath Jericho."

Emmanuel shook his head in disagreement. "Can't be. The symbols and the workmanship don't match. Any item that the Silver Scroll would've alluded to would be thousands of years old. The oldest piece we found in here was this." Reaching into the pile, he pulled out a small brass frame with a bronze etching inside.

Leah took the miniature work of art from Emmanuel's hands. She could barely make out the face that'd been carved into the background of a barren crypt.

She studied it carefully. A shaft of light came from a small window located at the top of the image. Within the shaft of light was a dark sinister shadow that resembled the figure of a man who was not supposed to be there. The eyes of a kind, masculine face were drawn on the rock wall of the tomb, as if watching the thief enter. It seemed like the figure was just waiting for his chance to emerge from the rock and smite the grave-robber where he stood.

Leah stared into the all-knowing eyes. A familiar feeling washed over her, but she couldn't put her finger on what it was. Placing the artwork back on the floor, she stared over at Gareth who was rifling through the piles of treasure.

Straightening up, he wore a look of utter disgust and anger.

"Himmler's *fortunes* of war," he seethed, holding up a glass jar.

Leah peered at the small nuggets of gold. "What are they?"

"Fillings ripped from teeth," he spat. "Souvenirs."

Emmanuel blanched. "From the people taken to the concentration camps?"

Leah's stomach revolted. "Jesus." She looked over at Emmanuel, trying to erase the images from her mind. "What else is in here?"

He shook his head. "We didn't go any further. Once we saw the treasure, we thought it best to get the hell out of here and call you guys."

"Why us? Why not have the University, or UNESCO excavate all this?"

He tore his gaze from the revolting jar of human remains. "Like I said, once the castle was taken over and the banners started to fly, I had a feeling this all had something to do with your friend Bauer. Wouldn't want to get any authority figures involved until we know what he's up to."

Gareth set down the repulsive jar and made the sign of the cross with his fingers, silently offering the victims of the horrible massacre a peaceful rest.

Without a word, he took hold of the torch and turned another corner. It seemed like the tunnel went on forever. After the treasure trove, there was simply nothing but rock and dirt from then on as they traveled the twisted path.

Leah could feel her panic start to subside. There was nothing she could see that remotely spoke of Daniel Bauer, or his presence in the frightening castle that loomed above the town. Maybe they'd been wrong. Besides the fact that they'd run across artifacts from a vile time in human history, there was nothing that shouted to her that a demon now occupied the land. Maybe a relative of Himmler's *had* come back to claim the castle and fly the blue and yellow banners just to make people angry. Maybe whoever it was thought it would be funny to put a little bit of unease back into the community at large. Maybe...

A deep, guttural scream came from Gareth and Leah raced down the tunnel to catch up with him. Her heart pounded inside her chest, as she prayed for him to be all in one piece when she got there.

The finely-sifted sand under her boots made her slip and slide around the corner. Her breath locked in her throat, and her dormant fear came alive once again as she inhaled the sickening stench of human blood.

CHAPTER 17

The huge swastika adorned each wall; four identical tapestries hung from floor to ceiling, completely suffocating the room with the wretched insignia and all the horror it stood for.

Leah put a hand over her nose and breathed through her mouth, focusing on the twelve empty chairs circling the large round table. The top of each armchair had a sterling silver nameplate announcing its owner and, on the back of each, was a royal family's coat of arms.

She stared at the center of the table where a huge gold bowl held a severed head swimming in a pool of blood. The skin was all but gone, and the eye sockets were empty. But the mouth remained open, as if its owner was caught in an unheard and never-ending scream for help.

Leah tried to block out the sounds of Emmanuel's retching.

Gareth turned her by the shoulders and stared into her eyes, completely dismissing the horrific scene. "You read about Hitler. What's all this?"

Leah shrugged.

Taking her hand, Gareth pulled her out of the room and back into the empty hallway. He rubbed Emmanuel on the back. "Someone apparently set that up just to welcome us here."

"That's one of the rites I told you about. The Odinic Rite, but more…"

"Graphic," Gareth finished. "A little performance art to make sure that anyone who might stumble across this scene would leave in a hurry."

"Why put it here?" Leah barely heard her own voice in her ears. "Wouldn't you put it before the room filled with treasure so people would run before they could get their hands on it?"

Emmanuel nodded. "That room was obviously here way before Himmler told Macher to blast-seal the cave. Obviously this was another thing Himmler didn't want the Allies to see. I told you he was into the whole 'knightly order.' Seems he even had his own Round Table built."

Emmanuel's face remained white as a sheet. "Remember those rumors that I said couldn't possibly be true? I guess they were true." He bent over at the waist and took a deep breath. "It's probably one of those sacrificial victims to Odin, or…"

"Or?"

"It's been said that Himmler used to have ceremonies with his own knights. They would have a candlelit procession into a spiritual area, where Himmler would then place a severed head of one of his own SS officers in the middle of the table."

"I thought he liked them?"

"He did. But if one died or got killed in battle, he'd have their bodies brought back and use the severed head to…communicate with the ascended masters."

"Oh, this guy just keeps getting better and better," Gareth remarked.

"You don't know the half of it." Emmanuel swallowed hard. "Kathryn ran across some old diaries of an SS officer at the University. He talked about how Himmler wanted only the best children for his Aryan race. And…he believed that if babies were conceived in cemeteries they would inherit the spirits of the people who'd passed on before. So he gave out a list of cemeteries that were good…breeding grounds."

Leah gasped.

Emmanuel shrugged. "Remember…these are all just rumors and hearsay."

Leah tried to block out the picture of the hideous room behind them. "Not anymore."

Gareth's voice grew louder, "Look, let's think of this as just what I said, a performance. Because that's what it really is. Someone staged this whole thing just to scare us away. We have to remember... Himmler and all his icky little friends are long gone. They haven't sat in those chairs for ages."

"Gareth." Leah's voice came out like a whisper, "The smell is pungent; the blood in that bowl is fresh. There's no way it's some leftover sacrifice Himmler used and someone else just set up. That head was…lost recently."

She tried not to be sick. Staring into the dark corner across from the ugly room, Leah squinted. There, sitting on the ground, was a small plate and cup. As she focused, Leah also saw a thin, ripped blanket lying beside the rotted meal, and the manacles imbedded in the rock above. It. Her mind clicked into gear and she struggled to swallow her scream. Someone had been held just recently in this awful place. Chained to the wall like a dog, the person would have had no choice but to stare at the horrific sight across the hall. "Fresh blood," she whispered.

Gareth looked over at her. He shook his head, as if trying to clear his mind of her truthful assumption. "Hitler was in on all this stuff too, I suppose. Where's *his* chair? Shouldn't it be made of gold and bigger than the others? He was, after all, the top scum."

Emmanuel stared at him. "Remember? I told you. There's no proof Hitler had anything to do with these ceremonies; there's no proof that he went anywhere near this castle."

Her mouth was dry; her head was spinning. "Could the man who most people still see as the sickest being of all time, actually have disliked his second in command?"

"Maybe he thought the guy was spending all his time playing demonic little games in his castle instead of working in the real world to save the Reich," Gareth surmised.

"*Heinrich Himmler was the perfect soldier!*"

With the sudden scream came the strong arm wrapping around Leah's waist and forcing her to turn around.

Daniel Bauer smiled at her surprised face. "Too bad he was also an idiot."

Gareth lunged at the strong man holding Leah in his grip. She felt her legs disappear from underneath her. As darkness took over Leah's vision, the last thing she saw were two silver lightning bolts side-by-side…heralding the bastard's second major victory.

CHAPTER 18

The blond German beer must've finally hit, Leah thought to herself. Her head felt like it weighed a hundred pounds, and strange images wavered in front of her eyes like an old, fuzzy movie reel being played over and over again.

She squeezed her eyes shut and then reopened them to the dimly lit room. As the world came into focus, Leah stared at the mural of a huge mountain towering over bleached white palace walls. Atop the huge hill sat a man with a crown of oak leaves resting on his head. In his hand was a gold scepter, and on his face was the smug smile of a man who had nothing left to achieve.

A strange looking merman stood beside him; his golden trident was raised high in the air. A woman with the eyes of a snake stood on the other side of the king, laughing. Her face would've been beautiful if not for the forked tongue protruding through her bright red lips. Her fangs seemed to reach out from the image, ready to send her venom spewing through the next unsuspecting victim who chose to climb the hill and invade their space.

"It's Mount Olympus."

Leah wanted to run from the voice, but the inside of her felt like jelly. She couldn't even turn her neck to see the familiar man, so she flicked her eyes to the comforting figure standing next to Poseidon in the portrait. It was the Hero's Companion. Athena stood there with her spear in hand and her trusty shield standing between danger and the mortals she chose to protect.

"The palace at the bottom of the hill belongs to King Minos. He was a son of Zeus and ruled over Crete."

Leah's throat was painfully dry and the words cracked through her lips. "I'm a librarian, asshole. I already know this. If you want to tell me a bedtime story, try 'Cinderella'. I've never heard that one before."

Daniel Bauer sent a small laugh into the room that made Leah's skin crawl. Hearing his footsteps walk toward the huge bed, she almost vomited when his figure finally appeared in her line of sight. Offering her a wide smile, he took a seat on the lovely settee located underneath the immaculate mural.

Daniel leaned forward and rested his elbows on his knees. "It *is* good to see you again. I told you that we weren't through with each other. I've truly missed you, Leah."

Raising her hand, she pointed to the large Grecian urn sitting on the table beside her captor. "Can you hand me that?"

"Why?"

"You make me want to puke and I don't wanna mess up the bed."

Daniel leaned back against the teal velvet cushions and folded his arms across his chest.

Leah closed her eyes. She had no desire to see the light brown hair and the golden-brown eyes of the Australian who haunted her life.

"I always think about the day we met; you, appearing at the top of the staircase of Herod's palace and falling into my arms."

"On second thought, I might need two urns," Leah mumbled into the pillow.

He chuckled. "Apparently, you don't remember our fortuitous meeting as fondly as I do."

"You're disgusting."

His smile never wavered. Leah used all her strength to roll her body over on the bed and prop her head up on the pillows. The ceiling above was just as amazing as the walls. Painted above her was a huge sun attempting to shed its light and warmth in the cold, drafty room. She scanned further, noticing the teal furnishings, oak armoire, and a set of strange looking chairs. Leah strained to open the card catalogue, trying to come back from whatever drug he'd injected into her veins. "Klimos," she whispered.

"That's right!" Daniel clapped his hands. "Fifth century! The Greek designers made the delicate back and legs just for women. Gentle curves so that they could sit more comfortably."

"You missed your calling," Leah sneered. "You should work at Home Depot."

Decorative objects, like incense burners and copper vases littered the tabletops. Leah's gaze met the large window to the outside world, and she could clearly see a blue and yellow banner flapping in the wind. "So you're Himmler's relation who stole this castle back from the district?"

"Stole?" He clucked his tongue inside his cheek. "No. No. It's completely legal, I assure you."

"So...what? You his grandson?"

"Sort of." Daniel smiled. "I was, shall we say, adopted into the family genes."

Leah raised her hand in the air. "Don't care. Forget I asked. I've heard enough about Himmler's genes to last me a lifetime."

"You don't think I agree with him, do you?"

"Well...he's been dead since '45, yet, in your cave, there's fresh blood. Are you telling me that's been sitting down there since the War ended?"

"Leah." Daniel's eyes beamed with pride. "I can't tell you how much I just love having you around. Smart as a whip, aye? And they say all Americans are fools."

She bristled at the happy-go-lucky accent. "A German Australian...interesting."

"I was raised down under, luv. That was one thing I never lied to you about. I only found out about my real family tree a little over a year ago when my father suddenly passed away. Although I don't agree with the mystical methodologies of the Reich, I certainly understand how someone would want a better race of people running the world. Besides," he said, with a wink, "this castle is very cool."

"Chicks dig cars, Bauer, not castles," she snorted. "If you were one of us rude Americans, you'd know that already."

Leah tried not to jump out of her skin when he stood from the small couch and moved quickly to the foot of her bed. Escape was everything. She wondered how fast she could get to the incense burner and cold-cock the insolent little shit. Attempting to flex her muscles, Leah tested her knees, but it was no use. The drug-induced numbness still had a stranglehold on her body. She groaned.

Daniel's brows furrowed on his forehead. "I'm sorry about the drugs. I certainly don't want to hurt you, but when you woke up you started throwing things at me, so my advisers thought it would be better if you remained calm."

"How long have I been here?"

"We got you and your friends out of the cave a couple of days ago."

"Where's Emmanuel?" The questions tore from her throat, as her mind slowly began to clear.

"The young man was taken back to his University. He'll be watched…until this is over."

Leah felt the fire burn in her soul. "You hurt him and I'll kill you. He's going to be a father."

Daniel's eyes lit up. "How nice for him. And how is your dear old dad?"

Leah cringed. It was too much. Not only did she have to put up with her father's lies and try to sort through the added family members that she'd known nothing about, but she also had to share her humiliation with a scumbag like Bauer. There was nothing worse than an enemy knowing your weaknesses. "He's fine. Thanks so much for asking."

"Off looking for your mother, I presume?"

Leah stared into the wide brown eyes. "You could just tell me where she is and save me the time and effort of beating it out of you. On second thought," Leah continued, "I wouldn't want to deny Gareth the pleasure of making you scream like a little girl."

Daniel kept his gaze leveled at her, like an assassin setting up the perfect shot. "What makes you think I didn't just come out of Eden and kill her? I knew you had the emerald so she would've been no use to me after that."

Leah snorted. "You'd never give up a bargaining chip."

"I have Lowery."

Leah shook her head. "No, you don't. You may have him locked away somewhere in this fortified mansion of yours, but you'll let him out."

Bauer sat back against the iron bedpost. "Why on earth would I do that?"

Leah rolled her eyes. "Because I won't help you find whatever it is you want me to find without him. We work as a team or we don't work at all."

"I don't need you to find anything for me. Just give me the emerald and we're square," he said quickly.

Too quickly, Leah thought. "Not a chance. Try this one on for size, Bauer—a trade. I want Athena's weapons back and you can have the stupid rock. Only then will we be square."

He smiled wide. "Leah…Leah…I am truly ashamed of you."

"That breaks my heart."

"You're only worried about some silly ancient weapons?" Tilting his head to the side, Daniel stared at her with mock confusion. "Does that mean if she does still exist I have your permission to kill your mother?"

Leah swallowed hard when his grin turned into a demonic smile.

"Because if I do…I'll make you watch."

CHAPTER 19

Leah's voice sounded cold and heartless in her own ears, but she certainly didn't want to give the bastard any more leverage than he already had. "My mother's in Connecticut, Daniel. I have no interest in some woman who abandoned me for something as stupid as a piece of jewelry. I took Athena's weapons and I need to give them back. That's what I want."

His laughter roared through Leah's ears. She knew it was real, as she watched the tears of joy flow from the corners of his eyes. Confusion danced in tandem with the drug and jumbled her senses even more.

"I don't believe it!" Daniel slapped his knee. "You have *no* idea what that emerald is, do you?"

Leah's skin grew cold, as she glanced down at the sapphire eye that clearly marked her as a protector. "Probably some sick and twisted Nazi thing. I could care less. Free Gareth and give me Athena's weapons. I'll give you the emerald and get the hell out of your way. You wanna' take over the world? Knock yourself out. Your ancestors were a bunch of weak-minded jerks that couldn't do the job and you will follow right in their pathetic footsteps."

He remained silent.

"You don't get it do you, Bauer?" She sighed heavily. "There have been people like you for thousands of years, and there will be people like you long after you're dead and buried. You want to be a king? There are still some fruit-loops in the world who'll follow you, I'm sure, so go find them. Gather at the Round Table, light some candles, drink some blood. Vampires are all the rage now, so you'll fit right in. I've got better things to worry about."

She continued; her skin boiling with rage, "You want to create a perfect race? Be referred to as Herr Bauer? You want blonde-headed knockouts? I suggest you try and recruit Kiefer Sutherland—hot guys like him, because if you start with uggos like yourself you'll just be wasting your time."

Bauer crossed his arms over his chest once again and stared at her like she was some kind of alien being. "You know, there have been studies done, and pretty much everyone in the world is a bigot of some sort, Leah. Hatred is not only acceptable, it's become downright normal. Everyone blames some race or nationality of people for their troubles."

"Funny," Leah remarked. "I only blame you."

Daniel leaned forward. "No. Really. Think about it, Leah. I guarantee even *you* will find a bigoted bone in that fantastic body of yours."

The strength of her convictions, her anger and her faith, blazed down her spine. She sat up straight in the bed and glared at him. "I do hate. I'm not perfect. And I'll tell you what I hate, Bauer. Ignorance. Whether someone's skin color is red, black, white or yellow, I don't care. Dumb is dumb. And that will always be unacceptable!"

The door flew open and a young, tall woman with bright blonde hair entered the room carrying a sterling silver tray in her hands. The Nordic beauty offered a stunning smile to Daniel and handed Leah a steaming hot mug.

"Mr. Bauer told me you love coffee and I was to bring you some immediately. I hope you enjoy it." The woman's eyes turned to blue ice inside their wrinkle-free homes. "I made it myself."

Leah offered her a wary smile, as she accepted the offering and brought it to her lips. She stared at Bauer before drinking.

"There's nothing in it, Leah." He smiled. "If you aren't going to fight me, there's no reason to keep you in a vegetative state. Besides, you're much more interesting when you're awake."

Leah took a sip and immediately spit it across the lovely teal bedspread. "Jesus, this is awful!"

Daniel took the cup from her and gulped the remains. "No. Just strong."

"Strong? It's mud."

"I'm so sorry, Miss," the woman offered a tepid apology.

Leah watched her clear baby blues stare at Daniel like he was a rock star. The yearning for him—the sheer happiness in her face as he complimented her coffee-making skills—was overwhelmingly sickening. "Were you ever a stewardess?"

The woman glowered at Leah. "Flight attendant, actually."

"Figures," Leah rolled her eyes. "You people never do like me."

Standing from the bed, Daniel walked to the door, followed closely by the curvaceous waitress. "Come down to the dining room as soon as you feel up to it. I'll give you a tour of my ancestral home."

"Where are my things?"

Daniel pointed to the armoire. "A leather jacket that's seen better days, to say the least; a pair of muddy leather boots, a wallet, a child's stuffed animal, and a handful of runes. However, no emerald."

"Do you really think I'm stupid enough to carry it with me?"

He smiled. "It wasn't at the University either. In fact, my people didn't even catch a glimpse of it in Athens."

Leah raised an eyebrow. "So the men in the silly looking suits do work for you. I figured. God, you are so easy to read that it's almost ridiculous."

A look of rage flashed across his face, distorting the calm exterior. "Trust me, Leah. After talking with you this morning, I can assure you there are surprises coming your way that not even *you* could imagine."

Slamming the door behind him, Leah heard Bauer whistle happily as he walked down the unknown hall.

She raised herself slowly off the bed and limped to the armoire. Opening the doors, she stared at the shabby contents and cradled the lamb in her arms. She squeezed the small animal against her chest and stared at her horrible, pale reflection in the mirror.

"I'm not the only one who'll be surprised."

CHAPTER 20

"Get Lowery," Leah demanded.

Daniel Bauer looked over at the man standing at attention in the corner of the massive dining room, before turning his gaze back to Leah.

She didn't blink. "I'm not a solo act, Bauer, I told you that. You want something from me, then you better go get him. Gareth is not a bargaining chip. He dies, I die with him, case closed. That's the way it works. If you don't bring Gareth in here, we're done. You should understand by now that I have no fear of death. I've seen Heaven, and I'm just fine with it."

Taking a deep breath that turned into a heavy sigh, Daniel finally nodded at the guard.

The man in black followed the silent order and marched out of the room. Daniel leaned against the straight-backed chair. "It's a shame. I so enjoy our alone time together."

Leah swiveled her head to stare behind her, and he followed her sudden movement. "What?" he asked.

"Just looking for another urn," she sneered.

Gareth's body burst through the door like a bullet from the barrel of a gun, and he raced toward Leah.

She stood carefully, still unsure if her rubbery limbs would support her. Sweeping her up in his arms, he held her so tight that her lungs threatened to explode.

"Thank God you're okay," he whispered.

"Ditto," she replied, trying to disguise the tears of relief that threatened to escape.

Gareth let her go and jumped across the table. Taking hold of Daniel Bauer's neck with both hands, he began to squeeze.

Immediately a flock of black-garbed men rushed through the double doors, pistols at the ready, and Leah screamed. She raced around the table and took his shoulders. "Gareth…stop."

Her angry hero kept up the pressure.

"Gareth!" Leah shouted in his ear, pulling on his shirt. "We can't win. Not here. Not now!"

Releasing him, Daniel fell to his knees gasping for breath as faint bruises began to blossom on his flesh.

Leah couldn't even imagine the horrific things that Bauer was going to order his guards to do to Gareth. But to her complete amazement, he simply stood back up and took his seat. Resuming his relaxed stance, all Bauer did was call out for coffee in a slightly raspy voice.

Gareth looked as confused as Leah felt, as he sat down beside her, and stared across the table at the eerie man.

"It's okay." Daniel waved his hand in the air between them. "If there's one thing I believe about you, Mr. Lowery, it's that you absolutely love this woman enough to kill for her. And loyalty like that serves my purposes."

A guard walked forward carrying Gareth's weathered khaki knapsack in his hands, and threw it on the table. Daniel smiled. "I must say, you two certainly travel light. A few books, a few clothes, some old metal object covered in rust…but no emerald on Gareth either. What'd you do, bury it at Stonehenge?"

Gareth shook his head. "I still don't understand why you need it. You must've taken a cache of…what? A *zillion* dollars worth of silver and gold out of Eden? You even have Athena's weapons."

Daniel's brown eyes grew black.

Gareth continued, "What good is an emerald when you can already buy the entire world if you wanted to?"

"You know, I never believed in the Bible."

Leah was taken aback by the strange statement. It was getting clearer and clearer to her that Daniel Bauer was well on his way to losing his mind.

"Excuse me?" Gareth said quietly.

Daniel raised his head. "Before we found Eden I didn't really believe all the ridiculous stories about God, His Son, etcetera, but with the path I've walked these past few years, I can hardly deny that some of this stuff actually exists."

Leah felt her stomach churn.

"I mean…the keys to the gate—the *actual* gate into Heaven; the staff of Moses'; the Ark…you've certainly proved to me beyond a shadow of a doubt that these things are real. I wish I could've seen them all for myself."

"You've been following us all along," Leah whispered.

"Of course." He smiled. "I needed to see what you were going to do with that emerald."

"You knew all along where it was," Gareth seethed through his clenched teeth.

"Actually, no," Daniel replied. "My father found out where it'd been stashed by your mother, Leah. It took forever to get that information from her, but she finally gave up the game. I guess that's when she resigned herself to the fact that she would become a permanent fixture in my father's life. After all, she'd already willingly become his lover after my mother passed away."

He stared at Leah. "Not going to scream at me for spoiling your illusions of a poor woman locked away in a dungeon by a mean old Nazi?"

Leah shrugged. "You're talking about a stranger."

He leaned his elbows on the table. "In this past year she and I have gotten to know each other very well. Your mother would read the runes and tell me about her children. She'd go on and on about the destinies that her offspring would have."

"You've spent time with her?" Leah felt the odd shot of jealousy erupt in her soul as she thought about her own mother throwing her to the wind, yet building a friendship with a psychopath.

He nodded. "My father held her for a very long time. When he passed away, I was given all the data of my very own destiny. She was nice to me, until she understood that I would carry out my father's wishes for her and continue his quest to find the missing emerald. Of course, he had no idea before he died that I'd already found you…and the gem." Daniel looked down at the marble table. "Shame. He would've been so proud that I accomplished something on my own."

Leah watched the slight shake of Daniel's head, as if he was banishing the thought from his mind. "Anyway, your mother and I bonded. I had to be careful, though. Neith was very smart. She reminded me of you, Leah."

"Neith?"

He nodded. "It's Egyptian for 'Divine Mother'. Funny, isn't it? She wasn't exactly divine to you. Hell, she wasn't even a mother."

Leah rolled her eyes. Struggling to keep her face passive and unreadable, she wanted to make sure that all her adversary would see was her complete boredom with the subject.

But the glint remained in Daniel's eyes, as he continued, "Like my father, she believed in the Odinic faith. She felt the gods were much closer to the truth than just the one that Christianity favored. She—like Himmler, actually—felt that we should honor the deities and their ancestors by having festivities, celebrations… even sacrifices. She's certainly not innocent in all this."

Leah tried not to give him the satisfaction of wincing at his words. She couldn't believe that she came from the flesh and blood of a woman who may have once sat around the table in that hideous cave and talked to a severed head.

Gareth spoke, "The Odinic Rites aren't what you've described, Bauer. Your…*people* just decided to make them as twisted as the rest of their ideas were."

Daniel gave a slight nod of his head. "Perhaps. I don't believe in purifying the world, believe it or not. I don't care who's in it as long as I get what I want."

"What's with all the banners then? What's with the new men in the old black and silver SS uniforms running around your castle? The swastika on your hand?" Leah questioned. "To me, it looks a whole lot like you're resurrecting their twisted ways."

"And you'd be wrong." Daniel sat back and grinned. "My advisers just want to keep some of the symbolism around that they grew up with. That's fine with me. They're older…stuck in the past; they can't see the big picture."

"And, that is?"

"Give me the emerald and I'll show you."

Leah saw the blatant need gleaming in his eyes, and shook her head. "What is it? Why follow that thing to the ends of the earth and back? Obviously my mother removed it from Cleopatra's mines a long time ago. It had to have *something* to do with King Herod, seeing as that it was hidden a hop, skip and a jump away from his disgusting palace. You can't possibly think that if you wear it on your head you'll become a king?"

Daniel winked. "Almost."

The Nordic blonde appeared in the room and placed the tray of coffee down before Leah. As the silver mugs rattled with the force of her annoyance, Leah looked up to witness the woman swiveling her neck back and forth between her employer and Leah's startlingly handsome mate, as if she'd died and gone to a heaven of hotness. "I don't *believe* this," Leah mumbled.

Gareth broke away from Daniel's gaze and looked over at her. "What?"

"Forget it." Reaching out, Leah poured as much milk as possible into the cup, attempting to dilute the wicked strong concoction. Taking a sip, she slammed the cup back down on the marble table. "You know? It's not like I'm asking for a soufflé, or pheasant under glass, or something difficult. The recipe is water poured over freakin' beans!"

Gareth attempted not to smile, as Daniel suddenly stood up and began to walk from the room. "I think it's time to give you a guided tour of my magnificent home," he said. Looking back at the hovering waitress, he offered her a sultry smile. "We'll all be dining in here in about an hour, my dear. Please have everything set up."

"Of course," she purred.

Leah stood beside Gareth and groaned, "I need another urn."

CHAPTER 21

Leah didn't want to admit it, but the castle was more than slightly impressive. Daniel had led them up the long winding staircase, back to the floor of bedchambers where Leah had begun her stay.

"The senior officers of the SS practically lived in these rooms. Himmler, my adoptive grandfather, decided to decorate all the rooms separately. Each one honors different heroes to the German people."

He threw open a door, and Leah looked at the huge bookcases stacked end to end. The murals on the walls depicted a familiar silver sword stuck in a huge stone. The red dragon banners hung proudly from the wide oak beams, and the well-known mystic who went by the name of Merlin, took up residence on the entire ceiling.

There was no way to scoff at the fantasy, thought Leah. She could remember the very real image of the legendary 'One and Twelve' standing together in the cave in Glastonbury. Being witness to that elite group had certainly proved to her that the legend had, in fact, been true.

Daniel closed that door and opened another further down the hall. "This was Himmler's chamber. It's dedicated to the Saxon King Heinrich the First. Himmler fancied himself a reincarnation of that mighty warrior who defended the Fatherland from the Eastern hordes."

The black and silver decorations gleamed. The multitude of

murals depicted warriors, broken and bloody on the battlefield.

"He used all period furnishings, and the bookshelves are full of documents and maps that his teams used to scour the globe for ancient artifacts."

Leah shook her head at the blatant signs of a twisted ego and stepped back into the hall. She turned away from Bauer's speech and stared at the painting hanging directly behind her. A mighty image hovered above a man lying flat on his back. The angel, whose face was strangely familiar to Leah, held a double-edged golden sword in his hand, and struck it down on top of the defeated human.

The victim was covered in black. His face was turned toward Leah, as if beseeching his artist to save him from the deadly fate. A dark crown lay twisted in the dying man's hand, and no matter how hard she tried, Leah couldn't seem to break her gaze from the slightly horrific sight.

Daniel came up behind her. "That was supposedly Adolf Hitler's favorite picture. The story goes that the Führer gave it to Himmler as a housewarming gift when the castle was completed. But according to a diary entry left behind by Himmler, upon gifting the art, Hitler told him to hang it upside down."

"So why didn't he?"

Daniel shrugged. "Couldn't tell you. Hitler never even came to this castle, as far as anyone knows. Maybe Himmler thought since his beloved Führer would never see it, why hang it upside down? Instead, he made sure to put it on this wall right outside his room, so that when he opened his door he could remember the generosity of his boss.

"Actually, the room you stayed in, Leah, was also an ode to Hitler. Supposedly the big guy wasn't into the stories of Odin and Norse mythology. He fancied Zeus and his Mount Olympus family much more. He sent team after team into Athens to find Athena's weapons, so it's quite a coup that I now own something even the almighty Führer couldn't attain."

"Get over it," she sneered. "When we go—and Gareth and I *will* go—those weapons will be coming with me."

"We'll see."

Gareth bumped Daniel away from Leah and took his place at

her side. "Moving on?" he growled.

Affixing the condescending smile to his face, Daniel led them to the end of the hall and pushed against a stone. A door opened up in the oak paneling, and he offered them a wink. "I've been over this castle with a fine-toothed comb looking for its secrets. It has many."

"You need a job." Leah sighed. "Too much time on your hands can make you go crazy."

He laughed. "Too late."

"My sentiments exactly," Gareth added.

Instead of walking up the small stone staircase found in the hidden chamber, Daniel waved his hand at them, calling them over to the large window. He pointed outside. "Do you see that small firehouse in the distance, and the water tower?"

Leah looked out and saw a small orange dome covering a tiny round building. "What's that?"

Daniel adjusted his focus. "That's just the security guard's station. There are stone steps in there that lead directly under us and back through the cave where you entered. This land is like its own little country, with all the roads leading in and out of Wewelsburg Castle.

"You see, this was originally planned as a city—an SS city where this castle would be the focal point. The grounds would be in the shape of a triangle, like an arrowhead, and the castle would be surrounded by houses, offices—even an airstrip and freeway access were planned for the Reich's soldiers and their families. They were going to flood the entire valley and wipe out the surrounding villages." He smiled wide, as if picturing the location of a lifetime. "What a complex it would've been," his voice turned dreamy. "Siegfried Taubert, Himmler's personal architect, was going to create the whole thing and call it 'The Center of the World.'"

Leah snickered. "He'd probably heard that Disney already called dibs on 'The Happiest Place on Earth.' "

Gareth pulled her closer to his side, and peered through the window into the forest. Leah followed his gaze and finally found the small red firehouse in the distance. "So…what is that?"

Bauer turned around and offered the most joyful look Leah had ever seen. "That's what remains of the concentration camp. Over three thousand people went in there and more than twelve hundred died; at least, those are the ones we know about. Two-by-two, they were led into the gas chamber."

Leah shivered, remembering the picture from the movie she'd played in the basement of her beloved library.

"Let's move on, shall we?"

Daniel bounded up the small stone steps that led deep inside the castle walls, as if he was nothing but a boy at play and not a captor who wished to keep an eye on his prey. Leah and Gareth quickly turned, but were met with a guard dressed in black, his pistol aimed at their heads.

Gareth whispered, "You heard the man. Let's move on."

"Do you have any idea what this crackpot is waiting for?"

"None," Gareth replied. "I woke up in some kind of dungeon. I figured someone would just show up and shoot me, but then they came in, gave me back my clothes—all cleaned and pressed—and brought me to you without a punch thrown."

"What the hell kind of game is he playing? And what does that *stupid* emerald have to do with it?"

"I swear," Gareth grumbled. "I'll never buy you jewelry again."

Leah stared into the only emeralds she ever wanted anywhere near her. As if an eclipse was taking place before her eyes, darkness clouded the intense color and she watched as Gareth suddenly resembled a man who was drowning in despair.

"What is it?"

"When I was in the dungeon I could've sworn I heard a woman crying. I thought it was you, Leah. I was petrified. I called out your name and the crying stopped, but you'd been in a bedroom up here all along."

Leah nodded. "That's where I was when I came to."

Gareth sighed. "Leah, I think your mother's here. I don't care what he's playing at, or what little innuendos he makes, I think she's still very much alive."

The guard stepped forward. "Get moving!"

Leah turned quickly, and Gareth followed her up the small staircase. Step by step they twisted and turned inside the castle walls, up and up, far above the dungeons that lurked somewhere beneath the evil home.

Dungeons, Leah thought, *that may just hold a woman by the name of Neith who she was destined to meet.*

CHAPTER 22

The symbol was enormous. It took up half the floor, like a huge spider sleeping in the center of the rock waiting patiently for its next unsuspecting victim to arrive.

Daniel gave a big smile and waved them inside. "You're now standing in the infamous North Tower. This room was called the Obergruppenführersaal. It basically means that this was the hall of the highest ranking SS generals. This is where the Round Table sat—the meeting place for the twelve heads." He smiled at his sick little joke. "They and Himmler would come here to discuss vital issues to the Reich."

High windows climbed up the tower. Twelve tall chairs came out of the rock pillars set against the wall, allowing all generals who sat down a bird's eye view of the dark shadow in the center of the floor. Leah also noticed the large chandelier hanging above her head with candles burning in twelve holders around a cast iron circle.

As she stepped forward to study the design imbedded in the gray marble floor, Daniel followed. "It's a Sonnenrad. People renamed it the Black Sun over time. You see, it's actually a dark green sun wheel; the axis is solid gold. It represents the World Empire of Germany."

"It's a swastika," Gareth corrected him. "An elegant one, yes, but a dirty swastika just the same."

Daniel looked up at him. "It's a symbol of Odin. However, this particular sun wheel was designed to match the SS victory runes because Wiligut wanted it that way."

"I thought you said Taubert designed the castle?" Leah asked.

"Wiligut was also very…ingrained in the Order. He was the designer of many things besides the Death's Head rings."

"Jack of all trades." Leah looked at Gareth. "Nice to have a skill to fall back on if being an elite, sadomasochistic freak doesn't work out for you."

For the second time, Leah could see the blood of anger and frustration turn Daniel's face a reddish hue. She grinned. "Something wrong?"

"You shouldn't make comments about things you don't understand." He turned around. "I think you're ready for the crypt now."

"Jeez," Leah said. "Take it personally, why don't you?"

Storming out of the room, Daniel headed back down the staircase.

Leah began to follow as Gareth caught her elbow, "Why are you egging him on? The guy's nuts."

"I'm getting to him. I don't even know how, but I'm getting to him. He's not unbeatable, Gareth, and he's certainly not some reincarnated god. Bauer's just a plain old mortal like the rest of us. All I have to do is push the right buttons and he's gonna spill his story. He's dying to tell us what he's got planned."

"And then we'll know," Gareth whispered.

"And then we'll know."

"Be careful."

* * *

The crypt…

All she saw was the chair placed in the middle of a sunken circle at the center of the room; the mammoth work of art was staggeringly frightening because of its size. It was far too fancy to be a chair of torture; it was rather a chair created for a ruler. Directly above it, looming like a vicious bird of prey ready to swoop down on the occupant and rip flesh from bone, was a golden emblem. There it hung; the most infamous image known the world over as

Hitler's swastika.

Leah's mind could only refer to it that way. She'd seen the mark displayed proudly by other cultures over time, including being stamped on Athena's weapons. But that was centuries before the Führer came along and turned it into something based on the worst, most demonic traits mankind could possess. And the gold symbol was definitely looked after, polished to a brilliant shine by someone who truly loved it and took care of it day after day.

Below the chair, set into the center of a gray marble circle, was a small blue pipe that was barely noticeable. But the sight sent Leah's heart rate into overdrive. She wondered if it was a device that would soon deliver the same deadly gas the Reich had used to kill millions. Perhaps here and now *was* the end…the moment that would turn her and Gareth into permanent residents of the castle of death.

Daniel stepped down into the sunken circle in the center of the floor and ran his hands lovingly over the mighty chair. He pointed at the central carving. "The 'H.H.' etched here is self-explanatory. This is only one of twelve chairs that were being made for Heinrich Himmler. Four were presented to him by the loyal staff and soldiers of the SS—the valiant Stormtroopers who guarded the Führer and his second in command with their lives. Karl Wiligut was, of course, the designer."

"There's that name again," Gareth whispered.

"I wonder if Himmler had a t-shirt that read; 'Adolf conquered the world and all I got was this lousy chair.' " Leah laughed, as the sarcasm once again hit her intended mark.

The fire of hate flashed in Daniel's eyes.

Gareth went along with her. "It doesn't even have a velvet cushion. Sitting on it must've been a real pain in the ass."

Leah snickered.

Daniel took a deep breath, clearly trying to ignore their taunting, and looked back at the chair. He ran his fingers down the left hand side. "As you can see, the victory runes of the SS are prevalent in the design. Then comes the swastika." He pointed lower. "This next one is the Hagel rune, which is quite interesting because it means; 'I destroy.'"

"That's original." Gareth exhaled, trying to sound as bored as humanly possible with the tour. "Not very creative blokes, were they?"

Without looking up, Daniel continued, "Then comes the rune of the Life of Man. You'll note the lifted arms of the man, signifying his birth into the world. The Rod rune is the strength of the male species. It's what truly makes a man, a man."

"I thought that was football." Leah smiled.

Daniel's voice sped up, "We then see the World Tree, which was also known as the Yggdrasil; it connects Heaven, Hell and Earth together."

Gareth whispered in Leah's ear, "That's the tree Odin hung from."

Leah nodded. She didn't like the room; it was very disconcerting. Their voices seemed to be swallowed up by the walls the minute the words exited their mouths. It didn't echo like a stone chamber should have; instead, it seemed to suck their souls from their bodies as they stood underneath the evil eye of the golden swastika.

Daniel kept stroking the huge, finely-carved chair. "And this is the Ring, or the Odel, which represents the strength and unity of life. The wood is oak; the seat is meticulously made with cross-caning rattan; and, the oak leaves you see on all the legs represent the crown."

Daniel's eyes grew black. "The crown that holds it all; the crown that will someday be worn by the one who is most deserving of the title."

Leah felt her heart race out of control at his words. She could tell his secrets were slowly coming to light. Lifting her hands, she began to clap. "That was a lovely presentation. I am telling you, you missed your calling. You would make a hell of an assistant manager at a furniture store in like a week." She snapped her fingers and Gareth chuckled beside her.

Daniel looked into her eyes with such hatred that Leah felt her body wither a bit underneath his contempt. She leaned against Gareth for support, as Bauer stepped forward.

"This is Himmler's crypt. Respect should be given. He believed that this would be his Valhalla when he died. As you can see, there are twelve seats in here as well. The SS elite would gather in this glorious space to pray. When one fell at the hands of the enemy, they would be placed inside this circle so that others could sit and pay homage to their lost comrade. I placed this particular chair in here myself, so I could sit and be a part of the mystical power this room still contains."

Gareth pointed at the floor. "What's the little blue pipe for?"

Leah leaned into him. "He wants to sit in some dead guy's chair and commune with the souls of Nazis? I'm gonna go for broke and say the little blue pipe delivers the happy juice that Mr. Freak-o has been sucking on for a while now."

Daniel smiled wide. His teeth were straight and white. So highly polished, in fact, that they seemed to possess an almost supernatural glow, like an obsessive compulsive vampire who'd been taught to brush religiously after every bloody meal. "Actually...Himmler was going to eventually add an eternal flame. The gas pipe was installed for that purpose only."

"Somehow I don't believe you," Leah said.

Walking forward, Bauer stopped an inch away from Leah's face. Gareth squeezed her arm, reminding her that he was by her side. She could feel him clench his fist, ready to strike their captor if he so much as sneezed on her hair.

But Daniel just winked. "Well...the pipe does actually have another purpose now."

"And that is?"

Bauer clapped his hands together so hard that Leah nearly jumped out of her skin. Head down, he checked the golden watch on his wrist. "Look at the time! We must go down to dinner so I can introduce you to my most trusted advisers. I've been monopolizing your time, dear Leah. Forgive me."

Taking one last look at the monumental chair holding court in the deep well carved into the rock, Leah's mind shot out a question. "Wait...the crypt and the meeting room. There are only two rooms in this whole tower?"

"No." Daniel grinned. "There are dungeons below that were actually used during witch trials long ago. Here, in Germany, they had to deal with the violence of their women when Satan took over their souls. They even built a courtroom down below to serve judgment." He smiled wide. "It's right beside the inquisition area where they beat the possessed ladies until the Devil released his hold on them."

Leah shivered in Gareth's arms.

"Unfortunately, most didn't survive the beatings." Bauer shook his head, and leaned in closer to Leah. "That pesky Devil is sure hard to get rid of, aye?"

"Really? I didn't find it difficult at all."

CHAPTER 23

Leah should've been hungry. Her mouth should've watered at the sight of the dining room table covered with roasted chicken in garlic sauce, steaming potatoes with rich brown gravy, and the huge bowl of pasta adorned with dark, hand-churned butter melting over it like hot fudge over a mountain of vanilla ice cream. But all her empty stomach did was revolt against the intoxicating scents.

Walking quickly to the sideboard, Leah picked up a crystal decanter of brandy and poured herself a huge glass. Her mouth was so dry and her brain so rattled that the soothing burn of the liquid banished at least some of the horrible images from her mind.

Gareth followed suit.

"We have *got* to get out of this town," she said to him, attempting a smile. "A little longer and you're going to have an extreme alcoholic on your hands."

Gareth grinned. "Bottoms up!" He downed the contents of his own glass in seconds and reached for another. "No idea why this is so creepy. I mean, we stood face to face with the real bad guy once, but somehow Bauer's making him look like nothing more than a confused Sunday School teacher."

"Please be seated." Daniel sat down at the head of the table. "We're very informal here, so there's no need to change for dinner."

"You mean you're going to stay you?" Leah said. "How unfortunate." Sitting down beside Gareth, she took in the delicacies

137

surrounding them. "Wait. This isn't German food."

"God, no," Daniel responded, sticking out his tongue. "The only good thing made in Germany is beer. I prefer American dishes. Much easier on the palette."

Leah took another slug of brandy.

"You should really be careful, Leah." Daniel's eyes shone with worry. "The drugs that I gave you probably won't mix well with that."

"Don't you fret in the least," she replied. "After another grueling hour of your company I'll just throw it all back up anyway."

He sat back in his chair. "I don't know why you're so disgusted with me. We're really quite the same, you and me."

She turned to Gareth. "Let the puking commence!"

"No. Really," Daniel continued, "we're both part of the Divine knowledge. You ate the apple from the tree, too. You and I are the only two people on the face of the earth who have that kind of power flowing through our veins. If you really stopped and thought about it, we could pool our resources and own the entire world."

Gareth cleared his throat.

Daniel bowed his head. "Of course, you'd have to say goodbye to our wonderful Mr. Lowery, here."

"Can't," Leah said. "He may not look like much, but he's seriously fun at parties."

"And I have a few gold cards," Gareth added.

"Good point."

Daniel shook his head. "I have more money than anyone on this planet, Leah. You saw to that by leading me to the Silver Scroll."

"Rub it in why don't you," she grumbled.

Bauer's hand flew across the table like a striking cobra, and grabbed her fingers. "Join me on this next adventure."

Gareth rocketed from his chair, as the double doors suddenly flew open and three men walked into the dining room.

Daniel stood up, backing away from Gareth's clenched fist and enraged face. He walked across the floor to welcome the new guests into his humble home.

Leah watched the men huddle together like the Four Horsemen of the Apocalypse getting ready to ride. One was a short little man with blond hair that'd gone gray at the temples. His nose reminded her of a raven's beak. His beady little eyes were a drab, dull blue, like someone had injected pollutants into a once perfect sea. His eyebrows were thick and bushy, and just looking at him reminded Leah of a Christmas movie Gareth had made her watch. The small man was an exact duplicate of the gruff, grumpy mayor of Sombertown who wouldn't be happy until all the toys were taken out of the hands of the village children.

The man beside him was his exact opposite in every way; this one was tall and lean. The pair looked like Laurel and Hardy standing side by side. Leah could see the gaunt man's ribs protruding from under his starched white shirt, mirroring one of the concentration camp victims who'd starved to death under Himmler's eager eye. His head was the shape of an egg, and any hair he'd once had was long gone.

He shook Bauer's hand. It looked almost like he was concealing Mexican jumping beans under his skin; every muscle, every nerve he owned, seemed to be dancing. His cheeks went up and down and his eyes winked and blinked like a set of chaotic Christmas lights. His fingers curled and uncurled, like a man who couldn't seem to grab on to the elusive brass ring that hung just beyond his reach.

Leah tried not to gasp when she focused on the third man. His eyes were yellow, with narrow black slits for pupils. They were the exact replica of the cat's eyes from the beer hall. The man with the red-painted face was now standing before her unmasked. His eyebrows were plucked and shaped like he'd just stepped out of the salon to attend this illustrious dinner, and his suit was cleanly cut, clinging to his tall body like a second skin of silk. The bright white hair was pulled into a ponytail that hung down his back, resembling a cold, hard icicle that would burn the flesh if you stepped too close.

His eerie eyes focused on Leah, and a smile came to his face. "Didn't I tell you that you would soon see Valhalla?"

CHAPTER 24

"Michael Hansen." He stuck out his hand to Gareth. "It's a pleasure to meet you."

"Gareth Lowery," he responded, ignoring the outstretched offering. "And the pleasure is definitely all yours."

The man gave a courteous bow, and re-focused his attentions on Leah. "Did you enjoy your tour of this magnificent structure?"

"Oh, yeah. I'd put it right up there with an invasive colonoscopy for pure enjoyment factor."

He laughed and waved the short, stout man over to the table. "This is my friend, Karl Williams."

The man with a permanent frown offered a curt nod and sat down hard in his chair, as if wanting to torture and break his own body.

The long, lean walking skeleton was next. He twitched his way over to the table and stretched out his bony hand. "Mark Wolf."

Leah took her seat, and Gareth slowly sat back down beside her. She was grateful for his strong, warm arm resting on the back of her chair.

Gareth spoke first, "Wolf, Hansen and Williams…all very American names, fellas'. I'm a bit disappointed. You're kind of spoiling the whole German experience for me."

Daniel took his place at the head of the table. "You shouldn't be disappointed, Lowery. Like I said, we are all partial to facets of the American culture. You have freedom. Not to mention, very beautiful women." He nodded at Leah.

Her response was a belch so loud and rude that the nuns at the local Catholic School down the road would be raising their wooden paddles right now and searching for the culprit.

Daniel laughed. "Beautiful and funny."

"Women should know their place," Williams announced loud and clear.

"And that is?" Leah lifted an eyebrow.

Williams smiled. "That all depends on what the woman is best at." He leaned his elbows on the table. "What exactly are *you* best at, Miss Talent?"

"Oh, please." Leah was disgusted by his visible leer. "You probably haven't dated a woman since Jesus was a boy."

"Be fair, Leah." Gareth laughed. "You've got Twitchy, Kitty, Baldy and Crazy, right here in an ancient medieval castle. I frankly can't understand why the women aren't lined up outside the door for these guys."

Daniel cleared his throat, as Karl's bald head turned bright red at Gareth's sarcasm. "You have to forgive our guests, my friends. They've had a hard day and haven't yet been given the opportunity to punch my lights out."

Leah mumbled, as she lifted the brandy snifter and took a big sip, "Day ain't over yet, pal."

"Can I ask why we're joined together here today?" Gareth sighed. "Because this is really boring."

Daniel smiled. "I wanted you to meet the men who will play a part in your demise, Mr. Lowery. They were so looking forward to meeting you both after I told them about your...adventures." He swallowed hard.

"Oh, man, I get it!" Gareth laughed out loud, and hit his fist on the table. "They don't *believe* you, Bauer. Your buddies think you made all this shit up."

Williams cleared his throat. "As a matter of fact, I *don't* believe it. Daniel has told us of the Silver Scroll and the Tree of Knowledge he found buried underneath Jericho, and I find it all a great deal to swallow. From what he's told me, I believe it was Atlantis that you stumbled across, not Eden."

The tall, thin man looked up from his pasta, and snorted disgustedly. "Because Atlantis was home to our Aryan ancestors?"

Williams slammed his knife into the table. "Do *not* laugh at me. You know as well as I that the continent existed over thirteen thousand years ago and was the home to our superior race."

Wolf wiped the butter from his chin. "You know as well as I that it's called Valhalla. And when the Ragnarok is fought and won, we will return there and finally be home." The strange man bowed his head to the table as if ending a silent prayer.

Leah couldn't stop her brilliant mind from engaging. "Ragnarok? You're talking about the Fate of the Gods?"

The man looked up from the table and stared at Leah liked she'd come from another planet.

Gareth turned to her. "Come again?"

"In Norse mythology, the Ragnarok is the final battle between the army of Odin and the army of Loki…more commonly known as Lucifer," she explained.

"Armageddon," Gareth stated.

"No!" Wolf and Williams shouted as one. The little bald man spoke quickly, "This is not the King of Kings against some silly Prince of Darkness. This is the *real* war; an apocalyptic conflagration where the entire world will be torn apart, and only the men who die honorably in battle will earn the right to go to Valhalla with Odin."

Gareth's brows raced up his forehead as he stared at the obviously insane man. "Okey-dokey."

Leah caught the eyes of the cat staring at her; the stare was not as intense now, just filled with humor. "You don't say much, do you?"

Michael Hansen lifted his stein into the air. "I enjoy the banter too much to interrupt."

Pulling her gaze away from his slightly intimidating smile, she stared at the angry bald man. She watched his bushy eyebrows intently. As his anger level rose, they seemed to grow in size. They now resembled spiders that might suddenly drop from his ruddy skin and take a swim in her soup. "The way you're saying it, with Odin in Valhalla where you meet him, he loses the war with Lucifer."

His beady little eyes faded deeper into their sockets. "Of course.

Everyone knows that. The prophecies state that the event will occur. But we are willing to fight bravely before succumbing to the chaos in order to go back to our homeland and *our* chosen people."

"The Aryan brotherhood?" Leah snickered.

"One way of saying it."

"You're very smart, Miss Tallent." Hansen finally spoke. "I figured you would be...after all Daniel has told us about you. But you believe in God and His Son. I don't blame you...it's a very good story. The Second Coming: He arrives—the King of Kings in all His glory. The good will win and the bad shall lose and be cast from the earth, like it was with Lucifer so many years ago."

Leah tilted her head to the side. "You are mistaken. Lucifer was cast *to* the earth—not from it," she corrected. "He's still here."

Michael bowed his head and smiled as if allowing her to win the battle of words. "When the end comes, Miss Tallent—and it *is* coming—the earth will tremble from the mighty beast; the ferocious bull will emerge from the cave and fire will burn in his eyes and leap from his nostrils; the giants will sit on their mountain and play harps as the warriors fight. The flooding will come, the tsunamis will hit, and a monstrous winter will grip the land."

Leah smirked. "That so? A bull, huh? Doesn't work for me."

He leaned his elbows on the table. "I'm actually surprised that any of this works for you, Miss Tallent. I didn't think such an intelligent mind would fall for such biblical nonsense in the first place."

She hesitated for a split second, knowing the agony she'd gone through in order to accept the faith that now burned inside her soul. "I've seen too much not to believe."

He grinned. "So have I." Hansen sat back in his chair, and cleared his throat. "The Prince of Light—not some King of Kings—will ride first. His golden helmet will be on his head; his spear will be raised high." He offered a nod to Daniel at the end of the table. "And his followers will go with him into the light."

Gareth looked from man to man at the ridiculous statement. "You think Bauer is the Prince of Light?" He laughed. "He's not even worthy enough to be the artist formerly *known* as Prince."

Leah looked at Daniel. "Oh, please. You're Odin in this cute little scenario? Taking everyone back to the land of the Aryan ya-ya-brotherhood?"

She felt the prickle that crawled across her skin when Daniel gave her a knowing wink. "What do *you* think?"

The familiar card catalogue stayed closed inside her head. In its place, was a steady hum that seemed to take over her senses. "I think that you didn't go through all this trouble just to commit suicide leading an army that's destined to lose."

He remained quiet as she turned back to Hansen's yellow eyes. "I also think that you should remember the fate of the wicked in your well-known Norse tale. It's not very pleasant for the ones who said they were doing what Odin wanted but were actually just doing it for their own gain. A hall of punishment called the Corpse Shore awaits those who enter Valhalla under false pretenses."

The oval pupils of Hansen's eyes narrowed. "Nothing could be worse than this life."

She swallowed, wondering what horrors he must've seen to choose some ancient prophecy of death and pain, rather than stick with reality. She continued, "It's said that the walls of the Corpse Shore are made of serpents that spit their venom, creating a very special river of poison that flows around the bodies of murderers… and traitors."

"Your King of Kings may just be stronger, Leah, but it is Lucifer who kills Odin," Hansen whispered. "Chaos will reign. According to the prophecy, Odin's followers will die, yes. They'll be the lucky ones—the saved ones. You know…the ones who died valiantly… and quickly for their king."

"Don't you mean Führer?" Gareth added with disgust.

Leah laughed at Hansen. "Hey, I'm not knocking your theory, guys. In fact, I'm on board. I think your entire group should definitely die and go to Valhalla. But can you speed it up and do the deed tonight? That way I can get out of this drafty old castle and get a good night's sleep." She turned to Daniel. "Just give me Athena's things, I'll give you the emerald, and you can be off to your little corner of hell and play Odin, with my blessings."

Daniel laughed. "We'll get to the weapons in a minute."

Williams spoke up; his voice was clearly annoyed, "Just give them to her. It's not like they're of any use to us. The prophecy about the spear was obviously dead wrong."

"Not quite." Daniel raised his hand in the air. "I believe that if it were put in Miss Tallent's hands the spear would work."

Hansen smiled. "I'd like to see that."

"We are not taking a woman with us," Williams replied.

"You forget your place. *I'm* in charge here!" Daniel glared at the man. "Once Leah finds what I seek, she can go with her spear. She won't use it for her own gain anyway, so there's nothing to worry about." He looked over at her. "She just wants to return it to its rightful owner."

"I want the shield, too," Leah added.

Daniel shrugged. "I might still need that one. And, unfortunately, you didn't retrieve her helmet. That would've come in very handy."

Leah looked down at the table, remembering the mighty helmet still hidden on the Acropolis. "It wasn't there. Obviously it was just a story tacked on to the legend of the Goddess."

Gareth spoke, "I've had enough. Why's the emerald so damn important to you?"

Daniel thought for a moment. Leah could see the struggle he was having. He wanted to remain silent, but his pomposity and pride were screaming at him to let Tallent and Lowery in on his plan. "It belongs to a great man," Daniel finally replied.

"Your beloved Himmler?" Gareth scoffed. "I highly doubt it. And what exactly is it that you want Leah to find for you?"

Daniel took a deep breath. He waited a moment, as if priming his audience for the awe they would feel with his monumental announcement. "A crown."

Leah spoke quickly. "That's easy. It's in Herod's palace underneath the pool. Knock yourself out. Are we done here now?"

"Do you really think I didn't go back there and look, Leah? That crown is nothing but a piece of broken tin, at best."

Leah's head swam. Anippe had told her that they'd brought the broken diadem up from the floor of bodies buried in King Herod's palace. Even her father had said on the phone how excited he was about the discovery; how he thought it was the missing piece to a puzzle that he and his first wife had tried to solve decades ago.

"Then what freakin' crown are you looking for? There's a bunch in the Tower of London. Check there."

She tried not to tremble as she remembered the Crown of Thorns safely secured inside the cave in Glastonbury. There was no way she'd go back to that place again. If Bauer were to find the mystical artifacts that rested there, she wouldn't be able to live with herself. It was bad enough she and Gareth had put Athena's power into his hands.

Gareth sighed. "This is so stupid. All of this just to start a battle you already know you're going to *lose*?"

Hansen stared at the befuddled couple. "You don't understand the concept of dying for what you believe in. The final battle is coming, and we need to be on the side that will be offered Paradise."

"Odin isn't in the final battle," Gareth shouted, backing up his Christian choice. "The Son will fight Lucifer and the Son wins, case closed."

"We'll see," Hansen smirked.

Leah shook her head. No matter how hard she tried, she just couldn't wrap her mind around the strange words coming from the fanatical guests. Raising her head, she stared at the short, stocky man. "Who exactly are you, Mr. Williams? Why are you here in the middle of this Nazi-villa?"

He raised one bushy brow. "Did you like the chair, Miss Tallent? Did you gasp at the intricately carved design of the Death's Head ring?"

The light bulb flicked on and swept the cobwebs from her brain. "You're a relative of Wiligut."

"I am." He nodded. "A descendant who dates back to one of the mistresses he acquired over time."

"Oh," she said. "You mean you're a bastard of a bastard."

"Of a bastard," Gareth added.

"Right."

Leah thought the man would break the table in two with the force he put on the handle of his steak knife. Her heart beat faster; she wanted nothing more than to break him first. "You know, I think I did read a little about old Wiligut. He's mentioned so briefly in Hitler's background, though. Wasn't he the schizophrenic megalomaniac who got locked up in a mental institution by his own wife?"

The man continued to seethe across the table.

"Yeah…yeah…that was him. Then he abandoned his family and was eventually hired by Himmler to head the Department for Early History, which was part of the SS Race and Settlement Office. Himmler thought he was a great designer. Too bad Hitler thought he was a loon."

The man gasped. "And, you?" Leah turned her attention to the man who resembled a toothpick. "Which nutbag do you claim as an ancestor?"

Wolf's fork shook against his plate. "I claim none of them. I'm simply a man who believes in the superiority of the German people."

"So…you're essentially a nobody? The fourth wheel?" Gareth grinned.

He raised his pointed chin in the air. "I come from a long line of military intelligence officers. My uncle was actually a spy during World War II, hired by the British Army to oversee their Psychological Research Bureau. He would feed them ridiculous information about astrological charts, convincing them that Hitler was obsessed with his horoscope, and actually planned his battles and attacks around what his astrologers were telling him." The man snickered. "The Brits were dumb enough to believe it. Paid him handsomely to head up their astrological warfare department."

"Another charlatan," Daniel whispered.

Leah glanced over at the faraway look in Bauer's golden-brown eyes.

Gareth pointed at the sleek, silent cat at the end of the table. "What about you, Hansen? How twisted is your family tree?"

Like an orator compelling his audience to hang on his every word, the man cleared his throat, stood from his chair, and prepared to speak. Leah felt strange, like she was watching a well-rehearsed play that made the actor performing it very, very happy.

"I am from noble stock. In fact, it was a close relative of mine who had Hitler's ear at all times. He went by the name of Erik Hanussen. He was an outstanding clairvoyant, occultist, and mentalist in the Reich's employ."

"Hanussen," Leah mumbled, trying to remember Emmanuel's words and the material she'd studied. "Wait," she chuckled. "He was the Jewish man who Hitler freaked out on and had his people kill. His body was tossed into the woods after he'd talked about the Reichstag fire that let Hitler finally seize power."

Gareth looked at her. "If he helped Hitler why'd they kill him?"

"Because he basically shot his mouth off. He claimed he predicted the victorious event because he was a master clairvoyant. But, Hitler had told him what was going down. Just for a little extra spotlight, the guy told the world about it. If anyone had believed him, Hitler would've most likely been arrested for what he'd done and the Reich would've been over before it began. They had to assassinate him because he knew too much and couldn't shut up."

She stared over at the strangely amused man. "Left him like a dog in a field on the outskirts of Berlin."

Looking over at their host, Leah continued, "So does this one know too much, Daniel? Is he going to follow in the footsteps of his relative when you're done with him?"

Daniel laughed. "Leah, you are by far the smartest woman I've ever met. But you are so far off the mark on this one, it's not even funny."

She crossed her hands on the table and leaned closer to her captor. "What's the emerald, Daniel? What's the crown? If these are your so-called advisers, they must know. Or, are you smarter than the ones who've gone before? Have you kept your secrets to yourself, or were you dumb enough to share?"

The table went quiet which made Leah's heart soar. There was mistrust surrounding Daniel Bauer; there was dissension in the ranks. Chinks were showing in the armor of Daniel's friendships, which meant there were gaping holes in his plan. And she was going to rip them wide open in order to beat him at whatever game he was playing.

"Zara?" Daniel called out, keeping his gaze directly on Leah's face.

The Nordic bombshell flew through the double doors. "Yes, Daniel?"

"I think we'll skip desert this evening. Mr. Lowery and Miss

Tallent are quite tired and they've had a little bit too much brandy. Perhaps you can have someone escort them back to Leah's room?"

With a snap of Zara's long, nimble fingers, the men in silver and black marched into the room.

CHAPTER 25

Athena stared out from her place on the mural. Her weapons were where they were supposed to be, at her side, as she stood next to her all-powerful father on top of Mount Olympus.

"They don't trust him," Gareth whispered; his warm body wrapped around Leah like a safety blanket.

She shook her head. "They shouldn't. I don't think Hansen trusts him at all."

"You think he's really psychic?" Gareth snickered.

Leah felt the panic spread through her limbs. "No. But I think he's playing his own game, even though he and Bauer are essentially out for the same thing. I just wish I could figure out what it is they're really looking for out of all this. I don't buy the Odin theory for a minute."

"Maybe they're working together…against the other two?"

"Not a chance. Bauer's out for Bauer, nobody else. It's like he's chosen to play a game of charades. With a flick of his wrist, he almost has these psychos believing that he's Odin—the god that will save them by letting them die and then taking them into Valhalla, which is basically Paradise. They worship him because they're probably dumb enough to think that he's the reincarnation of Himmler, except that Daniel got much further than his ancestor."

Gareth nodded. "He actually found Eden." His voice turned somber. "Well…we led him there, anyway."

"Don't remind me." Leah turned to look at her handsome hero. "But, come on, Eden...Valhalla? Gareth, I *know* there's no way Daniel's doing this in order to lead some Aryan army into the afterlife. This is a man who wants power in the here and now where he can lord it over everyone else. Apparently he thought that Athena's spear was the one that should fit in Odin's hand; the one he needs to change his destiny to become the victor, when he finds the crown he's looking for."

"What about that?" Gareth sat up in the large, comfortable bed. "Any leads in that stellar brain of yours on what crown he wants?"

"No idea." Leah shrugged. "Maybe he will want us to break into the Tower of London and steal the Queen's, or something. But the emerald's what's really bugging me. I mean, we know it has some kind of mystical quality. Just seeing it change shape when we picked up the seeds during our last outing showed us that. It's obviously some kind of vessel that holds the power to do...something. The question is...what?"

Gareth sighed and fell back on the pillows. "Tomorrow we get the answers, Leah. We'll find Athena's stuff, make our deal, and get the hell out of here. If he wants a crown, we'll make him one out of aluminum foil if we have to."

"Origami?" Leah laughed. "Why didn't I think of that? We could've had this whole thing all sewn up by now."

Confusion danced in Gareth's emerald eyes. "There's one other thing that bugs me. Daniel Bauer is *no* Nazi. He might have a background with Himmler, and he certainly thinks this castle is top-notch, but I don't think he gives one iota about the beliefs of the National Socialist Party."

Leah agreed. "Yeah, that guy is definitely a party of one. When he's done using those losers downstairs he'll cut them loose. He obviously dug around for a while to find the perfect little descendants, and then played on their lofty fantasies of creating the perfect race. For a Nazi wannabe, Bauer must seem like the new scion who has come again to pull the Aryan race out of the darkness and back into the light.

"He used them to get information about this castle, the cave... everything. And while he's searching for this crown, he knows he can't be everywhere at once, so he sends his little goons running across the world to watch us and see what we're up to. Maybe he does want to create a Fourth Reich based on his *own* screwy ideas, but not the ones from some long dead dictator. Bauer's concentration camps will destroy everybody who doesn't agree with *him*, not just certain races. This guy wants to cleanse the world and reincarnate it into something he can be in charge of."

"Isn't it nice to see progress? Bauer uses the past in order to make the future even more disgusting," Gareth sneered. He nodded at the mural. "He just wants to order people around from atop his very own Mount Olympus."

She stared into the eyes of the true warrior. "And all *we* have to do is figure out a way to knock him off his throne."

* * *

Leah felt like her feet were stuck in the La Brea Tar Pits. Her mind was fuzzy. The sun shone through a small window positioned high up in the cold, dark room. She tried to move her body, but it was impossible. She looked down; everything but her head was buried in a stone wall; only her face stuck out from the rock. Panic swelled in her tightened chest. Her eyes moved from side to side, and she suddenly saw an ominous shadow looming outside the open door. The man was coming in, and she knew she must free herself from the stone wall before it was too late.

Suddenly, a golden offering appeared in the rays of sunlight streaming through the window and hovered in the air in front of her. Leah wanted to reach out and take the handle of the glimmering weapon, but even with all her strength she couldn't pull her arm free from the unyielding stone.

The shadow was coming closer, crossing over the threshold. She could make out the strange glow as he entered the room, and spotted the glossy onyx crown perched on his head. It seemed to radiate power, making the foundation of the strange tomb tremble. When the sunlight lit the emerald in the pitch black crown, a scream burst from her throat that was so loud, it mimicked a thunder clap provided by the gods.

* * *

A silver tray slammed down next to her on the night table causing the Grecian urn to wobble on the edge. Leah woke up with a start, and reached out quickly to grab the rocking vase. She stared up into Zara's snooty glare.

Leah groaned. "Oh, great…it's you. Come to poison me again with your disgusting coffee?"

"It's time to get up and tour the library."

"Already work in the best one, but thanks for the offer."

The woman turned her gaze on the immaculately-shaped lump pressed against Leah's back. "Mr. Lowery is invited, as well," she purred.

"Mr. Lowery's seen enough libraries to last him a lifetime," Gareth mumbled behind Leah's head as if in total agreement with the statement.

"You'll both be out in the hall in ten minutes!" she ordered, marching to the door. "Or, a guard will be sent in to change your minds."

The door slammed behind her, and Leah once again reached out to stop the urn from falling off its precious stand.

"Damn, she's loud," Gareth grumbled, "I've always hated blondes."

Leah laughed. "Yeah, right. I think you just can't understand how a woman can even be *semi*-immune to your natural beauty and charm. What's *that* about, right?"

"Exactly. Blondes. I'm telling you, being semi-immune to my charm is proof enough that the woman isn't in her right mind." He rested his head on her shoulder, and smiled. "It's sad really…poor child. She's just been surrounded by these crazy little foreigners for so long that her mind simply can't adjust to the awesome strength and power of a real man."

Leah shoved her head into the pillow and laughed. "It's amazing. My stomach must be lined with lead."

"What?"

"Between the rancid coffee, Bauer's icky little friends, and your ego—I *still* haven't thrown up."

"You should get a reward," he snickered. "You want a carved chair to sit on? I know where I can pick one up real cheap. An artifact from the Third Reich, even. You just can't get any sweeter than that."

* * *

Leah threw on her leather duster. For protection or warmth, she no longer knew.

Standing in the open doorway, she stared across the hall at the portrait of the mighty angel—sword in hand—looking down at his crumpled victim. The work of art drew Leah in with the same magnetic force as Gareth's powerful emerald eyes. She stared at the mangled crown in the hand of the dead body, and sighed. Today was the day. Today, she would make the deal to get them home.

Daniel was leaning up against the entrance to the North Tower, staring at her. "You're in for a real treat, Leah. There's one more room in the tower that I think you'll just love."

"Look, Daniel, enough with the tour already. Let's talk business."

He held a hand in the air. "That's *exactly* what we're going to do, Leah. Today is the day. And I, for one, can't wait to see how it all ends up."

CHAPTER 26

The music was throbbing. Leah's ears actually felt like they were bleeding inside, and when the long, drawn out strains of the bow beat on the invisible strings, her eyes burned. She looked around as they stepped over the threshold; the room that held the mighty chair of Himmler was now behind them. Red velvet drapes were drawn tightly over the long, narrow window, and the opera music dipped low, right before another violent shriek from the string section pierced the air.

Leah's eyes danced left and right; she was half expecting the famous Phantom of the Opera, in his familiar white mask, to crash through the ceiling and take her hostage. She stared over at their captor and studied Bauer's closed eyes and lips that were turned up in a peaceful smile. Clearly he was enjoying the eerie ministrations of the hidden orchestra.

As if feeling her gaze, Bauer's brown eyes opened and stared back at her through the candlelight. He shrugged his shoulders and walked toward the wall, flicking on the overhead fluorescent lights.

Leah tried to adjust her focus as the room was suddenly bathed in light. She watched Bauer turn the round knob on the wall, thankfully lowering the offensive music to a silent hum.

He grinned. "The composer is Richard Wagner. He was obsessed with the Master Race, and Hitler was completely inspired by the magnificent man. Hitler once said, 'in order to understand the Nazi

Party, you must understand Wagner.' "

Gareth snorted. "Doom, gloom, and death; how original for the Nazi killing machine."

Daniel sat down on one of the long brown work tables and crossed his hands over his chest. "You know, Mr. Lowery, Hitler wasn't that far off. He believed the false virtues of conscience and morality were degrading, and that people should be free of all ridiculous emotion. They should be released from the oppression of free will and having to make their own decisions. Then they could rest easier at night, knowing that the responsibility for their lives would be borne by the men who had the balls to make the really tough decisions."

He took a deep breath. "Mankind would ultimately be saved if the masses would just let a superman lead."

Leah whistled through her teeth. "Then Krypton blew up and sent Clark Kent down to our world to save us all…while wearing tights."

Gareth smiled. "Yeah. And he lived in *America.*"

"Hence the red and blue wardrobe," Leah added. "And, as I've stressed on more than one occasion, Hitler was short. Can you imagine how god-awful he would've looked in that outfit?"

She stared at Daniel's slightly disturbed expression. "I think your oars have left the water, Bauer. You know what I'm saying? Hitler was a psycho, nothing more."

His hands balled into fists, and his voice grew louder with the strength of his anger. "People still very much believe in his ways and ideas. There are many out there who'll tell you right now that the world should be rid of certain…factions, in order for humanity to survive. Perhaps the focus is off Hitler's main enemy now, but the third world toilets that are decimating your very own country are coming into the spotlight. And no *American* wept when Bin Laden was cast to the sea, did they?"

"That's a very specific person," Leah said. "Not a whole race of people. The Koran is based on peace. Old Osama was just some other jackass like your beloved Hitler who decided to take the written word and twist it to suit his own purposes."

Leah shook her head angrily, as she continued, "If you want to die, be my guest. I said that last night. You want to idealize a terrorist or a ridiculous dictator—who both *lost*, by the way—knock yourself out." She snorted at his amused brown eyes. "But I don't think you have any desire to do it, Bauer. I think you want the power for yourself. All of it. Whatever that power may be."

Daniel tilted his head to one side and put a finger to his lips. He looked as if he was trying to decide what his next words should be. Taking a deep breath, he spoke, "Have you ever heard the story of the Dueling Crowns?"

Leah looked through the card catalogue in her brain, and finally had to shake her head. "WWF? The Undertaker versus Lucifer?"

Daniel laughed. "No, actually it's a very old biblical story."

Leah felt her stomach begin to churn, remembering her father's anxiety as he tried to warn her of the emerald's origin. "Oh, good," she mumbled. "Another bible story. I never get tired of those." She glanced at Gareth. "I swear this has got to be some kind of punishment for never going to Sunday School."

Gareth grinned and then turned to Bauer, "If you *read* the Bible, Daniel, you should already know that people like you always lose."

He smiled wide. "I've never read the Book of Revelation, Lowery. I don't like to know the end. In fact, a person with enough intelligence could alter the outcome of any story. All he'd have to do is figure out how."

"Let me guess? You know how." Leah sneered.

Daniel remained silent.

Leah sighed as the time ticked by. Frustration swelled inside her chest until she finally turned her gaze away from the silent, annoying man to study her surroundings. The walls were lined with large bookcases, end to end, filling every free space with journals, diaries, maps and pictures. Her eyes narrowed as she saw some familiar images amongst the mess.

Above one bookcase hung the picture of Mount Olympus etched in gold. Below the mighty emblem, a pile of notebooks and journals were scattered haphazardly across each and every shelf. In front of the case sat an island of computers. So many, in fact, that the black cords and cables resembled a mound of writhing snakes squirming across the polished stone floor.

Over the next humungous bookcase was the familiar sight of Petra. Leah stared up at the painting. It was clear to her that the red rock masterpiece had to have been created by the hand of a true artist. She shuddered when she saw the image of the Sapphire Staff hanging in the air above the red dirt like a Roswellian UFO.

Pulling out of her own mind, she walked to the mass of computers that were apparently assigned to the world of Petra. "What is all this?"

Daniel spoke behind her, "This is the work from the teams I have. These teams are, right this minute, scouring the land for the thing I want the most. This whole room, in fact, was once dedicated to higher learning. The mission of the people who once sat in here was to find and study ancient cultures; this room was where the Ahnenerbe was first set up."

Leah turned around. "The Ahnenerbe?"

"You know of it, I would assume?"

"The Ancestral Heritage Research and Teaching Society," she replied.

Pride, mixed with a disgusting look of passion, beamed from Daniel's eyes. "That's right. Himmler created the think tank in 1935. His partners were Hermann Wirth, a Dutchman who was completely obsessed with Atlantis; and Richard Darrè, who was the head of the Race and Settlement Office. They all believed in the spiritual prehistory of the Aryan race.

"Himmler took total control by 1936. He wanted to create a Germanic culture based on the Nazi belief system that would wipe out Christianity in Germany. They recruited researchers, astrologers, astronomers, scientists—all the very best in their fields to help them do just that."

"Recruited." Gareth snorted.

Daniel shrugged. "Some came willingly. Others…well…others had to be pushed into service."

"Wait a minute," Leah interjected. "I thought Himmler was obsessed with the Holy Grail? Even Hitler, after he annexed Austria, took a motorcade to Vienna and took possession of the Spear of Destiny that impaled Jesus on the cross. They *had* to have believed in *some* parts of Christianity."

Gareth answered, "The Spear was said to hold immense power, Leah. The person who held the spear and understood its power was said to hold the destiny of the world in the palm of his hand—for good or evil." He stared at Bauer's smug expression. "Christianity served the Nazis just fine, as long as it provided them with relics that would allow them to take over the world."

"Hitler would definitely not have liked the two of you," Daniel commented. "One of his most famous sayings was; 'How fortunate for leaders that the masses do not think.' Your brains would've been far too dangerous to keep alive."

Leah smirked. "Maybe we could've gotten jobs here in the think tank."

"Maybe." Bauer mumbled, "He did like to keep families together."

"Excuse me?"

Daniel walked toward another section of the room. Above this next bookcase sat a portrait of a regal looking female. Flames shot out around her braided head, seemingly engulfing the poor woman in a fire of mammoth proportions. Her mouth was wide open in a silent scream. "That's Hypatia." Daniel said, turning back to Leah. "I would assume you of all people have heard of her."

Leah blinked at the offensive picture, recognizing the large building that'd been drawn behind the burning woman. "She was the only female librarian in the Library of Alexandria."

"And?" he goaded.

"And they murdered her in the street," Leah's voice came out loud and angry. "They called her a witch because of her high intelligence. Amazing, right? That men would ever be so unsure of themselves they would have to murder a female who just happened to be far smarter than they were? They accosted her outside her house and stripped her skin off in pieces using sharpened seashells."

Daniel nodded. "Then they tied her to the back of their cart and towed her mangled body through the streets, ending their murderous rage by burning her. Too bad, if you ask me. She... *knew* a great deal."

"What's you point? Gonna carve me up and take me through the streets of Paderborn tied to the back of your pickup truck?" Leah spat.

"I wouldn't dare." Daniel put a hand to his chest in disgust. "I have the greatest respect for women. They're conniving, smart, and far more ruthless than men. They have the ability to set aside their egos where we, unfortunately, cannot."

"Oh, we're telling the truth today?" Leah said.

His gaze was intense. "Gareth will agree with me. We males want the quick fix, and if we don't get it or, God forbid, one of our enemies is doing better than we are, then we pick up our weapons and start a war. Women…well, women understand how to play the game and they have hang-time. They can lurk in the shadows; smile and flick their hair over their shoulders in the light; act dimwitted and innocent while listening to every word that's said around them while ingesting the information until they find just the right moment to show themselves as the smartest enemy and strike you dead." He scanned Leah up and down as he sauntered toward her. "They can so completely mesmerize the men around them that their victims never even know what happened until it's too late."

Leah felt her own sapphire eyes meet the level of his power. "I suggest you heed your own words, Bauer. I can bury you."

Gareth remained silent beside her but squeezed her hand, as if begging her to give him the go ahead to pulverize the repugnant man.

She gave a slight shake of her head, and squeezed back.

Daniel cleared his throat. "I know. I won't let my ego override my judgment with you, Leah. It would be a critical mistake that could, and most likely would, end in my death. There is only one way to get a woman under any man's spell, but unfortunately Mr. Lowery has already done that. Anyone else who tries with you would, unfortunately, fail. It's heartbreaking, and a regret I will have to live with the rest of my life." His eyes darkened with a craving that bordered on psychotic before returning to their natural shade. He continued, "Now…your mind is the asset I need in order to get what I want." Turning on his heel, he pointed to the other sections of wall space. "These represent teams who are digging in Babylon, Normandy—even Crete."

Leah stared up at the next painting. Colorful flowers grew on rocky terraces in the Hanging Gardens of Babylon. Her eyes went quickly to the next bookcase, focusing on the picture of a huge castle with a golden sword rising from its dome. Beside it, above the very last case in the room, was the picture of a humongous bull with sharp horns and a killer's face. He stood on two feet like a man; a bright star twinkled above his head, and an onyx crown sat at his feet.

Gareth walked over and removed a journal from one of the shelves dedicated to the work being done in Crete. "You have a team actually looking for the ancient Minotaur in the palace of Knossos?" He passed the book to Leah, and let out an amused laugh. "Talk about a huge waste of time."

"You never know." Daniel shrugged.

"A half-man, half-bull roaming a labyrinth waiting for its next victim? You have *got* to be kidding."

Daniel shoved his hands in his pockets. "Crete's a strange and dangerous location, Lowery. It was for Hitler, as well. It was the one and only place where he found a mass of people who stood up against him. Crete put up quite a large fight, killing thousands of Hitler's men. After it was over, Hitler decided never to use paratroopers again because of the monumental losses the Reich sustained in Crete."

Daniel smiled wide. "By the way, the Magi who are part of your faith believed whole-heartedly in the Minotaur, Mr. Lowery. Are you telling me your beloved wise men were fake too?"

Gareth shook his head. "You've watched *Clash of the Titans* one too many times."

"They once said the same thing about Athena, you know. She, too, was a myth. The Warrior Goddess: The owner of a weapon with power that was second only to the sword of the Archangel Michael."

Gareth searched the other cases holding the journals and diaries of unknown scientists who'd probably paid with their lives for the secrets they'd worked so hard to uncover.

Leah stared down at the open book Gareth had given to her. Each page was marked with a star. There were black and white photos of vases, statues of women with snakes writhing around their bodies, and a multitude of murals that spotlighted the half-man, half-bull who was goring helpless victims with his sharp horns. She noted that Knossos and its Minoan culture were not the only study that was written about in the strange book. Other data had been collected from the ancient sites of Rhodes, Troy and Pergamon.

Flipping through the index of the dusty, weathered book, Leah noticed that page after page was filled with names; both male and female listed in no particular order. Their ages, countries of birth, specific specialties in the world of science, had also been written in—a roster of the teams. She choked on the bile that began climbing up her throat, when she read the words in the far right hand column. It was a roster all right; a death book, like the ones that'd been kept at the concentration camps. The last day of their lives had been recorded right beside the horrific notation that stated what method had been used to murder each innocent soul.

Flipping to the end, Leah found a picture taped to the last page. The glazed stare of the man sitting on the remains of a temple was disturbing. White rocks were scattered all around him as he sat, looking totally defeated, under a large shade tree staring at his photographer. A huge amphitheater appeared in the photograph behind him, with rows of ancient seating circling the mountain. The site was incredible, but the man trapped inside its beauty broke Leah's heart. Even in the fuzzy image she could make out the flesh that was hanging off his emaciated arms. His hair was oily and flattened down on his forehead. Even though the color of his eyes was masked by the black and white technology, Leah could still see the hopelessness swimming in his weary stare. He'd probably been one of the thousands of researchers who'd had his future cut short by the Führer and his army of blood-thirsty killers.

She snapped the book shut. "Tell me what's going on right now or we walk. And don't think for a second that we wouldn't make it out of here alive. You should know us far better than that by now."

Taking just a second, Daniel reached behind him and opened a small door that led even deeper into the eerie fortress. "As you wish."

CHAPTER 27

She didn't make a move when Daniel disappeared into the next room. But when a light suddenly beamed through the opening, Leah took a deep breath and Gareth's hand as they walked forward.

She dropped the journal into her pocket—jostling the small, wooden runes that were still hidden in the depths of the well-worn leather. Following Gareth into the tiny room, Leah ducked her head to avoid hitting her skull on the small doorway.

When she once again was able to stand up straight, Leah found herself looking directly at Athena's spear and shield. She raced to the glass case and banged on it with her fists, trying with all her might to break the fragile tomb and set the goddess free.

Daniel laughed behind her. "It's bullet-proof, too."

Gareth stared at the overly-confident man. "You have two ancient powerful weapons and you keep them locked up like they're pieces in a museum?"

Daniel's eyes grew black.

Leah laughed; she saw the raw anger dance in the depths of his eyes. "The spear really *doesn't* work for you! Legend says that it's supposed to quiver in your hand right before the power of the gods is unleashed from its sharp point."

Daniel remained silent.

"But it hasn't done a damn thing since you stole it." Leah's smile grew wider as she reveled in the small victory.

Daniel's voice came out dismissive. His words were clipped; his tone was sour. "As I said, once I have the emerald and the crown I'll have no need for Athena's spear. However, considering the shield is supposedly unbreakable, it could definitely aid in my defense." He looked at the glittering objects. "But they are magnificent. The craftsmanship is truly divine."

Leah took a seat in the comfortable recliner sitting beside a small oak table. It was as if Bauer used this place to sit and stare at the first real artifacts he'd ever been able to get his slimy hands on. Here, Leah knew, was the place he came to dream—where the blueprint of his devilish plan had been drawn. She stared down at the center of the small table and peered at the tiny carving in the wood. "What's that supposed to be?"

Daniel walked to her. "That belonged to Hitler."

"I thought Hitler never came to this castle?" Gareth said.

"He didn't. This, along with the portrait that hangs outside Himmler's room, were the only gifts the Führer decided to bestow."

"A crappy painting and an old, broken desk," Leah mumbled. "He certainly thought very highly of his second in command."

Daniel slammed his fist on the table. "Hitler respected him more than anyone else in his organization. He gave Himmler the command of his elite guard! You can't get better than that. This broken-down desk, as you call it, was the desk where Hitler sat during the meetings of the Thule Society."

Leah cringed, as she focused on the small carved image of the all-seeing eye. It pained her to see the same symbol that adorned her own hand cut into a piece of furniture once owned by a madman. She glanced at the bright sapphire eye that'd long ago marked her as a protector, and shook her head; she was still trying to accept the fact that she could possibly be a descendent of the biblical Moses. It was as unbelievable to her as being the descendant of George Washington or Jack the Ripper, himself. To her, any and all were an impossibility for a no-name librarian who used to hide away from the world. Covering her inked hand with the other, she stared up at Bauer. "So someone twisted the meaning of yet another innocent and well-meaning symbol into something completely inaccurate in order to use it as their own. *Man!* You'd think Nazi's would've had at least a little creativity."

"Yeah," Gareth added. "For people who claimed they were the elite, you'd think they could've come up with at least one fresh idea. I mean…the swastika, the ancient runes…shows them for the lazy fakes they really were. They stole everything from people who were smarter than them."

Daniel smirked. "Hitler was a student of Dietrich Eckart who led the Thule Society. That powerful group actually boasts some of the greatest minds of the century." He looked over his shoulder at Gareth. "In fact, Aleister Crowley was a student of theirs. The self-anointed Beast believed that the members had to break through their small selves and live outside a world of morality. Rasputin was also a member of the team at one time, but it was Crowley who coined an interesting term; 'the gem of Heaven.'"

Leah's stomach churned as her life suddenly came full circle before her eyes sending her back into Crowley's creepy world. She had never wanted to cross his historical path again after the '13' fiasco, but it was beginning to look like everything she and Gareth had done thus far was just a small thread of a much larger web.

Daniel continued, "It was Crowley who talked about the existence of such a gem. He also threw out the beliefs of the god Odin and the idea of Valhalla; he dismissed them as pure crap. His idea was a new one that the Thule Society promoted quite vocally. Luciferianism was Crowley's brainchild. When Hitler came along, he was taught this idea under the tutelage of Eckart."

"We're getting somewhere," Leah said quietly. She stared into Gareth's emerald eyes, before glancing back at the excited freak. "So all that talk at dinner about how you're the reincarnation of Odin, and you'll fight the good fight, was basically horseshit. You have your…advisers believing that you'll be the one to lead them to the green grass of their personal paradise where you'll all sit—Nordic men who are ethnically superior—for the rest of your days."

"My advisers come in handy for certain…situations." Daniel laughed. "I like to keep them happy. They've used their extreme wealth to back me on all my archaeological digs. I've even been able to take up where Himmler left off in Crete, Normandy—all over, really. Those teams work for me now and they're digging for every treasure; every piece of power that the world has to offer. And it'll all be mine soon. Also, it quite helps that Williams sits in the office of agriculture and Wolf holds a seat of power in the government which allowed me to take over ownership of this castle."

"And Hansen? What exactly is *his* benefit?" Leah questioned.

Daniel shrugged. "We'll just have to wait and see."

"So you're the only fake," Gareth said. "They actually *believe* the Nazi drivel that Himmler spewed."

"Well, I must say that I bought into some of it after a while, myself. But my trip to the Boleskine house cured me of that thinking."

"Boleskine?" Leah trembled at the memory of that awful place; the very home of the self-anointed Beast. Aleister Crowley had held secret meetings there and, in the process, he'd opened a door before his death that'd allowed the Devil to walk straight through. The small house on the edge of Loch Ness had once possessed the orb of humanity—the thirteenth astrological sign that was needed in order to open the gate that she and Gareth had almost lost their lives trying to keep closed. In that house, stuck in a frightening Poe story come to life, Tallent and Lowery had met the worst of mankind…and she never wanted to go back.

What Leah wanted to do now was climb into bed and pull up the covers over her head, as she remembered a figure that'd been sitting in Crowley's basement. The Führer had most definitely been on the scene.

Shaking her head, Leah closed her eyes. She took the time to remind herself that the orb was long gone from that place and was now safely ensconced in the base of her favorite friend; hidden from sight in a creature that guarded the doors of her own paradise back in New York.

Daniel fell to his knees in front of the table and stared into Leah's eyes. "My journey has been right by your side for so long, and you haven't even known it. I've always been one step behind you until our meeting in Herodium…when I finally caught up."

"What did you see in that house, Daniel? What was in Boleskine that made you become this thing," Leah said quietly, dreading the answer.

"I saw ones who were everything I wanted to be, except I would be smarter. They had the right idea. They knew Lucifer would be the only one who could bring down the entire world."

"We beat him!" Gareth shouted.

"You only delayed him!" Daniel shouted back.

"The orb that you stole and hid away from the world," he continued, "which you hid very well by the way," he stared at Leah as if she would reveal the location by mistake, "isn't the only artifact capable of bringing Lucifer back. It was, however, supposed to be the easiest one to retrieve. My team still can't find it, even though they traveled behind you when you returned all the other orbs to their homes."

Daniel turned his glare on Gareth. "I don't need the orb now. With the discovery of Eden, we found another way into Heaven. All I have to do is put the crown on my head, go back to the Garden, and walk through the Tree of Knowledge. You saw the light coming from in there. You know the stairs inside will lead to the center of the world. I will take that world...and this one, too."

"Lucifer's crown," The answer hit her like a ton of bricks.

Daniel's brown eyes glittered like gold. "You do know the story of the Dueling Crowns."

She stared at the floor.

"The circle of thorns on the Son's head was one of the crowns which, of course, I know the location of after following you two into that cave in Glastonbury. But you forgot there's another crown out there."

An icy chill crawled up her spine. Leah remembered the blue flame that'd been lit inside that cave. She'd felt the masses lining up behind the Devil then, waiting to get back into Paradise and take it over for themselves. For so long she'd thought it was a figment of her imagination—that no one could possibly have been there except the quartet who'd fought bravely to keep the gate shut tight.

"You were behind me," she whispered.

Daniel smiled. "Behind you all the way. I wanted to talk to you when I saw you standing in the window of the Upper Room. I knew that story, too. About the man with the jug of water? I wonder sometimes if you got to see him in the flesh. I wonder what he said to you. Apparently, he didn't mention his crown."

Leah knew Daniel was referring to the demon who'd once worn the crown he was now searching for. The image of the haggard, wretched figure loomed before her eyes, and the words that'd flown from the serpent's mouth rang out inside her head. *I will be with you...always.* The Devil had made that promise to her and then disappeared from her sight.

She reached into the pocket of her leather coat and grasped the furry, white lamb, as another horrible thought rushed into her mind. "William Knight?"

Daniel clapped his hands excitedly. "Yes! He was one of mine, as well. He told me of your amazing journey to find the Sapphire Staff. The last time I heard from him he told me you were heading to Chartres. And then...nothing."

Gareth sent an evil laugh across the room. "Your boy bit the dust there, pal. Dead as a doornail."

"I'm sure he died because of his own ego," Daniel remarked. "As I said before, the male species can get drunk on power and completely overlook the superior intelligence of a woman."

"Yeah, it was a real shame." Leah grinned. "He could've handed you one of the most powerful weapons in history, but he didn't even care about it. All he wanted to do was turn lead into gold."

"And to think," Daniel sighed. "If he'd waited for one more adventure from the amazing duo of Tallent and Lowery he would've had all the gold in the world."

Leah leaned forward in her chair. "You make me sick."

"You should be proud of me, Leah. My teams are unearthing actual artifacts all over the globe. They are proving the existence of human races no one has ever even known about. They are rewriting history! The cultures, the architecture... I even had a whole team scour this castle when we arrived and they found some extremely interesting things, just not what I wanted."

Leah put her head in her hands. "You thought the crown of Lucifer had been given to *Himmler*? The guy was a second-rate fool."

Daniel paced the room. "I've gone everywhere, Leah. From Crowley to The Ripper, Rasputin to Bin Laden. I thought I had it at Herod's palace but it turned out that his was just a broken piece of garbage. But being so close to the mines of Cleopatra, I thought it *had* to be there."

"This crown you want is in the mines?" Gareth spoke.

"No," Daniel replied. "I figured out that the crown and the emerald had to have been separated from each other for safety."

"So the emerald is…" Leah swallowed hard.

"The gem of Heaven." Daniel nodded. "The emerald you wore around your beautiful neck is the centerpiece of Lucifer's crown."

CHAPTER 28

"That's just great," Gareth shouted, tossing his hands up in the air. "I work the last twenty-five years to finish the journey my parents had devoted their whole lives to and, on the way to Heaven, I just happen to *buy* Lucifer's emerald. This is freakin' unbelievable!"

Daniel ignored the irate man. "The emerald had been hidden in Athens. It took us a long time to find that out. My father worked day and night to extract that information from the woman who'd stolen it from the mines."

"My mother," Leah whispered.

Daniel nodded. "She was one of many people my father took when Himmler committed suicide after the War was over." He glanced at Gareth. "He, like you, was left a purpose in life, passed down to him by his ancestor. The only difference is that you wanted to find Heaven for mostly virtuous reasons, whereas my father wanted to find it in order to—"

"Destroy it," Gareth said.

Daniel tilted his head. "More like…own it. You see, in my family the Devil always wins."

He turned back to Leah; his voice grew soft and gentle. "You would've been very proud of your mother, Leah. I mean…eventually she lost it. But she kept her loyalty to your father for as long as she could. After she let us know what happened to the stone, she spent the rest of her days in the pursuit of true academia. She was a master at the runes. Once she began to work *with* my father, her knowledge of ancestral cults and doctrine helped tremendously for what he was trying to accomplish."

"She worked willingly for your father?" Gareth's voice was filled with doubt.

Daniel nodded. "But she did only wonderful things. She never had anything to do with the section for Scientific Research. When she joined the Ahnenerbe, she stuck to the things she knew best."

"And this research section does what, exactly?"

Daniel smiled at Gareth. "It's one of the older ones that my advisers chose to bring back. The section was originally funded by the SS; their job was to experiment on human beings. They would bring prisoners from Dachau, Auschwitz and other concentration camps to this castle, where they'd work on them while they were still alive. The medical men wanted to see what the human body could withstand…among other things."

"That was then," Gareth said. "What does it do now?"

He shrugged. "You just can't teach an old dog new tricks, Gareth. My advisers still believe in the Master Race. And they're still looking for the answers in much the same way as they did before."

Leah's skin crawled. She wondered how many bodies were writhing in pain inside the evil tower. "You keep using the past tense when you talk about my mother, but I know you didn't harm her when you came out of Eden. You pretty much confirmed that you needed a bargaining chip in order to get me to help you."

"Yes," he replied. "But you made it quite clear that you wouldn't bargain for the life of a woman who'd abandoned you. So I did take care of it. I wonder what could be learned from *her* dead brain. I can have her taken to Himmler's crypt so you can pray over her and say your goodbyes, if you'd like."

Leah swallowed hard. She grasped the stuffed lamb in her hand so tight she thought its head would fall off. "I want Athena's weapons."

"I want the crown."

"I have no idea where your stupid crown is," Leah shouted. "Until Gareth came along, I didn't even believe in any of this stuff. Even now I only believe in about half."

Daniel smiled wide and stared at Gareth, who was seething in the center of the room. "Well…then I guess it's a very good thing that you're not a solo act." Turning, he walked back through the tiny door.

Gareth rushed to Leah's side, and took her in his arms. "I'm so sorry."

Athena's weapons gleamed in the light of the room. Leah was in shock. Her real mother was dead; he'd called her bluff, but Leah held back her tears. There was no reason to cry over someone who'd never really existed in the first place. Taking a deep breath, she buried her head in Gareth's chest. "You'd think with all the crap we've gotten ourselves into over the years that we'd go to church more."

Gareth held her tightly, ignoring the sarcasm that flowed from her lips. He took a deep breath. "We have to find that crown."

Leah nodded. "And send it back to its real owner."

Leaving his arms, Leah began to pace the small room, as Gareth sat down in the chair. "Where do we start? Sounds like Bauer's already been to every place on the map."

Leah turned to the emerald eyes that held her future. "Hitler was at that table in Boleskine for a reason, Gareth."

He shrugged. "He was evil. Like the rest of them."

Leah shook her head. "There've been thousands of dictators. Hundreds upon hundreds of men have taken innocent lives for one stupid reason or another since the beginning of time. Daniel's only been focusing on Himmler. His ego got the better of him a long time ago."

"What do you mean?"

"Somewhere in the back of his twisted little mind he believes that since he has a link to the guy who owned this castle and mutilated scores of people, then he'll be the next hellish dictator who becomes worse than any other. But he's not. Himmler was always second, just like Bauer has always been second to us when it came to figuring all this out."

Gareth nodded his head. "The big Kahuna was Adolf."

"Exactly," Leah continued. "Hitler never came to this place for a reason. He simply didn't care. He might have given Himmler power,

172

but he took it back as soon as he realized that Himmler was going to give himself over to the Allies in order to save his own skin. He fell from Hitler's grace."

"Like Lucifer fell from God's."

She nodded. "Hitler's the key, here. *He's* the one Daniel should've been studying up on because if anyone would have possessed the most evil headgear in history, it would have been him." Leah's mind went into overdrive. "There were figures in Crowley's house. Crowley and The Ripper had direct attachments to the orbs; Hitler must be attached to the crown." An image of Rasputin floated in her mind's eye as she briefly wondered how the frightening monk who'd sat in Crowley's basement fit into all this.

"Did Hitler have his own castle?"

She shook the thoughts from her head. "No. He had a couple of houses. Even had a place called Eagle's Nest. I assume it's one of the ones Bauer has confiscated along the way. It was called Hitler's victory house."

"Maybe the crown's there."

"No. Hitler barely went there, either. He spent most of his time in Berlin."

Gareth sighed. "Leah, his house, the bunker…everything in Berlin is long gone. The Allies were all over that place like flies on a dead body."

"You're right." She continued to pace. "But there had to have been somewhere Hitler loved; a place where he felt like a god. A mountain like Olympus that he could stand on and address the warriors below who were fighting for him, holding out his arms to the huddled masses and—" Leah stopped dead in her tracks.

"What?" Gareth sat up straighter.

"A place where he could look down on them from atop his very own Mount Olympus; a place where he was Zeus, the strongest god." Her voice fell to a whisper, "Odin would've been a simpleton to Hitler—nothing but a weak god who could only lead his people to their deaths. In the end, Hitler would've thought Odin was a big, fat zero. Zeus was above all the rest. The strongest and most vile creature, he killed some of his very own children because he thought they'd take his throne away. He was that disgusting."

She looked at the golden gleam of the armor. "Until a daughter was born from his own head and became the strongest warrior ever known to mankind."

"Athena," Gareth whispered.

She nodded.

"So where was Hitler's Mount Olympus?"

Leah could see the old video running through her head. The banners were waving. The spotlights buried in the ground were beaming into the night sky, reaching up into the clouds to illuminate Heaven. The Führer stood on his podium with his hand raised in the air, as if blessing his army of mighty warriors marching below him. The band played. The masses cheered. And he, the devil, smiled.

She turned to Gareth. "Nuremberg."

CHAPTER 29

If she didn't get out soon, Leah was going to scream. The excitement she felt ran down her neck in tandem with the absolute hatred that she had for the man beside her. She tried to angle her body away from Daniel Bauer. She could feel the impatience radiating around the man like a nuclear cloud, and she wanted nothing more than to punch his lights out and make a run for it.

She stared over at Gareth. His worn knapsack was on the red carpeted floor between his feet. He sat straight and tall with his elbows tucked into his sides looking positively disgusted, trying with all his might to not let his muscular body make contact with the goons who sat on both sides of him.

Her stomach still revolted at the twin silver lightning bolts on the guard's shoulders. If it weren't for the sights and sounds of modern day life happening outside her gray-tinted window, Leah would've thought she'd traveled back in time and was a VIP attendee at one of the obnoxious rallies that'd been held here on the Nuremberg parade grounds.

The driver navigated the long car into the parking lot adjacent to the back of the Zeppelin Grandstand. As Leah stepped out—followed closely by Daniel and the pistol he held in his hand—she stared at the strange scene. It was in this very spot, not so long ago, where people dressed to the nines arrived in droves to pay homage to their leader. Now, thankfully, there were simply kids in shorts and t-shirts using the rear wall to practice their backswings. The tennis balls made an ominous sound as they thumped off the old marble façade; the hard projectiles slammed against the building like a barrage of bullets.

She twisted her neck to stare at the nearby Dutzendteich Lake. Carefree people were laughing, enjoying the brisk day as they cast their fishing lines into the ice-free lake. The paddle boats, covered with cheery yellow tarps, were lined up on the shore, and there were large wood ramps supporting a host of talented skateboarders. Looking like a flock of strange birds, they raced down the highly polished incline, up the other side, and flew out into the bright blue sky. Leah smiled to herself. Human nature was an amazing thing. This place, once used as a springboard for the worst ideas ever hatched in human history, now played home to hundreds of happy people enjoying their lives—free from the tyranny and hatred that'd once been their downfall.

Daniel gave her a push from behind and Gareth immediately appeared by her side with a growl. Her love was on full alert, and his eyes were glowing with the stark emerald fire of a man ready to start another war against anyone who even breathed on Leah wrong. She could see the wheels turning inside his head, trying to figure out the best way to disarm the evil freaks and get to safety.

Calmly, she rested her hand on his chest. "It's okay. The guy's just a worm."

"We could start screaming," he suggested.

Daniel's breath flowed in between them like a fetid wind. "I wouldn't recommend that. Not only will you not get Athena's weapons, but I'll shoot you right here on the spot."

Gareth smiled. "And you'll tell the police what? That you're a descendant of the Reich and came here to find the crown of Lucifer?" He snorted. "That should go over well."

"Don't be fooled. The world is full of violence. By the time someone turns around to see what happened, I'll be long gone. And don't forget, I have friends in very high places in the German government. You'll just be some American asshole who disappeared. But, Leah—" he stopped, grinning at Gareth's angry face. "She'll remain with me, unharmed, until I get bored doing exactly what I really want to do with her."

"Son of a—"

Leah grabbed Gareth's arm and led him into the old building. "Let's just get this over with."

"Do you honestly think if you find this thing for him he'll just give us Athena's stuff and send us on our merry way?"

Leah winced. "No. But at least we'll have a bargaining chip."

"Do you really think it's here?" Gareth calmed his voice and squeezed her hand tight.

"I have no idea. But it's the only place that makes sense. Hitler *was* at the table in Crowley's basement."

"What about Rasputin?" Gareth said casually, causing Leah to shudder as he once again seemed to live inside her own mind. "He was at the table."

Leah shook her head. "Our lovely host told us that he'd been all over Rasputin's territory already and found nothing."

"Then why would Rasputin have been there?"

Leah truly wanted to bury this subject and get on with their present theory. "Crowley worshipped the guy, and Daniel told us that this…Wiligut, the loony designer who worked for Himmler, was referred to as Himmler's Rasputin—Lord of the Runes. That could be the tie-in with the crown."

"Or he could have nothing to do with the crown. Maybe there's something else out there."

Leah sighed. "Bite your tongue. After this we're retiring to a nice, warm island."

"Deal."

Leah's brain tried to find reason. "It has to be Hitler. Remember? His image didn't even look at us in Crowley's house; we were too unimportant to even be noticed. He was the king, as far as he was concerned. He didn't hate us, he just didn't care. It was like he knew we hadn't come there for anything that belonged to him."

Pride was visible on his face. "Well, you're never wrong."

Leah rubbed the sapphire mark on the back of her hand. "I was. I involved Athena. That's why we're here in the first place, because I was dead wrong and I need more than anything to make it right."

* * *

The couple entered the back door, avoiding the accurate aim of tennis players all around them. As the metal slammed shut, Leah felt the fear slam against her chest. The air was cold, like an old tomb where the ghosts of innocent soldiers still walked, trying to find their way back to a world that'd held so much promise for them in their youth.

Leah walked hand in hand with Gareth and stared up at the mosaic ceiling. It twinkled above their heads, as if one ray of sunshine had gotten trapped inside the building and couldn't find a way out. She stopped and stared at the strange, glittering sight.

"This was known as the Golden Hall."

Leah could feel him before she heard him. Her skin crawled when Daniel passed by.

"The mosaic tiles are made of gold," he continued. "I thought you were completely wrong about this site, Leah. But now that I'm here, I can see this building is more like a house of worship than a place to simply hold parades. Albert Speer must have loved the Führer very much."

Leah swallowed her fear and let the calm, confident librarian living inside her clear the chaos from her brain. "Albert Speer," she repeated. "I've heard of him."

Daniel laughed. "I would certainly hope so, seeing as that we're standing inside his greatest achievement."

"Hitler's architect," she mumbled.

Daniel nodded. "It is really an amazing structure." He waved his hands in the dead, stale air. "This hall is over three hundred meters wide and eight meters high."

Leah felt the sarcasm creep through her body. "Kind of a waste of time when you think about it. After all, your beloved Führer was a munchkin. A hole in a tree would've been enough for him to stand comfortably."

Gareth chuckled. "And he could've helped out the little elves making the cookies."

"Exactly." Leah pointed her finger at him. "Then at least he still would've had a career path when the whole Reich thing fell apart." Leah and Gareth knew the hideous subject was nothing to joke about, but it made Daniel Bauer seethe with fury, which was exactly what they needed him to do.

Bauer's eyes flared. "I get so disappointed in you when you become like this, Leah; a bright, amazing woman of the world having to resort to childish sarcasm. It's just not a pretty side of you."

"I haven't found *any* sides of you that are worth a damn," she barked back.

Gareth held her close to his side. "Maybe you should look into that second career at a furniture store, Bauer. Just in case the whole, being the Devil, doesn't work out for you."

Daniel put the pistol into his jacket pocket. With this movement, the guards stepped forward, but he shook his head and pointed at the two doors across the hall. "Those are the staircases that led to the Führer's Rostrum. Hitler would choose one set of steps and walk up them by himself into the darkness. Himmler and the rest of his staff would take the other set of stairs so their leader could be alone to collect his thoughts."

Leah opened her mouth to let another jibe through, but decided against it. Worry and fear for the man she loved filled her brain. She still had no idea how far she could push Bauer before he snapped and decided to put a bullet through her true love's heart.

Daniel smiled when she closed her mouth. "See? You can be taught." He waved them to the staircase.

Leah opened the door, wondering why there were no locks in place to keep any potential sightseers out. Entering the small, enclosed stairwell Leah felt the breath leave her lungs. She didn't dare close her eyes, as she felt the unmistakable presence of evil dancing in the space around her. Hitler had stood here reveling in the sounds of a cheering, screaming, clapping, awestruck crowd, who'd traveled miles just to spend a few hours in his presence.

Leah could hear the rhythmic thumping of the avid tennis players outside. But in her mind the sounds of the innocent game transformed into the footsteps of a million marching soldiers, eager for their master to emerge and bestow upon them the pride and honor they so richly deserved. The black, red and white banners would've been flying when Hitler's foot hit the last step of the now blistering hot stairwell. The eerie strains of Wagner would've been throbbing in his ears inside this small space, welcoming the ultimate guest of honor to the massive rally.

Quickly Leah sent up a prayer, thanking her Friend for the warmth of Gareth's body behind her, as she tentatively walked in the footsteps of the Führer.

CHAPTER 30

The brisk wind cooled Leah's over-heated skin as soon as she stepped out on the grandstand. As her gaze adjusted to the bright sunshine, Leah took in the enormity of the site. Knowing her research, it was mind-boggling to see the place that was bigger than twelve football fields, able to fit over two hundred thousand people attending the mass parades honoring their twisted leader.

Leah watched others wander around the field. Some played sports, while others sat down with their picnic lunches to enjoy the snow-free winter day. And some, Leah noticed, had looks that mirrored her own. The other out-of-towners' mouths were agape as their cell phones took pictures, attempting to capture the awesome spectacle that'd been left behind by the Third Reich.

Leah peered over her shoulder at the guards who'd actually chosen to remain dressed in their black and silver outfits. "Do they really fit in here? I don't think these people would be too pleased with a reenactment."

Daniel's gaze grew frightened, as if he just noticed the seriously bad decision. Immediately he waved the guards back into the shadow of the staircase.

"My God," Gareth breathed.

"I told you it was stunning," Daniel said. "The Zeppelintribüne. Albert Speer put over one hundred anti-aircraft searchlights into the ground around this structure, enclosing the field in beams of light that looked like heavenly columns stretching into the night sky. That's what he called it…The Cathedral of Light."

Leah stared at the man whose voice began to quiver. She was shocked that he was truly crazy enough to be so utterly moved by the remains of this hell on earth. "Oh, for crissakes," she shouted. "They held *parades* here. That's all! It's not like the speaker's podium is a doorway leading into the magical world of *Oz*!"

She toasted her small victory when Daniel's eyes grew wide and his face turned beet red. He glared at her and clenched his fists at his sides. "The last rally held here was in 1938, and the attendance for that particular moment in time was over a million people."

Surprised at the statistic, she turned to Gareth. He smiled. "Nothing on TV. It was way before *Sleepy Hollow* or *The Walking Dead* came along."

She grinned. "No *German Idol*?"

Gareth winked. "Sure…Hitler was it. He worshipped the ground he walked on. And with only the one contestant, it made voting kind of a moot point."

Daniel sighed loudly. "Speer chose to construct the building out of concrete and brick. He then used shell lime slabs for the face. The creation is completely symmetrical. Speer liked using white and yellow rectangle stone facades that were so popular with the Roman Empire in most of his work. It's a wonderful tribute to Nazi architecture."

Leah raised an eyebrow. "Again…with your talents? Home Depot all the way."

The increasingly frustrated man continued, doing his best to ignore Gareth's laughter, "Hitler and Speer agreed that the ancient civilization knew what they were doing. They created their buildings so that even after thousands of years had passed, people would still be able to come and witness the perfection that'd been built by master craftsmen."

Leah stared at the speaker's platform. An iron fence went around the top of the balcony, and four concrete steps led to the dais where Hitler had performed. Looking around, she had to admit that the workmanship Speer had put into the building was quite remarkable, even it was made for the most evil of men.

"If it weren't for you rotten Americans it would look even better," Daniel remarked. He pointed up at the flat roof of the grandstand. "A large swastika once sat up there like a crown on Speer's glowing achievement. But on April 22, 1945, your army held its victory parade in this spot and blew the swastika up. They wanted the whole world to know that National Socialism had come to an end." He looked at Leah. "Your country seems to always want to destroy history. At least…any history that doesn't include them."

"Yeah, we're real jerks that way," Leah said. "How dare we march into this country and save people's lives."

"You really don't want to fight about this with me, Leah," Daniel said. "Your country is still doing it today. Walking into places where no one asked them to come in the first place and starting trouble."

Leah shouted, "Maybe they don't ask for our services but, boy o' boy, they take our money quick enough, don't they? All of you. You talk about how absolutely horrible we Americans are but everyone begs us for money, food, aid…everything. When anyone has a problem—oppressed by their regimes or starving to death in the streets—they like us a whole lot. And then, when everything's all smoothed out, they hate us again. So make up your mind!"

Leah took a deep breath, feeling the fire of loyalty explode inside her. "If Hitler didn't want us to notice what he was doing over here, and wanted us to stay the hell out of it, he should've called up Japan, found out their plans, and said, 'Dude, think twice. If you bomb them they'll eventually come over here and kick *our* ass.' "

Love beamed from Gareth's emerald eyes, as Daniel Bauer stood completely still before her utter rage at having her country smashed for doing the right thing. Surprisingly, a smile crept across his face. "You're fabulous, you know that? No political-correctness with you, dear Leah. Your opinion is your opinion and that's that." He threw a look at the tall, handsome man who was always by her side. "You're a lucky man, Lowery. I think whether this little adventure goes my way or not, I'll still have to kill you just because."

Gareth's eyes sparkled with glee. "I can't wait to see you try."

Leah stepped away from the manly threats. Daniel's statement had made her blood run cold. Without Gareth by her side she knew her present would not only crumble, but any future she could ever think of having would disappear in the blink of an eye.

Taking the small steps two at a time, Leah reached the speaker's platform and stared out across the field. Her stomach churned just thinking about the past. One lone man had stood right here and been worshipped by millions. That kind of ego-trip would send any sane person over the edge, let alone a twisted individual like Adolf Hitler.

"Can you imagine?" Daniel spoke behind her. "In 1909, a Zeppelin actually landed here on this land. Now the area is used for boating and swimming, car races and sports events. It's truly sad."

Leah kept her comments to herself. She let him take a walk through history, as she chose to engage her brain to try and find the one piece of the puzzle that seemed to be missing from Bauer's factual presentation.

Gareth walked up to her. "What is it?"

Her voice sounded desperate and defeated in her own ears. "He's right. This area has been ripped apart. Pillars were blasted off their foundations; the stone seating is crumbled and overgrown with weeds…everything's gone. If my hunch is right, that crown would've been buried here by someone who knew what they were doing. I have no idea where it would be now."

"Leah, there's something that really bothers me about this," Gareth began. "If Bauer's telling you the truth, your mother found that emerald in the mines. Even though your Dad says they never removed it, she must have gone back alone and done it. I remember what my parents said about the ongoing digs in Qumran. Most things were found after the excavations had been going on for decades, including those mines.

"Your mom had to have found that emerald in the early seventies, because your father said that's the time frame when she disappeared. That's when she told him to split you and Anippe up, and run. But the emerald had to have been placed in there from the time Christ walked the Earth—when Kind Herod's reign was in full swing.

"But this," he continued, placing his hands on the iron fence around the speaker's platform. "Speer built this in the 1930s. If you think the crown is actually buried here, then who brought it here?

Where did it come from? And where had it been buried since the time Lucifer got cast out of Heaven and walked the earth? If Adolf had it, someone else gave it to him. And if it was actually buried here before Hitler was ever born, who put it here?"

She smiled at the confused man. "All good questions."

He pulled her against him. "I just don't know how an architect in Germany in the 30's could've possibly known about Lucifer's crown being buried here. He couldn't have known where it was originally buried, or by whom."

Leah felt the frustration well up inside her soul. He was right. They were talking about a literal biblical artifact. All the others had been found in locations that had everything to do with the life and times of Jesus. How could a twentieth-century building be the final resting place of a crown that'd been cast from Heaven thousands of years ago?

The card catalogue inside her mind remained open. It felt like the index card she needed with the answer spelled out in big bold letters, was lost somewhere inside the over-crowded mess.

She leaned back against the metal railing and stared at their host. "Do you know what happened here?" she asked. "Besides the facts that are available on Google. Maybe the other descendants of the Reich had personal stories to tell that date way farther back than the Nazi regime?"

Daniel's forehead furrowed. The lines of intense thought were etched deeply in his tanned skin. "Hansen."

Leah's blood ran cold when an image of the man with the yellow eyes jumped into her mind. "What about him?"

"His grandfather attended the rally in 1938. He was a VIP in Hitler's hierarchy."

"Hansen came from a Jewish family."

Daniel smiled. "An incredibly *rich* Czech Jewish family who fully supported the Führer."

Leah felt like her eyes would roll so far back, she'd finally get a first-hand look at the storage unit inside her head. "Is there a point to this?"

Daniel's golden-brown eyes grew cloudy, as if he were the chosen narrator for a long-dead spirit who'd just taken over his body. "The parade grounds were stunning. The men and boys in their uniforms were crisp and clean, and so unbelievably young. There were stars in their eyes; they were actually grateful to be a part of such an amazing moment in history.

"But the *most* amazing part came when Hitler took the platform and began to speak; there were a million people but you could hear a pin drop. He was spell-binding. Hansen's grandfather said it was like Hitler had someone else inside his body when he opened his mouth—some powerful spirit that spoke through the Führer's lips. He transformed right in front of their eyes that night. Hansen's grandfather described it as a Luciferian possession—like the Devil, himself, was escorting Hitler up a ladder into Heaven."

Leah's breath came quickly; as she listened to Daniel Bauer tell the tale of a dead man.

Daniel blinked, and his face suddenly relaxed. He stared at Leah with a half-smile that made his lips twitch. His voice went back to normal, and the Australian accent once again fell into place. "That was one experience. I also read an article once about a defected Nazi. He said that watching Hitler speak was like a light appearing in a dark window. He said something along the lines of how strange it was to watch a little man with a comic mustache turn into an Archangel right in front of the crowd. Then suddenly the Archangel just flew away, leaving a short man down below with glassy eyes and sweat pouring off his face."

"Lucifer and the Archangel," Leah mumbled. She listened to the cards inside her head shoot from their box. "Albert Speer."

Daniel and Gareth stood silently staring at her. Confusion was prevalent in their eyes, waiting for Leah to continue her thought. She didn't.

"Albert Speer…the architect of the building," Daniel prodded her on.

"So he based *this* particular building on the Roman Empire?" Leah said.

"No," Daniel replied. "This particular one, if I remember correctly, was based on the Pergamon Temple. This is, or was, supposedly a mirror image of the real one."

Leah felt the puzzle pieces in her brain begin to click and snap together. "The Pergamon Temple. In the ancient Greek city of Pergamon?"

Daniel shrugged. "I suppose so."

"It's now called Bergama…in Turkey," Gareth added.

Leah nodded at her love. "A temple that was specifically built to honor Zeus."

Daniel chimed in, "But the actual temple isn't there anymore. It was moved to Berlin…to Museum Island. That's on the Spree River in the center of the city." He stopped. "I don't understand. The Pergamon Museum inside that complex holds the reconstructed Pergamon Altar. Did you want to see it?"

"The Pergamon Altar is in Germany?" Leah said. She tried to keep her voice calm as the answer stared her directly in the face. There was no doubt left in her mind—Leah knew exactly how the crown had gotten into Adolf's hands.

Bauer stared into her soul. "The Altar, with Zeus' podium, was brought here in 1910. It was excavated in 1904, shipped here, and rebuilt inside the museum."

"Leah…what's the matter?" Gareth asked.

She stuck her hand in her coat pocket and squeezed the small stuffed lamb inside. She slammed her boots against the concrete slab of the platform. "Albert Speer wasn't a diehard Nazi, was he?"

Daniel shook his head. "No. Some say he was hiding the fact that he was a devout Christian. When the Nazi war criminals were put on trial—just down the road from here, in fact—he was the only one who showed any type of remorse."

"Remorse?" Leah felt the clouds of fear slowly disappear, as a plan began to form inside her mind.

Daniel nodded. "I couldn't believe it either when Hansen told me about it. Speer was the chief architect, and later the Minister for Armaments during World War II. He was one of very few people who had the Führer's ear. Yet, when he was sentenced to twenty years, he was actually grateful for the justice he felt he deserved. Speer went down in history as the only Nazi who ever said he was sorry."

A light bulb flicked on inside Leah's brain and she immediately aimed her eyes at the ground.

"Leah…speak," Gareth begged.
"We're gonna need a sledgehammer."

CHAPTER 31

The sledgehammer was apparently too simple for the determined Australian. Leah couldn't believe how fast he'd mobilized once the words had come from her lips.

Bright orange dump trucks appeared out of nowhere. The familiar guards changed out of their requisite silver and black into the battered jeans and plaid shirts of a hard-working German road crew. Leah noticed, as they marched toward her single file with their expressionless faces set in stone, that they just didn't fit the costumes of normal everyday citizens. She was an American, after all. The superhighways of the United States were littered with the annoyed looks of road crews. Whether sweating in the blistering hot sun, or freezing in the horrid winter weather, the men and women stood stoic, signaling drivers to stop or frantically waving at them to move on. And most of the time drivers were too into their cell phones to pay any attention at all. But the reincarnated Stormtroopers had no trouble making people stop. When they'd appeared in the parking lot, one look from them had even sent the avid tennis players running back to their homes.

Leah shielded her eyes from the setting sun that now looked like it was on fire; a warning, perhaps, from the real power above that they were about to unearth something that needed to stay buried. She pulled her jacket tighter around her shivering body as the winds changed back into the familiar deep-freeze of a January evening.

Her eyes followed the workmen as they came up the steps. Their heavy boots were buffed and shined, like good little soldiers, and their steps were quick as they marched up the two staircases leading to the podium. The group proceeded to drop large orange cones around the Führer's dais, marking their territory so they could follow the orders being given from the next leader in line for the throne.

The sledgehammer was a distant memory; Leah covered her ears when the jackhammers sprang to life. She looked over at Gareth, who was staring out at the now empty field. The happy faces of the people were gone; the friendly picnic gear had been picked up, and the tourists' cameras had been silenced.

Daniel stood beside the guards and stared into the hole where the concrete had been split open. His eyes were huge. Leah waited to see his tongue drop from his mouth and begin salivating over the still undiscovered crown. Elbowing Gareth, she pointed her finger at the door.

Gareth took one last glance at the men huddled around the now broken landmark, and followed Leah inside.

The metal slammed behind them and Leah quickly marched down the steps, intent on getting away from the evil that she swore was still alive inside the stuffy stairwell. As they exited into the open space of the Golden Hall, she took a deep breath.

Gareth took her in his strong arms. "Are you okay?"

"How did he—?"

"I don't know, love. He probably has his own million-man army on standby just in case. One call on his cell and he made the world disappear."

"This place." Leah shuddered. "The evil that came out of here. The evil that *stood* here. It's like all of it remains locked inside this…"

"I know."

"It's not even Bauer who scares me. It's the fact that he seems to be building up the kind of power Hitler had."

Gareth laughed. "I wouldn't say that, Leah. The guy is, at best, a really distant copy of the demon that used to speak here."

"The demon who looked like an Archangel had taken over his body," Leah repeated the strange description that'd come from

190

Daniel's lips.

Gareth leaned back. "I know. I wouldn't exactly put those two beings together in one sentence."

Leah shook her head. "There's something about that line that really bugs me."

"Because it's sick?" Gareth continued, "The Archangel comes to this earth to protect the innocent, fight for the people who can't fight for themselves. It is the angel's job to watch over you and make sure no danger is nearby."

Leah stared into the emerald eyes. They were so soothing. She could get lost in the power and the love that always seemed to glitter inside them. Gareth was such a strong man, but she still couldn't get over how big the heart was that beat inside his chest. She smiled up into the face of the man who never ceased to amaze her. "You must be an Archangel."

He raised an amused brow. "Nah. Celibacy doesn't work for me."

Hitting him in the chest with the palm of her hand, she rolled her eyes at his sad attempt at a joke to ease the moment. "Seriously. You've already proven you were put on this earth to protect people, to fight for the ones who aren't strong enough to fight for what they believe in. Kathryn and Emmanuel, Anippe…me."

He laughed loudly. "*You*? Not strong enough? The woman who hunted down almost every object of God and His Son in order to protect *Them*? Beings she didn't even *believe* in? A woman who figured out every puzzle left behind by some pretty sick and twisted wingnuts? And let us not forget, you're a descendant of Moses… which means you and the Archangel Michael have some history."

Leah felt her mouth go dry. "What?"

"You know, Michael being Moses' guardian, and all." Gareth grinned. "Well, maybe *you* wouldn't know. Kathryn and I learned all this in that place called Sunday School."

"Okay…tell me a story," Leah whispered.

Gareth's eyes suddenly narrowed, as if finally noticing the serious look in the sapphire eyes. "In the Epistle of Jude the Archangel Michael was the one who fought the Devil over the body of Moses." His voice sped up as he continued, "In the Book of Joshua, Joshua looked up and saw a man standing in front of him with a weapon in his hand in…Jericho." Gareth paused.

"*What* weapon did he have in his hand?" asked Leah.

"It was described as a golden, double-edged sword."

The image of her dream—the sword hovering in the light—raced back into her mind. But she'd been completely encased in rock. There'd been no way to reach out and grab the weapon. And there had been no way to stop the horrible crown-wearing beast from entering the tomb and killing her. "Michael didn't have a spear?"

Gareth shook his head.

"Not *ever*? Not even in *one* story?"

"No."

"Someone's trying to tell me something, Gareth. If the Archangel was close to Moses and watched over him then maybe, because of the link, he's watching over us, too." Her heart beat faster. "Unfortunately, he's not the one who looked in my eyes and said that he'd always be with me."

Gareth swallowed hard. "The Devil told you that in the Upper Room." He reached out for her hand. "Love…think of it this way. If you'll excuse the pun, there's not a chance in hell Lucifer's crown is going to be buried in this twentieth-century building. Maybe Crowley would've put it here, but he was only involved with hiding the orbs."

Leah nodded, remembering the artifacts. "Well, Crowley hid one half; Steiner got the others."

"Wait a minute." Gareth whispered, "Rudolf Steiner."

Leah looked up at her suddenly pale-faced hero. "What?"

"I researched those orbs for years before I met you."

"I know. After you found those six 'good' ones, you came to the library to find Crowley's map to the 'evil' ones." Leah waited. "And?"

"Steiner gave a lecture in Zurich in 1917. Thousands attended. My mom used to talk about it because her parents had been there. Steiner talked about a momentous event that once took place—a battle of the Powers of Darkness against the Powers of Light."

"So?"

"Leah, he said the battle ended with the Archangel Michael overcoming the Dragon…Lucifer—not the Son overcoming him."

She could barely breathe. "Daniel wants the crown worn by Lucifer because the Crown of Thorns won't stop him."

Gareth's muscles strained against his coat. "Bauer told us that if he got the emerald and the crown back together nothing could stop him."

"He's right, Gareth. If he puts those two things together, Lucifer's power will be reignited. The orbs, the words of the Son, the Sapphire Staff…he won't need any of it because we brought him underneath Jericho and led him right into Eden already. He knows where it is. With that crown on his head he could travel between Heaven and Earth, back and forth, taking everything and everyone with him. He'd have it all. And the Second Coming wouldn't be a worry because Bauer is just a guy, he's not Lucifer. He'd just have the power of that crown."

Gareth choked on his words. "And the only thing that can destroy the power of that crown—the only thing that ever conquered it—"

"Was the sword of the Archangel Michael." Leah hit herself in the head with the palm of her hand.

"Wait…Leah…there's still the huge fact that the crown being here is highly unlikely. It just wouldn't make any sense."

"Gareth, *everything* makes sense about this. There have been wars forever. There have been demons forever. The Greeks referred to them as giants." Her brain swirled with information. "I may not know my theology, Gareth, but I definitely know my mythology. In every time period, every decade on earth, there's been a giant. These demons would stand on the shoulders of others and force them down with their power. Their gift was the ability to make people afraid. And they preyed on that fear every chance they got.

"King Herod was a giant. So was Rasputin, and even though in today's violent world Jack the Ripper seems abysmally normal, his power once had people scared to death. These were actual demons. And *Hitler?* Hitler went way farther than the rest of them. He almost had it. He was actually the culmination of all the wannabes. Think about it. We're standing in a place where one man held a million people in the palm of his hand. They were beyond sheep, Gareth. They would follow this guy—and *did*—to their deaths without question. Today, nobody can figure out exactly why they were so taken in by him but, back then? In a world that was hungry and needed someone to stand up for them he must've seemed like a god. He said all the right things at exactly the right times. An Archangel didn't float into his body when he spoke—Lucifer did."

She wanted to stop talking. Leah was so frightened by the look on Gareth's face that she wanted more than anything to comfort him and tell him she was wrong. But the last thing she could ever do was lie to him.

Taking a deep breath, Leah felt the gears of her mind engaging; each cog clicked into place. "The biggest demon—the *biggest* giant— has walked the earth since he was cast out of Heaven. We know chances are he's been hitching his star to anyone who showed even the tiniest ability to resurrect the power and place it back into his hands. The picture outside Himmler's room that Hitler gave to him *shows* Michael standing above Lucifer. His sword is in his hand and a broken crown is beside Lucifer's body."

"Hitler wanted Himmler to hang it upside down," Gareth remembered.

Leah nodded. "Because if reversed the outcome would be different." She paused. "Gareth, the crown in that painting had no jewel. It was a simple pitch back ring, like the silver had been burned in a fire, or something."

Gareth bit down hard on his lower lip. "So quite possibly the crown wasn't anything but headgear and all the power was in the emerald."

Leah shrugged. "That gem probably holds the Divine knowledge of Heaven, which Lucifer warped into something evil. It made the crown powerful, and Michael took that power away."

"By extracting the emerald with his sword," Gareth whispered.

"Exactly. That emerald was probably buried in those mines forever. Would anyone ever really look for it there? Something with that much power relegated to a pit? The evil coming off that thing was what produced wolves and scorpions—its own demonic army that would keep it safe just in case someone did stumble onto the scene. Whoever did take it out of there had to have had protection to get it. And then, when I showed up with it around my neck, the demons couldn't touch me because I was already wearing the thing that'd made them in the first place."

"But how could Lucifer's emerald have held the seed of the actual Son? You put that in there, Leah."

Leah remembered how the stone had grown in size in order to hold the seed that would uncover the location of the true Garden. "The Son is watched over by the Father, Gareth. And since any power Lucifer had could never even come close to God's, anything belonging to the Son would have been automatically protected by the Father. Therefore, the seed had no trouble being inside the emerald."

Leah's heart filled with sorrow. "The 'good' seed was hidden in a place where no demon would ever be allowed to go—the Garden Tomb. And they hid the 'evil' seed where no good person would ever enter—Herod's palace of death. They split them up so you would need both sides of the puzzle in order to locate Eden."

"Just like we needed the good and evil orbs in order to open the Gates of Heaven," he added.

"We did it again!" A scream erupted from her throat. "Why don't we *ever* just leave well enough alone?"

"Leah, your father had been kidnapped. They would've killed him."

"I sacrificed the location of another doorway to *Heaven* to save one man?"

Gareth sighed. "Leah…he's your *father*. I sacrificed the location of Heaven because I wanted to finish my parents' work, remember? I wanted to honor their memory." He bowed his head and stared at the marble floor. "What about the seed of Athena? That was the third one. What did she have to do with all this? The Archangel Michael was the warrior in this little scenario, not a Greek goddess."

She shrugged. "I don't know. They needed a woman?"

Gareth sighed.

Leah's head felt like it would burst when the answer appeared before her eyes. "No. It *was* the seed of the Archangel…*protected* by a beloved woman. Like Mary was to Jesus, Athena was the warrior whose spear protected her male counterpart. That's it!" She stared into the emerald eyes. "The powers that be wanted us to have that spear."

"But why? It can't kill Lucifer. It can't even break the crown."

Leah offered a silent apology to the Son for all the mistakes they'd made. "Aren't you the one who always says, have faith? The spear *must* do something."

Gareth stood up straight. "Whatever you do, don't let him get that emerald."

"Gareth," she whispered. "We can't let him get that crown."

CHAPTER 32

"I've never loved a woman more in my entire life."

Leah's heart shattered when she watched Daniel Bauer arrive victorious in the Golden Hall carrying a sterling silver crown in his hands. When he placed it on top of his head Leah's stomach finally revolted.

Daniel's face glowed. He reached up and ran his fingers over the polished crown. He caressed the carved images that'd been etched into the metal. "Oak leaves. I didn't think it was possible."

Gareth joined Leah. Turning, he bent over and retched.

"I don't know what you're both so upset about." Daniel laughed. "I think it makes me look good."

Leah pushed the strands of sweat-soaked hair away from her face, and tried not to look at his smug expression. Instead, her eyes went directly to the center of the crown. A gaping hole sat there waiting to hold the missing gem. "I think you look like the fourth-runner up in a Miss Dumbass pageant."

"Tsk, tsk." He smiled. "Is that any way to talk to a newly crowned prince? You should be congratulating me. This is a *big* day. I've accomplished something that no one else in history ever has."

Gareth wiped his mouth on his sleeve and stared at the ridiculous man. "Prince of the Fourth Reich. Congratulations."

"Please," Daniel snorted. "I told you, I've used the past only as a stepping stone to get to my future. I have no interest in leading

Germany or anyone else, for that matter. I have much higher goals than that. Besides," he continued, "I rather like the States. Maybe the West Coast. I like the sun and, after all, I'd be right at home now in the City of Angels."

Leah gagged; she wouldn't be surprised to see her lung fall out on the floor.

Daniel stared at her. "How did you know?"

She remained silent.

"I have to know, Leah. You have to tell me." He snapped his fingers and two of the guards—who'd changed back into their silver and black uniforms—appeared from around the corner at the end of the golden hallway. "I'm afraid I can't take no for an answer."

"It was Speer."

"The architect?"

"You said Albert Speer built this monstrosity to mirror the Pergamon Temple."

"So?" Daniel prodded.

She stared into his golden-brown eyes. Anger swept through her body like a raging inferno. "I may not know religion, Daniel, but I have one thing on you."

"Which is?"

"When we were at the castle you said you'd never read the Book of Revelation, remember? You said you didn't want to read about how it all ended…how the Son of God wins the final battle. You wanted to change the outcome."

He nodded.

"That was the one I did read. Being a librarian, I may not like a book—may not understand, or want to learn the subject matter—but I definitely want to know the end. That way, if anyone ever asks for my opinion, I can honestly tell them what I thought. All the best parts; surprise endings, unmasking the bad guy—everything is always saved for the last page in the final book."

She turned to Gareth's confused face. Reaching out her hand, she caressed his overheated cheek. "In Revelation, Pergamos was where Satan's Throne was. The Pergamon Altar was a large open-air marble podium with four steps going up to it. It was forty-feet high and had a ton of sculptures, but the biggest was a frieze called, 'The

Battle of the Giants.' It was dedicated to Zeus, but another had sat there and used it for his throne, as well."

The emerald eyes filled with tears, as she continued, "I'm so sorry my brain didn't get there sooner. I could've stopped all this."

Gareth shook his head.

Daniel's voice echoed in-between them. "*Sooner?* My dear, Leah. You have a mind that even the gods aren't worthy of. Add to that your Divine knowledge and, good Lord, you could actually be the smartest person in the whole world."

"If I'm so smart, why are *you* wearing *that*?"

Daniel offered a sympathetic pout. "Because I gave you no choice. I took your family, I threatened your friends…I was horrible to you. I found your fears—"

"And preyed on them," Gareth spoke softly. "It's not your fault, sweetheart. We've gotten out of so many messes, we've beaten so many demons, and we'll beat this jerk, too."

Daniel laughed heartily. "That would be something to see, Mr. Lowery. My ego isn't big enough to make me the fool. After seeing you in action these past years, I don't count you out. However, I sincerely hope I'm not dumb enough to even give you the chance to *try* and beat me."

The uniforms came out of nowhere. There seemed to be hundreds of them, like a horde of locusts had been sent down from above to punish them for what they'd done.

Leah screamed when a large arm wrapped around her waist to restrain her. Gareth pummeled the pile of men, but their numbers were too great. Screams tore from Leah's throat when bright, red blood poured from Gareth's nose and mouth. The lids closed on his emerald eyes, like a curtain falling on a life not yet completed.

She pulled and kicked against her attackers, but it was no use. It would take the Archangel, himself, to save her from the army of brute force that surrounded her.

Daniel took a step forward. His hot breath scorched her flesh. "Now…lets you and I talk about that emerald, aye?"

CHAPTER 33

Was it a relief to be dead? The pressure, the tension, the stress—all the things that made up the bad parts of life were gone. Her shoulders actually felt light as air now that the worries were far behind her. But there was still fear. She couldn't deny it. Not only had she fought against faith for years, but she'd also been the one to help Lucifer regain his power.

Leah laughed to herself. That's definitely one sin that probably didn't come with an automatic forgiveness policy. She could Hail Mary all she wanted, but it wasn't going to help.

Anguish filled her soul. No Hail Mary could erase the fact that she'd brought back 'Heil Hitler'. She'd done that with her stupid, sarcastic brain. A quiet librarian who'd wanted nothing more in life than to sit in the confines of her library far away from the outside world, was going down in history as the woman who returned Satan to his throne. Great. How had this happened? How had she gotten so far away from what she'd once cared about?

Gareth.

No. She shook the mutinous thought from her head. He was the only right decision she'd ever made. The heart, the mind, the love that he gave her unconditionally, was priceless. Yes. That was the word. There were no conditions with him. She could make mistakes, trip over her tongue, be scared of children, name a cat a swear word—it didn't matter. Find Lucifer's crown? Well…maybe that one mattered a little.

It hurt so bad; the knowledge that she would never see him again felt like a deadly virus crawling inside her. If Daniel's army had killed him and tossed his body into the forest, Gareth would be long gone by now. He'd be in some great glass elevator shaking hands with the Son as he walked through the Gates, back home.

She was happy for him. He'd be able to see his mother and father again. Boy, would he have stories to tell them. Leah hoped he wouldn't tell them what she'd done—the enormous mistakes she'd made. Even though she'd never have the chance to meet Mr. and Mrs. Lowery, she really wanted them to at least have a semi-good impression of her. Above all, though, she wished she could at least get the chance to tell them how much she had loved their son.

Leah felt herself hovering in the air. She swallowed hard, waiting for the moment when the angels with their checklists discovered who she really was and threw her into Hell where she belonged. Of course, Hell didn't really matter now. Without Gareth Lowery, Satan could do his worst and it wouldn't hurt, her heart was already gone.

"Leah?"

She didn't want to answer. Maybe she could make up a name... say she was someone else. *No*, she chastised herself. Lying probably wouldn't be the best idea, considering how much they frown on that in Heaven.

"Leah!"

"Crap," she breathed. She cringed at her own choice of words. Maybe it was better to go down below. God had to know that there was no way Leah could stay quiet, and no screw-ups were allowed inside the Pearly Gates.

Taking a deep breath, preparing herself for the horror to come, she opened her eyes. A face swam in front of her. The eyes were sapphire and the hair was black as midnight. The clouds in her mind suddenly parted. "Anippe?" She began to cry. "Jesus. He got you too?"

She nodded.

"Oh, my God," Leah wept. "But how can *you* be here? You didn't do anything wrong."

Anippe craned her neck from left to right and stared, completely confused, at their surroundings. Leah's skin was freezing. "I thought Hell was supposed to be hot?"

Finally, Anippe grinned. "We're not in 'the' hell, Leah. But if you ask my opinion we're damn close."

Leah tried to sit up but her muscles screamed out in agony. She raised her hand and felt the layer of sticky blood that was drying over her scalded skin.

"He burned your tattoo off," Anippe whispered.

"It's okay," Leah mumbled. "I didn't deserve it anyway." She took both hands and touched her face, searching for any other open wounds.

"I think he may have bruised your ribs," Anippe said softly, "but nothing else. I think when you passed out you killed the guards' fun, so they left."

"Good. The last thing I want Bauer to do is have more fun at my expense." She grunted, reaching out her good hand to Anippe. "Help me sit up."

Taking her cold flesh in her warm hand, Anippe pulled as gently as she could.

Leah wanted to scream when her ribs cracked and snapped under her sudden movements. Resting her feet on the floor, she placed her head against the damp wall behind her. "Where are we?"

"The witches' dungeon," an elegantly-accented voice replied.

Leah opened her eyes and stared at the new narrator in this twisted play. Heavy dark circles framed a set of weary eyes that glistened with tears. The long black hair was matted down the older woman's back, and her skin sagged from her bones, like she hadn't had a good meal in years. "Who are you?" asked Leah.

The woman bowed her head to the floor, as Anippe sat down beside Leah. "Her name is Neith. Apparently...she's our mother."

Anger and hatred tried to rage inside her broken body, but the knowledge that Gareth was no more had already blackened her soul. Nothing mattered. Leah stared at the defeated figure slumped against the wall. "Well...if it isn't the beloved mother."

The woman leveled her stare at Leah, not even cringing at the cold, lifeless tone of her daughter's voice. "I've wanted to meet you for a long time," she spoke calmly. "This is a dream come true for me."

"Really?" Leah snorted. "How ironic. I would call it a nightmare."

CHAPTER 34

Leah did her best to ignore her newest acquaintance, and turned to Anippe. "Where'd he get you?"

She could see that Anippe wanted to include the quiet female sitting in the corner in their conversation, but the harshness in Leah's voice kept her from doing so. "Herod's Palace. Some people dressed in black showed up. They told me it wasn't the real crown. They said I was wasting my time. Then they threw me into the back of a car with some man." Her eyes grew wide. "He was frightening, Leah. He had the yellow eyes of a cat and bright white hair. But he seemed no older than Gareth."

Leah felt the knife blade slice her in half at the sound of Gareth's name. She struggled to speak, "His name's Hansen; some psychic extraordinaire who hangs out in Bauer's circle." She sighed heavily. "Don't worry about him. He's just another useless wannabe. Bauer must've put an ad in the newspaper."

Anippe shivered. "He smiled at me the whole trip. It was like he knew a secret—something he was dying to tell me."

"He did," Leah replied. "Daniel probably called him up to let him know we'd found the real crown."

Anippe practically jumped off the stone ledge. "You found it? Where?"

"Nuremburg."

The woman spoke from across the room. "In the

Zeppelintribüne?"

Leah kept her eyes on Anippe, but offered a curt nod in reply.

"How did you guess that?" Anippe finally turned to Neith.

The woman opened her mouth, but Leah cut her off, "She helped Bauer's father ages ago. She told him where to find the emerald, but probably didn't give up the crown in order to hold on to her disgusting life just a little longer."

"That's not true," Neith stated.

Leah flicked her wrist in the air and winced in pain. "Whatever." Closing her eyes, she spoke to Anippe. "Where's dear old dad?"

"He'd already left."

Leah nodded, trying to block out the scalding pain that she knew she so richly deserved. She prayed for death now. She prayed for Hell. The bruises and breaks were nothing compared to the shattered heart inside her chest. She just wanted it to end.

"He left?" Neith's voice finally broke with emotion, and her thin face turned red. "You were at Herod's Palace and he just...*left* you there alone?"

Leah's eyes immediately popped open. "I wouldn't throw stones if I were you, *Mommy dearest*. You haven't exactly proven yourself to be an award-winning parent either. Neith, is it? Means, beloved mother? Boy, someone had a sense of humor on your side of the family."

Neith ignored Leah, apparently choosing to speak to the lesser of two evils. "Where's your father now?"

Anippe flicked her eyes between the two women. "He's at the Coptic Museum...with my uncle."

"Aaron is there?"

Anippe nodded. "Yes. He raised me. We work at the museum together."

A small smile crept slowly across Neith's face. "I'm glad it worked out."

Leah was stunned. She finally understood the phrase 'demonic possession' when the power of bitterness overtook her. "I see there's no apology forthcoming."

Neith stared at her. "There's so much to apologize for I wouldn't know where to begin."

"Give it a shot." Leah's voice remained calm; she knew that nothing would faze her anymore. She could stand up, grab a knife, and thrust it through the woman's chest without even a thought. Unfortunately, the witches' torturers had left no implements behind.

Leah pointed to Anippe. "She never even got a family. She's lived her whole life thinking her parents were dead. Not to mention, she had no idea there was a sister out there. What the hell is wrong with you?"

Neith swallowed hard. "I did what I had to do in order to save your lives."

"Don't romanticize it, lady," Leah snapped. "You disappeared in the middle of the night to grab some stupid stone. You got caught, and then sent word to your supposedly beloved husband to split up his *children*, make a run for it, and live a life of complete and utter lies. You're no better than Bauer."

"Leah," Anippe whispered.

"No," Leah continued her calm tirade. "Scratch that. That's not exactly true. Bauer's actually a step above you on the scumbag meter. At least he's open about being a jerk. He doesn't try to mince words about what he wants and why he wants it. He's just your average power-hungry idiot. He wants his fifteen minutes…that's all. But… you? *You* make it sound like your some kind of saint…sacrificing your life to walk in the footsteps of biblical people who may or may not have even existed. Put simply, you decided to protect their family instead of your own."

Neith put her back straight against the wall and folded her hands in front of her. Leah noticed the large burn mark on the top of her hand, and Neith followed her gaze. "I was marked—same as you sister—with an eye of emerald." She sighed. "From almost the day I was born, I was asked to be a protector of secrets…of families. You hate me, Leah. But in the end you're just like me."

Leah covered her own blackened hand. "My mark was sapphire."

"The Magi." Neith's eyes grew wide.

Slamming her boot heel against the ground, Leah felt the overwhelming need to cause the woman pain. "I *never* asked for this. And *I* never accepted the job. I'm *nothing* like you. In fact—" She tried to stop herself from choking on her own shame. "I pretty much just dropped the First Family into the lap of a psycho in order to save my father. I chose *my* people first."

Neith shook her head. "No."

"Excuse me?"

"The world is in upheaval again, Leah. It was coming. And this time it may be much worse than anything the Führer could've become. Demons are coming out of the woodwork and evil is taking over. You were chosen because of this. All you've done is fought for *Them*. You've discovered the pieces and risked your life to hide them away so no one will ever find them. What I began, you're finishing. You're in the battle of your life, and I know you'll win. The runes have said so."

"Great." Leah turned to Anippe. "We're not only from liars, we're from loons. Our stock is falling every day, kiddo. Better get yourself a good man while you still have your looks."

Anippe grinned. "You already took the best one."

Leah cringed as she felt the call of death. "I didn't deserve him."

"I've heard great things about him," Neith chimed in.

Leah would kill her with her own hands; she was definitely not good enough to speak his name. "Cast the runes, did ya?"

"As a matter of fact, I did."

"You didn't even know him."

"I have friends on the outside who've risked their lives to bring me information about you and your sister."

Leah snorted. "Great, more stalkers. Between you and Bauer, it's a wonder Gareth and I have had any alone time whatsoever. Had…" Leah bent at the waist, forcing her broken ribs to stab her even harder.

"He's not dead, Leah," Neith said quietly.

Leah's head came up so fast she heard another crack echo from inside her body. "What?"

Neith bowed her head. "I just wanted to be sure you knew that."

Her ice cold blood suddenly ran hot. "Lady, I know everything about Gareth Lowery. I don't need you or your ridiculous magic to tell me that he's okay." She settled back down. "He's always okay."

A small brown object flew through the air and landed in Leah's lap. She stared down at the small symbol⎟ etched on the wooden tile.

Neith spoke, "That is Isa. This is the one I always pull when I cast for your love. He is surrounded by challenges."

"No shit."

"Treachery, illusion, deceit, ambush; he must exhibit great courage in order to get past the frustration he feels. Right now he needs to come to a standstill and wait for things to unfold."

"I wouldn't count on that." Leah smiled.

A huge crash sent the metal door flying off its hinges, as Daniel Bauer marched over the threshold and into the dungeon. Without a word, he walked to Leah and pulled her up off the ledge, slamming his fist into her stomach. "Where is he?"

Leah could hear orders being shouted in the distance. Strange voices cried out, "Find him!" Through the mist of pain, Leah heard the frantic words echoing off the walls.

Bauer released his grip and she fell to her knees. As she stared up at her enraged enemy, laughter suddenly came through her tears. "Gareth's gone."

"I said…where is he?" The man seethed through clenched teeth. "The door to his dungeon was locked. Guards were posted outside. I can't believe the trouble you've caused! I was even kind enough to pull my guards off your brother-in-law and let him meet his pregnant wife in Crete. I've been kind to your extended friends and *this* is how I'm repaid?"

Leah laughed harder, ignoring the ferocious pain.

"Even his bloody knapsack is gone!" Bauer screamed, sending a hard kick that connected with her jaw.

Anippe screamed out. But Leah just opened her eyes and stared up at the gold swastika stuck in the stone ceiling. She smiled. "Fuck you."

Daniel stomped back through the door. A myriad of colors suddenly flew past Leah's head like a flock of birds that'd bombarded the cell. The bars slammed shut and the metal door on the outside banished the world from her sight.

He yelled from the other side. "I thought you girls could use a little company."

"My God…Khait!" Neith cried.

Leah stared past Anippe's body to see their surprise guest. A warning bell resounded in her skull, as the mysterious tour guide from Athens appeared before her eyes.

CHAPTER 35

Anippe helped Leah off the floor and set her carefully on the seat of stone. She whispered, "Isn't that the woman who showed us around the Acropolis?"

Leah nodded.

"What's *she* got to do with all this?"

Leah's sapphire eyes marched up and down the woman's sobbing figure. She looked afraid, but her hair was straight and shiny—her clothes clean and wrinkle-free—like someone had marched up to her on the street no more than an hour ago, thrown her into a car, and whisked her away to their dungeon.

Leah felt her skin prickle. "Why is it you don't even look slightly confused?"

Khait stared over at her. Her eyes were wide as saucers; it was as if this were the first time she'd noticed there were other people in the room. "What are *you* doing here?"

"I asked you first," Leah said, spitting the warm blood from her mouth.

Neith spoke, "This is the woman who I mentioned before; she is the person who has been bringing me information on all of you. Khait has spent most of her time in Athens watching over the emerald that I'd given her to hide."

Khait choked on a sob. "Until that horrible little woman came from England and bought it. I had stepped away from my post for

210

only a moment, and it was gone."

Neith shook her head; her face filled with shame. "And the runes never even warned us that could happen."

Leah had the overwhelming desire to follow Bauer's lead and kick both of them square in the face. "That's what happens when you use pieces of magical wood instead of your *brain* to live your life." She looked at Anippe and rolled her eyes. "Un…freakin… believable!"

Anippe undid the belt from her jeans. Reaching under Leah's arms, she wrapped the wide leather strap tight around her ribcage.

Leah squealed. "What are you doing?"

"If anything's broken you'll need the pressure to make sure it won't get any worse."

It was a shock to Leah's system to see the true respect and love for a sister swimming in Anippe's eyes. "Thank you."

Anippe smiled.

"Those are my girls."

Leah heard the emotional whisper. "There's *nothing* about us that belongs to you."

"Are you always this insolent?" Khait practically shouted, as if backing up her friend.

Leah glared at the well-kept woman. "Yes."

"You aren't much like your mother, after all."

"I'm the rude American version."

What looked like a sneer crept across Khait's face. "Ah, yes… truth, justice…"

"Exactly," Leah stated. "As opposed to lies, deceit, treachery…"

"America is full of those traits."

"I'm not," Leah snapped.

Khait sat back against the wall. A confused Neith sat still beside her and watched the conversation; her eyes were filled with questions. "You're hardened for one so young. Your sarcasm has made you bitter," Khait remarked. "I've been through hell and back—so has your mother—but we can still love."

"Congratulations. I'm so happy for you both. When's the wedding?"

Khait turned to Neith, and her voice transformed back into a soothing whisper, "Don't worry about it. My child, too, was against me for a long time. But along the way he finally understood that I was right about everything."

Leah turned to Anippe. "Do you ever think maybe people should have to pass a psychological exam before being allowed to breed? I've been thinking about that an awful lot lately."

Anippe couldn't stifle her giggle. "But you hate kids anyway, don't you? You think they're—"

"Icky." Leah conceded. "Well…except for one."

"Mary?"

Leah placed her hand on Anippe's shoulder. "You like her, too. Don't you?"

Anippe looked confused as she stared down at the forceful hand squeezing her shoulder. "I do. Very much…I was extremely happy to see her."

Leah nodded.

"Who is this child you speak of?" Neith said.

Leah flicked her chin at Khait. "You didn't tell her about Mary? You should know all about her…if you've been following us around since we got hold of the emerald."

"I only met her recently in the marketplace…when you went to wash her hands." Khait said, "I haven't followed you around. I kept track of the stone, that's all. I knew you'd eventually come to Athens."

"So the runes told you we'd visit Athens, but not the fact that the emerald would be taken out of the store in the first place? Interesting."

Khait's eyes turned black as pitch. "You shouldn't mock something you don't understand."

Leah grinned. ""I don't mock the ancient runes. In fact, I just gave a book about them to Mary so she could study up. She's getting pretty good at it. But, of course, *she* understands that the tiles are just a path…a path you can always alter, even slightly, to change the whole outcome."

Khait continued to stare at her. "Well, I'm happy to hear that you're being nice to this little person. It's a true joy to raise a child." Her eyes turned gray, as if clouds were forming in a midnight sky.

Anippe whispered in Leah's ear, "She seems sad. I wonder if

she lost her child?"

Leah raised her voice an octave, "Children and parents grow apart. That's what you just told Neith, didn't you?" Leah continued, "I remember you saying back in Athens that we all have to help the ones who need us. No matter what, it's their happiness that comes first."

Khait nodded strongly. "And I have done so for your mother for a very long time. She's my friend."

"Uh, huh," Leah spoke, turning her attentions back to Anippe. "How was Mary when you saw her in Qumran?"

Anippe shrugged. "A little afraid, I think of…what you asked her to do. When she got there she threw up all over the place. I felt bad for her."

Leah felt a pang of guilt, but the pride she had for the young girl who idolized her made her heart grow. Leah laughed inside. Talk about irony. A child—a creature that made Leah squirm—had ended up being her hero.

Neith spoke up, "My goodness, what on earth did you ask a little girl to do that would make her so afraid?"

"None of your business," Leah snapped. "I'd left something somewhere and I needed her to get to Anippe so they could return it to me." Leah looked out of the corner of her eye and registered the small grin that raced across Khait's face.

The metal door swung open and Daniel Bauer once again appeared before them.

Anippe turned to Leah. "Oh, God. They killed Gareth."

Leah stared into the eyes of her captor, filled to the brim with hatred. "I wouldn't bet on it."

CHAPTER 36

"Let me guess?" Leah smiled. "It doesn't matter, anyway. Isn't that your favorite phrase when you lose?"

The corners of Daniel's mouth twitched violently. "I simply came to say goodbye to you, Leah."

"Oh, good. Can I hope that this is goodbye forever? Or, would that be asking too much?"

Daniel glanced at the golden swastika over their heads. "I would do anything for you, Leah. You know that. Hope has nothing to do with it."

He walked toward her as the other three Horsemen of the Apocalypse filtered in behind their leader. Leah was revolted at how happy Williams looked. His bushy eyebrows were practically bouncing up and down on his forehead, like dueling caterpillars. Between his pasty white ears, those thick black brows, and bright red face, he could've passed for the Nazi flag.

The long, lean Wolf stood beside him, staring at Leah and Anippe. He, too, was filled with a euphoria that beamed from his wide eyes. He bowed to both of them. "I want to offer my thanks. Because of you the Master Race will eventually rise and take their place beside the other perfect nations."

"In Valhalla," Leah snorted. "How nice for all of you. When you get there tell Odin I said, hi'ya."

He smiled. "And you do the same for me…when you stand

before your god."

Leah hid the shivering of her limbs beneath her long, leather coat. Moving her gaze to meet Hansen, she watched him stare around the dungeon like a prospective buyer, reaching out and placing his hands on the strong, sturdy rock.

His creepy yellow eyes focused on Leah and Anippe. "It's amazing how unalike you are. Except for the eyes, of course...the sapphire orbs of power." He chuckled. "But I must say, Leah, with your dark red curls as their frame, the effect is like a beautiful sun setting over an ocean of blue. You can really pull it off."

"Gee...thanks," she sneered. "Maybe when you get to Valhalla you could open a salon. You know, do up those white guys with some signature coiffeurs."

Laughter shot from his lips so fast that the bright white ponytail hanging down his back jumped as if a bolt of electricity had struck it from above. "That's my truly favorite thing about God's children... their sense of humor."

Anippe whispered, "He scares me." Leah took her trembling hand.

Hansen finally calmed down, and wiped the tears from his eyes. "Ah...I really like you, Leah. And I don't like anyone."

"What can I say, Michael? Can I call you Michael? Mike...I'm honored." The room swam in sarcasm, and she flicked her gaze back to Daniel. "Seems all you nutbags are attracted to me. I must be some kind of magnet for crazies."

Hansen spoke before Daniel had the chance, "You know there's a huge part of me that hopes wherever Lowery is right now he'll come back and save you. I would very much like to meet you again one day."

"I'll be sure to look you up."

"I'll look forward to it."

Daniel slapped Leah across her already bruised face. "Wherever Lowery went it was definitely out of this castle. And even he isn't quick enough to get back in."

Anippe shuddered.

Daniel turned to the older women. "Well?"

Leah took a deep breath as she focused on Khait in the corner.

She felt no shock or surprise whatsoever when the woman got up and walked toward her. Khait reached her hand deep into the pocket of Leah's leather coat and extracted the white stuffed lamb. She tossed it into Daniel's hands. "The emerald's in there."

Neith gasped. "*What*? Khait…what are you doing?"

Khait turned and blew Neith a kiss. "Goodbye my friend."

"*What?* Wait!"

Leah watched her mother struggle from her seat and fall to the ground; the starvation had finally caught up with her.

Anippe jumped up and raced to her, pulling her off the cold, stone floor. "I got you."

Standing carefully, Leah tried with all her might to straighten her back like the warrior she felt burning inside her soul. She faced Daniel, as he tore off the head of the child's toy and extracted the large, round gem from inside. His eyes glittered with happiness as he stared at the priceless stone sitting in his blackened palm.

He looked at her, and smiled. "It's still warm. You've been saving it for me…protecting it until I could hold it in my hand. Thank you," he said through his visible tears. "I wish I had more to give you. I wish…we had worked out."

Leah remained silent, listening to the sobs coming from her mother's throat.

"But even if Lowery had never been in the picture," he continued, "Your brain would have ended up destroying me. The intelligence you have isn't good for you, Leah. What you need to learn is that sometimes in life, it's much better just to be a follower."

Hansen's long arm snaked around Daniel's chest and he snatched the emerald from his hand. "I'll carry it. You can take the crown."

"Why?"

"You shouldn't put them together until we are far away from here."

Daniel nodded, as he stared into Leah's eyes. "You're right."

Leah watched Wolf and Williams disappear into the hallway, and gazed at Daniel Bauer one last time. "I guess that's it then."

He shrugged. "Tell you what." A fleck of gold beamed in his brown eyes. "The weapons of Athena are still inside the castle and I have no desire to take them with me, because…well—"

"Because they don't matter, anyway."

"Exactly." He grinned. "At least you'll die knowing that the warrior's weapons are safe. I give you my word that I won't come back for them. I won't let anybody come back for them. Soon you'll be gone, and then the guards out front will supervise the workmen. I'll have someone come to blast-seal Wewelsburg for good. And this time, *my* demolition man will know what he's doing."

"Why not just blow up the castle around us?" she asked.

He shook his head. "As I said, Leah, you can't teach an old dog new tricks. Some traditions are just so beloved that they're hard to let go of."

Her heart felt like it was going to explode; she tried to use her unmatched brain to figure out what terrifying form of torture they were about to experience.

Waving at Anippe, Daniel escorted Khait out of the dungeon. "Come on," he said to her. "It's time to go and celebrate our victory… as the elders did."

"Khait?" Neith stuttered.

The cell door slammed in Leah's face, and she wrapped her hands around the unyielding metal bars to stare into the eyes of the cat that lingered behind the rest of the troop.

Michael Hansen stepped closer and stared at her through the rusted metal; his thick gloves wrapped around the bars. "By the way, Leah." He smiled wide. "Nice crown."

Panic and confusion ran through her veins, as Hansen pressed his face through the bars and gave her a kiss.

She jumped back from him, listening to his laughter as he slammed the outside door, closing her off from the world for the very last time.

Neith wept on Anippe's shoulder. "I don't understand. She's my friend."

"No," Leah said, turning to face the females of her family. "She's Daniel Bauer's mother."

CHAPTER 37

Leah walked slowly to her place on the rock ledge, and sat down.

"What did you say?" Neith's voice was nothing but a shocked whisper.

"Khait is Bauer's mother."

Anippe leaned forward, her eyes wide. "How do you know that?"

"When she came in here she didn't have even one bruise. It was a setup. She talked about how hard it is to raise children and that her only child—a *he*—was against her for years. Daniel said his mother died and that Neith, over there, became his father's lover."

"I would never—" Neith began to voice her denial.

Leah held up her hand. "But there wasn't any anger in his words. And considering what an egomaniac he is, if his father had soiled his mother's memory by schlepping you, there would've been."

Neith took a deep breath to calm her anger, as Leah continued, "When Daniel talked to us about his father's death, and how he was given his destiny to follow, there was sadness in his eyes." She sighed heavily. "He also told me how much he respected women; how good they were at playing games and being conniving. No one would know what they were doing until it was too late. His harsh words uncovered a hatred for a mother who was supposedly already dead. It didn't add up."

She stared at Neith's desperate face and watched a smile curve her lips. "You *do* have the Divine knowledge, Leah."

"No. I just listen, watch and record. Although if you ask Gareth, I've always been a genius."

Anippe's sapphire eyes grew dim. "Where do you think he is?"

Leah shrugged. "I don't know. As long as he's alive, that's all that matters."

"How did he get out of a locked dungeon?" Neith asked. "Does he claim genius status, too?"

Warmth rushed into Leah's soul. "He's a genius, alright, but he didn't need to bite an apple to get there."

* * *

Time was ticking away so slowly that Leah wondered when the other shoe was going to drop. Not to mention, how heavy that shoe was going to be. Anippe paced around the small cell, and Neith held her head in her hands, defeated and afraid.

"I can't believe I didn't figure it out," Neith sighed. "I've known Khait since 1970. She was with me through both of your births. She absolutely loved David."

"Did you?" Anippe's words were quick and honest.

"What?"

"Did you love our…father?"

Leah laughed at the young woman's hesitation. "Yeah, come on, *Ma*. Give us the juicy details of a true love. It's not like we have anything else going on. Show us the kind of person you *really* are."

Neith sat back against the wall, with the gleam of challenge beaming in her eyes. "I *still* love your father. Very much, in fact. I was young when he came to Egypt." Her face grew softer as the memories floated back. "In the sixties, the digs at Nag Hammadi were still going on. The researchers had been there for decades and would end up looking for decades more. I was working with my father, who was a wonderful man. It was he who met your father first.

"David and Aaron were working on the dig. Young, strong, strapping young men who my father decided to hire. They helped him code and catalogue items that we found. David became my father's favorite very quickly. He would bring him home to have dinner with us, and when he took me out to the sites, your father would trip over his own two feet to be nice to me."

Leah tried to stop Neith's words from melting the ice cold veneer that'd grown over her heart when it came to the woman. She tore her gaze away from the once beautiful Egyptian and stared at Anippe, who was absolutely riveted. In fact, her sister looked like a VIP ticket-holder to the reunion of the Beatles. She hung on every word, visibly thirsty for any information she could get.

Leah felt bad for her. Anippe was just like her beloved Gareth, in a way. Both had spent years without their parents. One had lost them in a vicious accident; the other had lost them the day she was born. Leah still didn't feel that way. She'd had her father and her three annoyingly beautiful sisters every day of her life. And her mother…step-mother…had tried. Well…maybe not very hard, but she'd at least been there.

Neith took Anippe's hand and continued her trip down memory lane, "We became very close. Your father understood that I was marked. He understood that I was a protector and he wanted to be the hero who stood by my side. Much like Gareth is to your sister, I would assume."

"Gareth's the hero. I'm *his* companion," Leah corrected quickly.

"Are you sure?"

Mulling over their adventures in her mind, Leah replied, "Very sure."

Neith smiled. "Well…let's just say your father and I fell in love quickly and married young. My father was absolutely thrilled about it. Then we were blessed with Leah." She raised her gaze. "You were our savior…our shining star."

Leah turned away.

"With that auburn hair and those sapphire eyes, you were… are, a carbon copy of your father. He certainly could never say you weren't his."

Anippe's voice cracked. "Probably why he chose to bring Leah with him."

Leah's heart hurt for the sorrow-filled girl who felt severely jilted. Her voice spoke volumes about her deepest desires. "He wanted to take both of us," Leah said. "Mom over there was the one who told him to break us up and send us away."

"Leah," Neith began. "When we found that emerald I knew what it was. I'd studied with other protectors for years. I knew people were after me, and I had to get it out of there."

"People were after you because your beloved best friend, Khait, sold you out! She was married to a man who wanted to bring back the Master Race, for crissakes! And he passed that lovely duty down to his creepy little son."

Neith's eyes filled with tears. "I never thought she was a liar."

"Don't you know the old saying? Takes one to know one, *Ma*. You should've had her number in a second and a half." Leah's harsh, biting words flew across the cell and connected, knocking the wind from Neith's chest.

Neith shook her head; tears glistened in her eyes. "I know you'll never forgive me, but they were going to kill us all. They knew who I was and they knew the destiny that my children were born to have. I didn't know which one it would fall upon, so I sent you both far away from it."

Anippe's eyes grew wide. "I knew it. When my uncle and I were in Petra, I knew we were Moses' descendants. And then when Leah got there…" She stopped and stared into her mother's eyes. "We're a real part of history."

Neith nodded. "You come from a long line of protectors. And you've both proven yourselves to be strong warriors for the men and women who watch over us all."

"I knew it was true," Anippe cried. "I knew we were special."

"Well." Neith hugged her close. "You're both very special to me. I've missed you so much. I was hoping for so long that I'd just die in here."

"You might still get your wish," Leah muttered.

Neith looked over at her. "There's the one thing I don't understand. Khait was the one who buried the emerald for me. She knew where it was all along. If she'd known what it was, why didn't she just take it and give it to her husband years ago and start up their Fourth Reich immediately?"

Leah shook her head. "They needed the crown. Without the

right setting the emerald's useless. The two have to come together in order to work."

"And now they have them." Neith shuddered.

Leah and Anippe answered in unison. "No, they don't."

* * *

The small hissing sound crept into the dungeon, like an angry cobra had been unleashed under the door. Leah could barely hear the new sound. It was as if a lover was whispering in her ear. She stared up at the gold swastika on the ceiling and could just make out the faint drops of mist that hovered in the air before falling to the floor.

"Jesus," Leah whispered. Her head began to spin as the image of the victims walking two-by-two into the horrific building materialized inside her brain. Some had been smiling, completely unaware that the shower they were about to take would be their last.

"What?" Anippe said.

Leah could barely see the small blue pipe curled around the Nazi emblem. "Looks like Daniel was right. There's one tradition they wanted to keep." Closing her eyes, she tried to stop the poisoned air from entering her lungs. The metal door was shut tight; the high windows were closed and caulked.

Prayers echoed in Leah's brain as her body was slowly surrounded by the fatal air. The truth was overwhelming, knowing that she was about to die in Daniel Bauer's very own gas chamber.

"This can't be happening." Leah heard Neith whisper from the other side of the dungeon. "This can't be happening."

Leah groaned. "This is like one of Gareth's stupid horror movies."

Suddenly, the swastika fell from the ceiling and smashed to the ground in front of her. The familiar muscular form rode down the rope like Tarzan swinging comfortably from his favorite vine. The blue pipe had been turned up and out of the newly formed hole, stopping the deadly poison.

Gareth landed in front of her and pulled her into his arms. "Did I hear my name being said in vain?"

Leah stood…stunned, relieved, and grateful in his comforting grip. There was no pain anymore. Everything was right as she pressed her face against his strong chest and let the tears of relief flow from her extremely grateful heart.

CHAPTER 38

Neith struggled up through the hole in the ceiling, as Leah and Anippe pulled from above and Gareth pushed from below. Her withered body crawled over the stone floor, as she pulled herself up into Himmler's chair.

Leah took Gareth's hand and helped him through. When they were all once again on solid ground, Gareth aimed the blue pipe back into the dungeon and turned to the women around him. He raced to Neith's side. "Are you okay, Ma'am?"

Neith stared into the beautiful green eyes that reminded her of the sunrise over an Irish moor. "So you're her true love; the companion's hero."

Gareth smiled. "Or the other way around, depending on the day."

Neith laughed. "I've seen you in my dreams, Mr. Lowery. I'm so happy to have you in my reality."

Leah's voice echoed behind them, "What is it with the women in this family? As I told my new and slightly annoying sister already, I called dibs on the guy first."

Gareth winked at Neith and turned to Leah. "I happen to like the women in your family. I've never seen a bloodline that has such absolutely perfect taste in men."

Leah rolled her eyes. "Can we go now, please? Call me silly, but I have this aversion to blowing up."

"Blowing up?"

Anippe's worried voice broke through the chatter, "That's right! Gareth, he's sending someone to blast-seal the castle. He's going to destroy it."

Gareth stood up and grabbed Neith under her arms. He looked into her exhausted eyes. "Can you walk?"

"Running would be better," Anippe said.

Neith nodded.

Leah gave a kick to Himmler's ridiculous chair and raced to the door, forgetting the pain in her own body. "You guys go. I'm not done in here yet."

Neith was placed at Anippe's side, as Gareth took off after her. He shouted back over his shoulder, "Anippe, there's a small guardhouse outside with an orange roof. Get into it and wait there. I already got rid of the two goons Bauer left behind." He raced out the door. "We'll meet you there!"

Neith looked into the sapphire eyes of her youngest child. "He certainly is something, isn't he?"

Anippe smiled. "Leah's very lucky."

Neith pat her on the back and attempted to speed up beside the frightened girl. "Your Gareth is coming, my dear. I promise. Those runes that Leah hates so much already told me so."

* * *

Leah ran down the narrow staircase and into the second floor hallway. Putting on the brakes, she stopped outside Himmler's bedroom door. She stared at the strange addition to the painting of the Archangel slaying the worthless demon. Her heart stopped and her brain engaged, wondering why Daniel Bauer had taken the time, after finally getting his illustrious emerald and crown, to come back here and turn the painting upside down.

Gareth jogged up behind her. "I thought you were going for Athena's things? Why did you come down here?"

Leah pointed at the picture. "There's something wrong with this. It's bugging me."

"Well, let's just take it with us. You can study it on the way."

"Look," she said, pointing to the red light blinking behind the frame. "It's rigged. If we move it, it'll blow."

"Why the hell would he rig a painting?"

Leah stared at the upside down canvas. "Because there's something here that someone doesn't want us to figure out."

Gareth shrugged and his voice grew louder, "We have got to get out of here, Leah! It's just hung the wrong way. Looks like Hitler got his wish after all."

She shook her head. "No. Look closer."

Sighing, Gareth searched the eerie canvas and spotted the small red lines someone had drawn on the priceless painting. A pencil thin smile had been placed on the Devil's face who now lay above the Archangel Michael. Gareth shook his head. "That's sick. You'd think the guy would've had more on his mind than vandalism… considering."

Leah's palm brushed the Devil's side. "This doesn't make any sense."

Gareth tugged on her sleeve, as he heard the sound of a distant motorcade coming closer. Running to the window, he watched the line of black and silver military vehicles enter the long, winding driveway at the bottom of the hill. "We're officially out of time."

Leah took one last look at the troubling scene and ran back to the wall. Pressing her fist against the stone, the door leading back into the tower slid open. They raced up the narrow steps and burst into Himmler's crypt. Into the old Ahnenerbe they ran, past the tall bookcases holding priceless history. Hitting the button to open the tiny door, Leah raced into Daniel's private room.

"Damn it!" she screamed.

Gareth was right behind her. "What now?"

The case stood open and Athena's spear shone under the light. The gold was polished from arrowhead to hilt, but the shield was gone. Leah stepped forward to read the small white note that was impaled on the tip of the warrior's weapon.

"What does it say?"

Her brain was ready to burst with frustration. "See you soon."

"Damn right the little shit will see me soon! Try to gas my wife and get away with it. My face will be the last thing that bastard sees.

Count on it! I'll send him to Valhalla in a Ziploc bag!"

Leah took the spear from its mount, and turned to Gareth. "The note's not from Bauer."

The face she loved turned white as paste as he stared over Leah's shoulder. Turning on her heel, she swung around fast, searching for the monster that must've appeared behind her. But all that met Leah's gaze was the bright red light blinking on the wall where the spear had hung. "Oh, crap."

Gareth took one large step forward, grabbed her hand, and ran from the room.

The blood was pumping in Leah's ears as they flew past the journals and diaries, over the marble floor, and down the narrow steps into the dark tower. She could hear what sounded like a cannonball echo in her ears, as Gareth pulled her past the painting and down the hall. The duo took the wide steps of the staircase three at a time. Throwing open the huge oak door, they raced toward the small guardhouse with the orange dome.

Leah felt the ground shudder and quake. She threw a look over her shoulder, as the huge North Tower cracked in two and began to crumple to the ground. The humongous chunks of rock were flying at her, like a catapult that had been specifically aimed to send her and Gareth straight to a fiery hell. Her legs felt like jelly, and the screams came barreling out of her mouth like machine gun fire.

Gareth stopped and wrapped a hand around her waist, throwing her through the small door of the guard house. Once inside, he raced forward, towing her behind him as they flew into the small, dark space and entered the tunnels.

Panting, Leah tried to catch her breath, as she listened to the mighty castle collapse up above. It sounded like huge, heavy raindrops were pummeling the ground above them; a gigantic avalanche of hailstones sent by the gods to finally destroy the castle of death once and for all.

Gareth pushed her against the wall. "Are you okay? Are you hurt?"

Shaking her head, she clutched the spear in her hands.

Gareth brushed her cheek, as his eyes moved up and down her body, taking in the spots of blood that were growing bigger with each move she made. The pain she saw in his eyes made her heart sick, as he carefully touched the dark purple bruises on her face. "I'm going to kill that son of a bitch."

"*We.* … *We're* going to."

CHAPTER 39

Gareth slowed their frantic pace, and supported Leah as they walked back through the underground labyrinth. Leah could hear the soft cries coming from up ahead, and as they moved closer, she caught sight of her mother weeping in the corner.

Leah wanted to help her, but her legs wouldn't move. Gareth knelt before the distraught woman. "You're all right now, Mrs. um…"

"Neith," Leah offered.

He nodded. "It's all over now, Neith. We're leaving."

Anippe stood stoic and scared, staring at the horrible remains of a Nazi-decorated sacrifice. She whispered, "Is that a…is that somebody's…head?"

"Don't look at it," Gareth said.

Anippe turned and stared at him. "Why do this? Does it glow? Come to life? Lead you to another planet?"

Her slightly sarcastic voice made Leah laugh. "Hey…look at that! Maybe we really are related, after all."

Anippe shrugged. "I can't believe I ever thought that little slime was handsome!"

Gareth pulled Neith to her feet. "Let's get you away from here."

"I'll never be away from here," she whispered. "I sat down here…" she pointed to the plate of rotten food sitting beside the rusted manacle hanging from the wall. "Right here…every single day…for years."

Leah felt the bile rise in her throat, as she noticed the bright red line of hardened blood circling Neith's wrist. It was clearly visible through the torn flesh that'd been rubbed raw from years of imprisonment. "Jesus."

"They left me here. Sometimes they'd come down and give me food. But, mostly I only saw other people when the parades came."

"Parades?" Anippe whispered.

She nodded. Pressing her palms into her eyes, the woman looked as if she was trying to rip the horrible memories from her brain through the sockets. Her voice was strained and angry. "They'd be all dressed up. Bauer's father would lead…then, lately, Daniel. They'd come down here, sit around the table, and chant. They always had some poor man or woman with them. They'd scream…until one of them slit their throat. They'd take an axe and put the head…"

Gareth pulled her into his arms. He stared over the thin woman's head into Leah's disgusted eyes. "I guess it *was* recent. You were right."

"Sorry," Leah choked.

"I'm used to it," Gareth smiled warmly at her.

"No," Leah began again. Taking a step forward, she touched Neith on the back. "I mean, I'm sorry you went through all this. If I'd…we'd, known, we would've come sooner. I swear we would've come no matter what the past was." She looked over at Anippe. "We all would have. Even Dad."

Neith raised her head from Gareth's chest. "I know that."

Leah took a step back, afraid that a hug might just send her straight into permanent insanity.

"He still loves you very much," Anippe added.

Leah pressed down the lump of bitterness that seemed to have taken up residence in the base of her throat. "That's true. He left my mother to come find you when Bauer let it slip that you might still be alive."

Instead of the happy face Leah thought she'd see, Neith stared at her with an apology shining in her eyes. "Then I'm sorry, too, Leah. Sorry you had to go through that. I'm also sorry for your…

mother." She nodded, acknowledging the woman who'd raised Leah in her stead.

Giving a small smile, Leah limped as quickly as she could around the corner. She reached down into the large pile of war souvenirs and pulled out the small painting that'd come alive inside her dream. She stared at the face of the man encased in rock. The sun shone down through the small window, illuminating the shadow of a man creeping into the tomb. She broke the frame against the stone wall and took the small work of art. Folding it, she put it deep inside her pocket, on top of the journal that she'd confiscated from Ahnenerbe. She pulled out the old, weathered book.

"What's that?" Gareth said, rubbing his hand softly over her bruised and battered back.

Leah shrugged and dropped it back into her pocket. "Just the journal you handed me back in that room. I forgot it was in there."

She froze when she heard the distant voices of men in the corridor.

Gareth took Neith's hand, and Leah reached for Anippe. Forgetting the pain, they raced past the millions of eyes gleaming from the Death's Head rings, until the cold wind hit their lungs. ... And they were safe.

* * *

When the last person had climbed out of the entrance, a winded Gareth sat down beside the Externsteine formation. He breathed heavily, staring across the top of the valley of trees to witness the smoking rubble of Wewelsburg Castle. "And he said *Americans* ruin everything. So far the guy's racked up the Zeppelintribüne, and now this. Doesn't seem to give a shit what *he* destroys."

Leah sat down beside him, and thrust her burned hand into a pile of cold, wet snow.

Neith leaned against her other daughter, trying to adjust her eyes to the light of the real world that she hadn't seen in decades. "Why did you say that Daniel didn't have the real emerald?"

Gareth stared at Leah. "What?"

Shaking her head, she pointed at Anippe. "You tell them. Every time I breathe in, it hurts."

Gareth placed his hand on Leah's stomach and sighed. "I am so sorry."

"Trust me." Leah's hand came up to stroke the face that she now knew she could never live without. "You're here. I am just fine."

Their gazes turned to her blue-eyed sister who seemed happy to be the center of attention. "When you were in Athens and ran into Khait, Leah knew something was wrong."

"You knew she was working for Bauer even then?" asked Gareth.

"Didn't have a clue." Leah shook her head. "But I don't believe in coincidences, remember? And after meeting you…" Leah snickered. "I never will again."

Gareth laughed.

Anippe put her arm around her mother. "Leah called me and told me that Kathryn was coming to Qumran with Mary before heading to Crete. Mary was going to be bringing two white lambs with her. One had the emerald—the real emerald—inside it." She stared at her mother. "You see, Leah knew the emerald protected people who went into the mines. She'd worn it around her neck when we went through there for the first time, and the scorpions and wolf couldn't touch her. It made some type of strange shield, or something."

Neith's face was a mask of confusion.

Leah held up her hand to stop Anippe. "Actually, what about that? You went into the mines and took that thing *out* of there. How did you manage to avoid getting stung and mangled by those critters?"

Neith shook her head. "There were no scorpions or…wolves, was it?"

Anippe nodded.

"There was nothing like that in there when I went in. When I took the stone, the evil must've grown up around the spot where it'd last been. I've heard that. Power that's so dark lingers behind when the actual vessel is removed. Darkness breeds darkness."

Leah swallowed, remembering how the emerald had turned to ice once the seed of the Son had been removed. The emerald had grown to an enormous size considering how small it'd started out.

"That's not good," she whispered. "I wore that thing around my neck for two years…at least."

Neith smiled. "The bad can't touch you, child."

Leah rubbed her bruised cheek and stared down at her burnt hand. "You really want to stick with that statement?"

"When it comes to the Devil, Leah, like all unholy demons, he has to be let in. If you don't allow him to enter, then his power… his evil…can't touch you."

Leah stared at Gareth, as they remembered the Gates of Heaven located deep inside Tor Hill. That peaceful location remained safe because of the choice Gareth had made.

He sighed. "Thank God I didn't let him in either."

CHAPTER 40

They should've gotten out of the freezing wind, but Leah, like the others around her, was enjoying the cold, as if it somehow reminded her that they were still alive.

Neith stretched her back, as she paced back and forth in front of the exhausted bodies. She stared down at Anippe, who'd taken a place beside Leah. "So you took the emerald out of the stuffed lamb and went into the mines?"

Anippe shook her head. "Actually, no. Dad wouldn't let me."

Neith's eyes closed with emotion. "I thought he left you?"

"That was after we were done. Leah told him over the phone that she and Gareth believed Herod's crown had nothing to do with the emerald, but he thought she was wrong."

"Everybody's first mistake," Leah mumbled.

Gareth wrapped his arm gently around her. "True. I'm the luckiest guy in the world. I'm the only man on earth who gets to sleep with a genius."

"Except for that boyfriend I have on the side," she laughed.

Picking the spot with no bruise whatsoever, Gareth kissed her hard on the lips. "I'll take him out."

Rolling her eyes, Anippe continued, "Dad put the emerald in Herod's broken crown, but the metal didn't change. It stayed broken. That's when he knew Leah was right. So he decided to go into the mine and steal another emerald. There are millions in there. It took some time, but Dad was able to find one the same size and the same green, marble coloring. Then we put that one in the lamb and sent it back to Leah in Paderborn."

Leah nodded. "I knew they'd done it because the lamb wasn't cold. The real emerald can turn anything close to it into a ball of ice."

"See?" Neith nodded. "It was shutting you out of its power because you wouldn't let it inside."

"Daniel didn't even notice." Leah wondered out loud, "Which is strange…because he tried to rip it from my neck back in Jericho. The emerald is what mangled his hand in the first place. Maybe the first time around it killed all the nerve endings so he just doesn't feel anything anymore. Or he *is* just a ridiculous jackass. I don't think the whole Divine knowledge did squat for him."

Leah was taken aback by the giggle that burst from Neith's lips. "You're a librarian, yet your grammar is just…extraordinary."

Gareth grinned, and pulled Leah closer. "She's great, isn't she? She can repeat word for word the creative manifestations from almost every literary genius who ever walked the earth, and still cuss like a drunken sailor on shore leave. I'll tell you, Neith, she's a keeper."

Leah couldn't help the laughter that bubbled up inside at his words. She punched him playfully in the shoulder. "It's your turn, Houdini."

He raised an amused eyebrow.

"You want to tell us how a person as imposing—"

"Don't forget devilishly handsome," Gareth added.

She rolled her eyes and continued, "As you are, disappeared from a locked dungeon with no windows, protected by guards?"

Gareth unhooked the green knapsack from around his neck. "Elementary, my dear Watson. You weren't the only one who was hatching a plan underneath the brilliant Athens sun." He reached into the green bag and pulled out the golden headpiece.

Leah's heart beat hard inside her chest, as her fingers flexed around the matching spear, "Athena's helmet."

He grinned. "When Emmanuel and I took off after lunch, we went back to the Acropolis. I went inside the Erechtheion and took it. I couldn't believe it was still there. I thought, after what we saw, that it would be gone. But I had to take a chance. And, like before, the wood kind of split open and I grabbed the helmet."

Leah shook her head in wonder. "Man, we have serious dues to pay to the Warrior Goddess, you know that? We've, like…stripped her of all her worldly goods."

"I'm not sure I understand," Neith said. "What does her helmet have to do with getting out of the dungeon?"

Gareth smiled at her. "The legend is that when Athena wore the helmet it gave her the gift of invisibility. In times of great need, the helmet would allow her the ability to sneak up on an adversary and take him out."

Anippe stared at the headgear with awe. "It really works? Put it on."

Gareth placed it on his head.

Anippe frowned at the still visible green eyes.

"It only seems to work in *actual* times of need. Like in the dungeon. I wasn't sure it would work, but I tend to have a lot of faith." He winked. "And, sure enough, when the soldiers opened the door to shoot, I put it on and waltzed right out of the cell. They didn't see any part of me."

Leah snorted.

Gareth put the helmet back in the knapsack, and stared at her. "We'll get her shield back, too."

"I know." Leah nodded.

"How? We don't even know where Daniel went." Anippe offered in a frustrated voice.

"I do," Leah replied. "And he's *so* not going to be happy when he finds out the emerald's a fake."

"Not to mention, he can't come back here and beat the truth out of you." Gareth pointed at the smoke in the distance. "As far as he's concerned, you three are all piles of dust."

Leah smiled. "I can't wait to see his face when he realizes he's been had."

"Where to now?" Anippe joined in with the happy pair.

Gareth looked over at her. "I want you and your mother to go back home."

Anippe began to protest, "Now, just wait a minute—"

Leah held up her hand. "You need to watch over that stone. It's the most important card we have to play, and it's only a matter of time before he realizes that the real emerald had to have been hidden by me in a place where he wouldn't find it. He'll comb through everything that he and all his goons—Knight, Dorsey, all of them—had their hands on. And when he gets to William Knight," Leah said. "He'll think of you, Anippe. He'll go over everything and everywhere you've ever been to hunt for that stone. It's your job to see he doesn't get it."

Anippe let out a huge sigh. "Fine."

"The emerald's in Egypt now?" Neith asked.

"In the Coptic Museum," Anippe answered. "Dad and Aaron are there watching over it."

Neith wrung her hands in front of her. "Oh."

Leah's voice came out soft and calm, "It's about time you two saw each other again, don't you think?"

"And continue to let my daughter risk her own neck while I sit and do nothing?"

Gareth stood and helped Leah stand. Walking toward Neith, he hugged her. "Don't worry about her neck. I'll make sure nothing happens to it."

Anippe turned to Leah. "Where are you two going to look for him?"

Gareth joined Anippe. "Yeah. Where *are* us two going to look for him?"

"Daniel said he wanted to go celebrate his victory…like the elders. I told you about it once. Hitler had a lot of property. One was called the Kehlsteinhaus, also known as the Eagle's Nest. It's a chalet built by the Nazis and given to Adolf for his fiftieth birthday. He hardly ever went there; probably because he didn't have that much to celebrate. But I remember from the videotape I watched, that Mussolini presented him with a fireplace that he had installed in the main reception room where Hitler could entertain dignitaries. They could all sit around with their feet up talking about the millions that they killed. It was supposed to be used as a throne for the most powerful men around. There's no *way* Daniel could ignore that."

"I've heard about that place," Gareth said. "Dwight D.

Eisenhower, Commander of the Allied forces in Europe, said that the U.S. was the first to take Eagle's Nest even though there are plenty of other groups that said they'd been there first."

Leah laughed. "Yup. I watched some newsreel footage back home of the U.S. soldiers sitting on Hitler's patio and drinking his wine; which is yet another reason why Daniel wouldn't ignore the place. As far as he's concerned right now he's the one man who took it back from us rude, thoughtless Americans." She turned to Gareth and rubbed his shoulder. "Ready to see the German Alps, sweetie?"

"That depends…do I have to yodel?"

Leah smiled and kissed his beautiful mouth. She could feel the strength of the weapon quivering in her grip. It was time to end this. It was time to send Daniel Bauer to his precious Valhalla on the sharp point of Athena's golden spear.

CHAPTER 41

There should be another word for winter, Leah thought; *mind-numbing, blistering, Hell on Earth…something*. 'Winter' just wasn't a strong enough word to describe the harsh blowing winds that rattled her teeth in her jaw. Her lips felt like they'd been blast-sealed with ice. Her eyelashes were coated with freezing rain, making them stick to her cheeks like heavy curtains that'd been hung with crazy glue over her eyes.

She envied Anippe and Neith, flitting back to the warmth of Egypt, playing in the bright sun that was used to worship the gods of their land.

"You okay?" he screamed

She heard Gareth's question over and over again, as if his words got caught in an icy tornado that kept circling her head. He was still worried about what the doctor had said after he'd demanded she go to get checked before heading off on yet another leg of a nightmare that never seemed to end.

Using a well-concocted story of a skiing accident, the medical man had no doubts whatsoever. And, thankfully, only one rib had been fractured, with the rest being just a mass of swelling and bruises that would heal over time. Gareth wanted nothing more than for her to rest, leave Bauer to screw things up on his own. Considering he didn't have the real emerald anyway, Gareth argued that they had plenty of time to destroy him, *after* Leah had healed. Seeing as that they were now heading through a hideous snowstorm, it was clear who had won the argument.

"I asked if you were okay." Gareth shouted again, barely covering his frustration with the woman he loved.

"Why is it that bad guys never go anywhere warm? Seriously, is it too much to ask for just one psycho to live in Palm Springs or, better yet, the Caribbean? Or is that just for the Mob?"

She thought she heard Gareth laugh, but it could've just been his teeth cracking under the deep freeze. "Maybe next time we'll go after an old pirate legacy, or something," he shouted over the tremendous winds pummeling the vehicle.

"Next time? No way. Unless the Devil is found posing in Macy's window, I'm not going anywhere," she yelled back.

"You've saved both your parents, Leah. There can't be any greater feeling in the world than that," he reminded her.

"Yeah, well…that's two. Anyone else can just fend for themselves."

Gareth gunned the motor of the high-tech snowmobile he'd purchased when they'd arrived in Berchtesgaden. Considering the astronomical price tag, Leah thought the ridiculous machine should've been encased in a heated bubble.

The guide had warned them not to go. He'd said that the mountain pass had been closed because of the weather. Not to mention, the tourist attraction had been shut for an indeterminable time period. Some Board of Directors said they needed to update Hitler's Nest because of the precarious shape it was in. A group had arrived and closed the mountain down, allowing no sightseer access to the Kehlsteinhaus.

But Gareth, as always, would simply not obey rules that he hadn't set up himself—especially when Leah had told him she wasn't about to wait to bring Bauer down. Leah still wasn't quite sure what allowed Gareth to gain access to anywhere he wanted. With women, especially beloved flight attendants, she knew exactly what asset let him do whatever he wanted. But with men she was beginning to see that those gold cards were the most efficient way to open any closed door.

So, with no real great concern for their welfare, the German guide ran the illustrious card, beamed with glee at the outstanding commission he'd just received, and most likely had run home to celebrate the once-in-a-lifetime sale. At least he was warm, Leah grumbled, as she gripped the spear across her lap. With the weapon in hand, she wanted nothing more than to go to the salesman's warm, cozy home and run him through.

Up the treacherous mountain they went. The guide had said how absolutely spectacular the 6.5 kilometer drive was during the beauty of the summer season. The lovely road had been built using the strong backs of slave labor, most likely, and had cost the Nazi regime over thirty million Reichsmark to build. They should've gotten a gold card, thought Leah. *Just think of the frequent flyer miles old Adolf could've banked.*

Even the expensive machine began to whine when it passed the old information center built at the foot of the hill to remind tourists of the unbelievable cruelty that was dispersed at the hands of the Third Reich. Gareth shut the motor off as they came to a stop in front of a tunnel. The old entrance looked as if it had once been used by trains to pass through the mountain on their way to someplace warm.

Gareth bent down on one knee. He barely saw the other tracks that'd recently led up the horrific mountain. The snow had made them almost invisible, covering up the arrival of the twisted group of men. …Almost.

Leah could no longer feel her fingers through her leather gloves and had to look down to make sure the spear was still safely in her grip. "Now what?"

"Now…we go up," Gareth said.

Leah stared at where he was pointing. The chalet roof was completely covered by the heavy snowfall, as it hung precariously over the ledge. She groaned, "Tell me we're not going to climb a rock face covered in ice. I mean, I want to get this guy, but not *that* bad." She looked over at the love of her life. "Maybe you were right. Maybe we should go back to Berchtesgaden and get a room in one of those nice B&B's and wait for the snow to melt. He's *gotta* come off the mountain eventually."

"Okay," Gareth put his hands on his hips. "Please tell me you're serious."

Leah offered the smallest shake of her head in apology.

He sighed. "You are such a pain." His lips were purple, but his bright green eyes lit the way into the dark tunnel. "Let's go, love. Because after this, no matter what you say, I am taking you to some warm, exotic place with white sandy beaches and a massive bed. I'll drug you and throw you on a plane if I have to."

Leah smiled wide. "No need. I am completely on board!"

* * *

As they stepped into the tunnel, Leah was surprised to see a set of large metal doors. "What's this?"

Reaching out, Gareth placed his hands on the rocks surrounding the opening. "An elevator, I guess. The builders must've blasted through the mountain."

"Of course. We wouldn't want the Führer to have to walk."

Locating the button, Gareth and Leah held their breath. But as the doors slid open without a creak, squeal, or whine to announce their presence, they exhaled.

"Guess someone's oiled it since Hitler fell from the throne," Leah remarked. She covered her eyes with her hands as the bright light spilled into the dark tunnel. "What is *that*?"

"Polished brass," Gareth muttered. "Looks like whoever oiled it also kept it shiny."

He stepped in; Leah followed. "Won't someone notice that we're here when the box lifts?"

Gareth nodded. Reaching up, he pushed on the access panel above. "But we're not going to lift, we're going to climb."

Leah rolled her eyes. "Oh, good. I haven't had nearly enough exercise today."

"You wanted to come," he reminded her. He sighed, trying to bury the frustrated boyfriend inside. "It'll be an adventure."

"*It'll be an adventure*," she repeated sarcastically. "Sometimes I really miss my boring life."

Gareth stared down at her and Leah suddenly caught sight of guilt and hurt within his gaze. She spoke, "I would never change a single thing about these past years. You are the best thing that's ever happened to me, and I learned in that dungeon that I can't be without you. And I don't want to be. I love you, Gareth."

The vow was true. The kiss was quick, loving, honest, and real.

* * *

As they stood on top of the glimmering elevator, Leah stared up into the dark, foreboding shaft. The cave was damp and cold, a perfect home for the bats that needed warmth for the winter. Leah peered into the darkness to look for any eyes staring back. Gareth reached for the spear and put it under his arms, as he began to climb up the cable. Leah watched him from below, her mind analyzing the odds of whether or not they would actually live through this particular event.

"It's not far," Gareth called down. "There's a side access through the mountain, probably built as an escape route if the Allies happened to show up. Which, of course," he continued, with a chuckle, "we did."

"Any dead Nazi's in there?" Leah called back.

"Nope, just rat droppings and a bad smell."

Leah shrugged. "Sounds like Hitler's kind of place. I can't believe he didn't visit more often."

Struggling to follow the enchanting voice which represented the only peace she'd ever known, Leah crept up the cable and reached out for Gareth's hand. She lodged herself into the crawlspace and continued to follow behind him. It was quiet, too quiet. The scratching noises were driving her crazy, as she waited for the rats or other vermin to attack her from behind.

Then, suddenly…silence became a memory. The strains of that horrible Wagnerian music filled the small tunnel and made her head pound. It was as if the tunes had been created for the simple pleasure of torturing people into madness. "Must go faster."

Gareth groaned from up ahead. "I'm a little big for this place… apparently."

"I told you," Leah said. "The guy was *seriously* short."

What seemed like hours inside the small space finally ended when Gareth reached up and unhooked a rusted latch. A small trap door fell inward and let the dim light of winter spill into the hole. Gareth got on his knees and poked his head carefully through the opening.

She could hear his muffled voice. "Looks like a pantry."

"Good," Leah responded. "I could eat." Her stomach grumbled and her back screamed in protest, letting her know in no uncertain terms that she would soon have to find employment as the understudy for the *Hunchback of Notre Dame*.

She scrambled out of the hole behind Gareth and stood up quickly on the cement floor. She tried to arch her back, but her bruised ribs screamed at her to stop. She doubled over.

Gareth's hand was immediately on her shoulder. "You need to stay here, Leah. You're hurt."

She grabbed Athena's spear from his hand. "Forget it." She thought of her mother's tears—her years of sitting in a tunnel where her only entertainment was watching screaming people get their heads chopped off. "I want this guy."

"Get in line."

* * *

As they continued their quick scan of the pantry, Gareth pointed at a small desk sitting in the corner surrounded by modern day cans of food and vintage bottles of wine. Leah stared at the carving in the wood; the all-seeing eye looked back at her as if it was mocking the fact that her own symbol had been taken away by one of *them*.

"Hitler's desk," Gareth said. "Wait…the guide gave me a brochure."

Leah snorted, as he dug into his pocket and took out the four-color advertisement. "I bet even the bathroom at Graceland has a brochure."

Gareth smiled. "Yup. Socialism, out. Capitalism, in. Here it is. Hitler's small study is now a store room for the cafeteria."

He peeked through the circular windows of the double doors to search the next room for any bad guys who could be waiting.

Leah stepped forward. "Let me guess? The cafeteria?"

"Those brochure fellas' really know their stuff, don't they?"

Gareth grinned.

"Too bad they didn't leave behind a brochure to a lost city of gold. *That* would be cool."

Stepping closer to the wall, Leah read the graffiti that'd been left by the armies who'd celebrated their victory in this place. She smiled at the soldiers' words. She was so grateful to the men who put their lives in danger so that the short, little freak and his ridiculous crew could be wiped from the face of the earth. Of course, things hadn't changed much. She found herself praying every night for the men and women who were still sacrificing everything they had in order to discover a way to peace.

She sighed as she touched the writing on the wall. With all she and Gareth had been through, Leah knew that peace was one thing that could never be. Everyone would always fight over who was right instead of accepting the fact that they were all headed to the same place. Call it Valhalla, the Great Beyond, Heaven…whatever. It was all the same place; one that offered a chance at forgiveness to people like Daniel Bauer, which was still one thing Leah couldn't understand.

Gareth pushed open the double doors and stepped carefully into the cafeteria. Leah glanced down at the pistol in his hand. "I hate that thing."

He shrugged. "Even with ancient weapons and magic, Leah, sometimes modern technology is the way to go. Speaking of that," he said, turning to face her. He reached into his backpack and took out Athena's helmet. "Wear this."

She laughed. "I don't want to be invisible."

A fire lit in Gareth's emerald eyes. "For the very first time, I don't care what you want."

"Excuse me?"

"Leah," he sighed, placing his forehead against hers and closing his eyes. "You're bruised, battered…your insides are probably mush and may be bleeding at this very moment. You've been thrown in dungeons, gassed… Really. For me. Please just put the damn thing on." His gaze grew soft. "I love you."

She nodded, unwilling to make the man she loved more afraid than he already was. She raised the helmet to her head and watched

Gareth's face harden when she continued to exist before him.

Reaching up, Leah touched his smooth, warm face. "See? Even Athena doesn't think I'm in mortal peril."

"Athena's dead."

Leah's brow furrowed on her forehead. "We're supposed to have faith...right?"

Gareth rolled his eyes. "God...I've created a monster." He put the helmet back in his worn knapsack, and gripped the pistol tighter in his hand. "Can I at least go first?"

"Of course." She smiled. "I may not believe in coincidences, but I definitely believe in age before beauty."

"Funny."

She felt the warmth of their familiar banter float away, smothered by the thundering winds outside and their own thundering hearts. With a deep breath, Tallent and Lowery walked into the nightmare house that'd once been owned by a true devil.

CHAPTER 42

Leaving behind the empty cafeteria that catered to tourists, they stepped into what could only be described as a dream. The hallway was carpeted in a stunning dark red wine color that screamed royalty. The walls were lined with pictures of summer meadows; churches that sent their tall spires high into the majestic blue skies; and, huge, fluffy dogs whose faces were loving and carefree as they offered a smile to their master standing behind the lens.

The wretched scent from the elevator shaft was gone. Inside, there was incense that spoke of heady dreams and quiet interludes shared between lovers. Her head began to swim. From the pain or the pungent oils, at this point she really didn't know. Leah's stomach screamed at her to go back to the cafeteria and raid the pantry. She truly needed to replace the energy she'd lost so many days ago. Leah yelled inside her brain, ordering her ribs to stop aching and her feet to keep moving.

There were doors scattered along the great hall. In one, was a luxurious bathroom with a built-in spa. It had obviously been updated for its new owner to allow him to indulge in the marvels of the twenty-first century.

In the next room, a large desk sat in the center of a royal blue carpet. Statues of gods covered the polished oak tables, and oil paintings of far-away places decorated the dark blue walls.

Gareth stopped at each door and surveyed the rooms, but the

notes of Wagner were not coming from any space they'd walked by. They continued down the hallway. Gareth peeked into yet another room, and his gun fell to his side. He looked behind him and took a step back toward Leah.

Her heart skipped a beat, as she craned her neck to see what atrocity could've made him turn so pasty in an instant. She shot him a nervous grin. "Another severed head?"

As she leaned in, Gareth reached up and covered her mouth quickly. As Leah's eyes focused, she could not hold in the scream.

She breathed the scent of Gareth's skin into her nostrils, trying to avert her eyes from the hideous scene. There, before her, in a darkened room, sat two well-known figures—one at each end of the long table. The china settings were in place and the golden silverware gleamed, waiting for the dinner guests to begin. The two men sat and stared at each other across the mammoth table. One was Williams, the man with the bushy eyebrows. Once animated characters on the man's forehead, the clumps of hair were now shedding like dead animals; flat and frozen against ruddy skin.

Across from Williams sat the long, lean body of the man they'd called Wolf. His eyes were glazed over. His hand was suspended in midair, holding a golden fork dripping with blood. Leah stared at their plates and watched their hearts give one last beat on top of the elegant dishes.

She swallowed hard, staring at their clothes. Not one drop of blood stained their shirts. Unlike The Ripper, there was no blood left in their bodies where the hearts had been. They just looked... surprised.

"How—" Leah began.

Gareth shrugged, staring at the impossible image. "Are you sure the emerald Daniel got was a fake?"

Leah nodded. "Positive."

"Huh." Gareth's face turned back into a mask of determination. "Well...that's two we don't have to worry about."

Leah nodded; her eyes hurt from how wide she was keeping them open. "Guess they made it to Valhalla."

Gareth offered a crooked smile. "Godspeed," he said, and took off down the hall.

Leah followed, burying the atrocious sight deep inside the card catalogue of her brain. Looking over Gareth's shoulder, she stared at the plate-glass window up ahead that framed an absolutely amazing view. It was as if the chalet were flying over the snow-covered Alps, far away from the pain and sadness of normal life. She could see why this had been a gift—a beautiful one—but couldn't understand why Hitler didn't spend every waking moment of his life staring out at the view from atop his very own Mount Olympus. "My God, look at that!"

Her body shuddered, as the sound of Gareth's bullet entering the chamber brought her back to reality. There he was. Daniel Bauer was standing in the grand living room…all alone. But instead of savoring the sight that he now owned, he was staring into the roaring fireplace.

Raising his head slightly, he turned toward the sound of the pistol. Instead of surprise, fear, or anger, Daniel Bauer offered them only a huge smile. There was no bitterness gleaming in his brilliant brown eyes, Leah noted. There was only a look of sheer resignation—complete defeat—that came from the depths of his soul.

He stared at Leah, who stood with the spear in her hand. "I knew you'd do it." Grinning, he gave Gareth a thumbs-up. "I don't know how. I don't know why. I just knew that you'd save each other again. It's a shame really, considering the amount of talent or…luck that you two have, that you couldn't find it in your hearts to join me."

Leah gasped at the broken crown that dangled from his fingertips. The silver oak leaves had melted. The metal was twisted, like it'd been tossed into the blistering heat of the roaring fireplace sitting in front of him.

"It's not the real one," Daniel said, staring at Leah. "Nothing was real. Was it?"

She remained silent.

"I'm pretty sure I know how you switched the emerald. You had plenty of time for that. But I can't understand how you knew a fake crown was buried in a spot where Hitler stood back in the thirties. I can't figure out how you would be able to bury a bogus crown, and then lead me there without me knowing about it. I had you watched *all* the time."

Leah looked at Gareth's face. Surprise was beaming from his eyes. Turning back to the broken man, she spoke, "Daniel...I actually thought it was the real crown. I didn't bury anything."

"Sure," he chuckled. "Then, who did?"

She shrugged. "People have been hiding that thing forever, probably."

"Or, maybe not," Gareth added.

Daniel looked up at him. "What?"

"The emerald had to be hidden because that's the thing that carries the power of the Divine. It came down from Heaven when the Devil was cast out. The crown was just a piece of metal. They might have let Lucifer keep it—like a parting gift, or something. Without the jewel, it was nothing more than a shiny baseball cap."

Daniel nodded. His golden-brown eyes dulled to a lifeless beige hue. "Maybe I just wasn't the one meant to have it."

"Apparently not," Gareth agreed. He walked slowly around the glass coffee table, searching for a better aim. "We saw Huey and Dewey down the hall. Care to explain?"

Daniel turned back to the fireplace. "Did you know that this is made out of real red Italian marble? It was presented to Hitler by Mussolini." He turned to Leah, and laughed. "Actually, *you* probably did know that."

She gave a slight nod of her head, watching the man step away from the heat and sink into the couch.

Gareth continued, "Are you going to give me an answer about your friends?"

He waved his hand in the air. "They don't matter—"

"Anyway," Leah finished.

Daniel grinned. "Absolutely beautiful, you are. Red hair...like Mary Magdalene, aye'? Divine color given to the Divine female."

"Yeah, she created the color," Leah snorted. "We redheads get together every Thursday to worship her; her and Miss Clairol, of course."

He stared over her head. "The Divine female. I wish *you* were the female I'd had on my side."

Leah followed his gaze. The scream left her throat so fast, that she was afraid the plate-glass window would break and they'd all be sucked out by the howling winds. She stared at the body suspended from the large beam over their heads. Khait swung back and forth like a pendulum out of control. Around her neck was the emerald. The stone had been imbedded in the slit of her throat; a glittering emerald eye framed by her bright red blood.

Leah looked away.

"Jesus," Gareth muttered. "You killed your own mother because you didn't get what you wanted?"

Leah's eyes focused on the crown still grasped in Daniel Bauer's hands. His head hung low.

"No," Leah whispered. "He didn't touch her. Hansen did."

CHAPTER 43

Gareth looked over at her with a surprised face, but Leah kept her gaze locked on Bauer—a mere mortal who was innocent of the crimes that filled the doomed chalet. "Right?"

Bauer grinned. "You know everything. It must be so difficult to be you."

"It's no picnic lately, I'll tell ya."

"Michael Hansen." Daniel sat up and put his knees on his elbows, tossing the crown onto the glass tabletop. "The descendent of a Jewish magic man…Ha!"

"Supposedly," Leah added. She touched the spear, knowing in her heart that the note attached to the arrowhead had been written by the so-called psychic.

Daniel gave a crooked grin. "He was so excited when we got here. I wanted to place the emerald into the crown and see everything I ever wanted spread out before me. But he just held the stone in his hand and laughed. He took off his glove and pressed the gem between his palms. The look on his face was almost…euphoric. But then—"

"Nothing happened," Gareth said.

Daniel nodded. "I don't know what he expected it to do, but he threw the stone at my mother. He put his hands around her neck and started screaming at her that it was the wrong one—that it had no power. I went over and picked it up, I put it in the setting of the crown, but he was right. The metal just…broke, and the emerald just fell on the floor."

"So he killed them all," Leah said.

Gareth looked as if he was about to get sick. "How the hell did he cut out their hearts? There were no…wounds."

Daniel shrugged. "I don't know. After he exacted his revenge on my mother, he just walked out the door and down the hall. I heard the screams, but I stayed here. There was nothing left for me to do."

Leah shuddered, wondering what kind of sick power had been passed down to Michael Hansen from his twisted family tree. "But, why did he leave you? Why would he let you, the ultimate leader of this party, stay alive?"

Daniel laughed. "He told me…that's the way it's done. Disappointment, he said, was all he felt for me. And now he knew what the others before him must have felt, too. He said that no matter where he went or how hard he tried, there were two things in life he hadn't been able to find yet."

"And those were?"

"A person evil enough to help him, and—" Daniel stopped and looked up at his accusers. "And an adversary worthy enough to beat him."

Leah felt panic rise in her throat, as she once again found her eyes glued on the broken crown. Fraudulent, a fake, a charlatan's crown worthy enough to rest only on the head of a second-rate fool. She placed her freezing hands inside her jacket and brushed her fingers against the folded up picture. Her brain brought forth the upside down painting that was now buried beneath the rubble of the castle.

A red light seemed to blink in the corner of her eye, like the VCR in her mind was running out of steam and had to be plugged in before the picture faded to black. She shook her head, trying to get rid of the annoying spot.

A sudden bolt of fear struck her in the chest, like the gods had sent a lightning strike directly into her body. "Gareth," she whispered.

He remained still; his pistol aimed at the desolate man.

"Gareth!" Her scream jarred him from his stance.

Turning to look at her, Leah pointed to the small red blinking lights. They framed the plate-glass window like a Christmas decoration.

"Move!" he shouted. Grabbing Leah by the wrist, he pulled her down the hall. Bodies moved through her vision; the two dead men looked like they were really enjoying their very own Last Supper. Running back through the cafeteria and straight through the double doors, they threw their bodies into the open hatch and scrambled back though the crawlspace.

Wagner's orchestra followed them, prodding them, pushing them onward. The music stayed with Leah, interrupted only by the distant sounds of Daniel Bauer's hysterical laughter echoing from the living room.

As the violins grew louder, they jumped from the tiny crawlspace. And as the drums arrived with their deadly beat, Leah and Gareth flew down the cable and landed hard inside the polished brass box.

As the horns blew their desolate calls, like ships that were about to sink in the cold, black ocean, they raced out of the tunnel and pole-vaulted over the expensive, ice-covered toy.

Gareth jumped into a snow pile and threw Leah's body into a huge snow bank that would completely cover her. Righting herself, Leah raised her head and stared up at the precarious roof; it seemed to shimmer like a wall of gold in the waning light. Holding her breath, she watched Daniel Bauer step forward. He offered a wide grin and blew her a kiss from the balcony of the Führer's birthday gift.

Gareth's hand appeared on the back of her head, forcing her deeper into the pile of snow.

And then...

The explosion was deafening. The flames were so hot that the ice began to melt above Leah's immobile body. Rivers of freezing cold liquid found the chinks in her leather armor and raced across her flesh. A wall of glass rained down. Feeling like the sharpened claws of a pack of wolves, tiny shards pierced her skin.

When the world stopped moving and the ground stopped shaking, Leah carefully raised her head to check that the man she loved had made it through the deadly storm. Gareth's green gaze met her own. A line of bright red blood flowed from his forehead where one blade had found its mark when the snowmobile had flown over his head, but he was fine.

The tears wouldn't come—she wouldn't allow it. In fact, Leah was slightly afraid that the salty tears would form a mask that would somehow freeze on her face for all eternity.

Pushing her aching body across the melted snow, Leah buried herself in Gareth's arms.

CHAPTER 44

They ran. Well…limped, was more like it, down the long winding road of the no longer scenic mountain. They avoided the flashing red and blue lights that were trying to fly past, in order to discover what kind of brute force had caused their village down below to be shaken from its foundation.

They wanted more than anything to stumble into the bed and breakfast, but their massive cuts and abrasions gave them away as the bad guys in the scenario playing out on top of Berchtesgaden's beloved mountain.

Gareth broke a Commandment. Leah let him know that, as he smashed the window of the small car and started it up. Roaring out of town at a frantic pace that wouldn't even register on the old speedometer, Gareth finally sighed with relief. Leah pulled the cell phone from his pocket and dialed.

* * *

The plane was so warm. Maybe too warm, considering the pain that Leah now felt in every inch of her body. With the winter weather behind her, the numbness in her limbs had started to fade allowing the blood to flow more freely, and the broken and battered bones now screamed at the horrible treatment they'd received.

Leah let out a squeal, as Gareth administered the iodine and alcohol to her open wounds. She bit her tongue as she, too, got into the act and cleaned and bandaged what seemed like Gareth's entire body—relegating him to an ancient mummy.

They sat back against the leather seats of the luxurious plane that'd been rented with the card of gold. No stewardesses flitted about. Only the invisible captain was anywhere near them, and he had the common decency to stay far away. Apparently he didn't want to ask too many questions about his strange fare that resembled two walking corpses.

Leah lifted the fork to her mouth and attempted to chew, wanting to get something into her stomach before her body completely fell apart. She groaned at the effort.

Gareth continued to gaze worriedly at her. "When we land you'll see another doctor."

She raised an eyebrow.

"We'll see a doctor. We'll tell them we've been in a plane crash, or something." He grinned.

The card catalogue spit out an image from the recent past. "I was thinking more along the lines of seeing a priest."

"Last rites? Jesus, I must *really* look bad."

"No. I just think you should make good."

"Make good?" Gareth sat, completely confused at her statement.

"Back in Himmler's castle you referred to me as your wife."

The emerald eyes took on a look of surprise, as Gareth leaned his elbow on the chair and reached for her hand. "Did I say that?"

"Well, I've been through a lot these past few years so I could've imagined it, I suppose."

He planted the softest, sweetest kiss Leah ever received on her sore lips. "No, Madame Librarian. You, as always, are right on the money."

She smiled.

"Do you think pilots are like ship captains? Maybe we could get married right now."

She laughed. "We'll save the ceremony for later."

He grinned. "Okay. Do you?'

"You bet. You?"

"More than you could possibly imagine." His voice came out

strong and serious.

Leah felt the shudder run through her. The amazing amount of emotion that was beaming from the depths of those eyes made her feel like she could fly without the benefit of the wings outside. "I love you."

Their kiss was deeper this time, solidifying the intimate vows in their own minds, as strongly as if their promise to each other had been followed by the music and good wishes of family and friends.

Gareth leaned back and heard the audible cracking sounds of his wounded body. "Dear God."

Leah laughed. "I think we should postpone the wedding night too, handsome. I wouldn't want you to break anything I might want to use later in life."

He patted her on the hand. "Bless you. You will find a place in Heaven for this."

She stared at his amazing profile. "I already achieved Heaven, Gareth. You're right here."

His eyes suddenly filled with desire. "Forget it. I want the wedding night. There are all kinds of surgeries available now. If I break anything, they can just rebuild it."

Leah pushed him back in the chair. "Nope. I like you the way you are."

He groaned.

Laughing, she picked up the remote.

"We're married two minutes and already I'm so boring you're tossing me aside for the television," he mumbled. "That's just not right."

Smiling wide, Leah hit the button. She was interested to see if the other prayer she'd made would be answered by now. The small wooden doors slid apart and the big television set roared to life. She flipped through the many channels of nonsense until a smart-looking newscaster with intelligent eyes began to speak.

The story she was looking for unfolded when the Coptic Museum came to life on the screen. Leah tried to smile, but the broken, chapped skin that covered her lips was too much to stand.

Anippe was front and center. Her skin was tan and her long black hair gleamed in the sunshine. In fact, it was so unbelievably bright, Leah could almost feel the balmy Egyptian temperature radiate from the screen.

"We feel so honored and very lucky to be the recipient of such an amazing find." Anippe's lovely voice matched her elegant dress. "It takes a very giving person to understand that the past must be looked after."

The reporter babbled on, as Leah watched her father appear on the screen. "It was actually found in Qumran," he said. "It was buried in the old emerald mines of Cleopatra, herself. We here at the Museum feel very blessed to have a pair of such wise and intrepid explorers working for the protection of antiquities across the globe."

Gareth spit the food from his mouth, and turned to Leah. "Intrepid explorers?"

Leah laughed. "Yeah…cool, ain't it? You don't think he means us, do you?"

"Nah. Then he'd say; 'two imbeciles who keep making up shit as they go.' " He laughed. "Why, exactly, did we want to announce to Michael Hansen where the real emerald is? Shouldn't we have wanted to keep that a secret?"

"We couldn't have." She sighed. "Hansen knew who the players were when he walked into that cell…or, maybe even before. It was only a matter of time before he showed up and tried to torture Neith and Anippe in order to get them to talk. This way, we've announced to the world that something as noteworthy as the Hope Diamond is on display in that museum. And, hopefully, the whole world of ancient fanatics, *Indiana Jones* wannabes, and the bevy of tourists who just wait for something new to see, will be all over that place. He's gonna have to jump through an awful lot of hoops to get at it."

Gareth nodded.

"Besides," she continued, "he already knew that the crown was bogus. He basically told me. Which means—"

"He knows what the real crown looks like."

She nodded. "Which means he may just—"

"Know where it is."

"And if he does—"

"We want him to go after that emerald so we have time to find the crown."

"Exactly. Without the setting, the emerald doesn't work, and vice versa. So, what we know for a fact is that Hansen either knows or has some inkling of where the crown is buried. We also know that he knows what it looks like, since he has the ability to spot a fake. As far as he's concerned, he's comfortable on the crown part of the puzzle. The emerald is in our hands and will be watched over by a circle of powerful protectors. While he's wasting his time trying to get that—"

"We'll destroy the crown," Gareth finished.

"Maybe Athena's spear will destroy the crown if the power of the emerald isn't in it. The Archangel's sword may only be necessary if the two things are combined."

"The spear comes alive in your hands. I've seen it," Gareth said, in a hushed voice.

She nodded. "And there has to be a reason for that. Unless they just wanted to give me the opportunity to wade into a pond and learn how to fish."

"The shield?" Gareth's eyes grew dark.

She shrugged. "Can't do anything about that one right now. Hansen must've taken it with him. He probably knew the power of the spear. I'm sure he picked it up and tried to bring it to life, and it didn't happen. But the shield gives him protection from it."

"But why not just take the spear and destroy it? That way, if you did manage to get out of that gas chamber, there wouldn't be a chance in hell that it would end up back in your hands."

She leaned against the seat and watched the reporter babble on about a stone that he would never understand. "I think Bauer was right. This guy is salivating for a worthy adversary. I suppose he wanted to give it a go…see what we were made of. Maybe he's bored. If there's no risk for the reward, what's the point? There's no satisfaction in an easy kill."

"And he probably had no idea that your freedom would also free another powerful protector who he never counted on joining the game."

Leah followed his gaze to the screen and her breath caught in her throat. Neith stood beside David Tallent; her hand was locked in his. Her face was infused with the healthy color of life, and the once gaunt, defeated eyes now shone like polished onyx.

Leah sent the fork crashing to her plate, and she turned to Gareth. "That's it."

"What's it?"

She reached into the pocket of her coat and took out the small painting. Her bandaged hand snagged on the corner of the old journal that was also hidden in her pocket, sending the small book and the small wooden runes scattering across the thick carpet. Ignoring the trinkets, she unfolded the picture and handed it to Gareth. "Look at the crown."

Gareth squinted at the small painting. "So?"

"Remember how the painting outside Himmler's room bugged me?"

He nodded.

"It was because of the crown that'd been painted beside Lucifer. It was black, Gareth. Pitch black. Just like this one." She flicked the picture with her finger. "I thought it might have been burned silver or something, but it's not. The crown that we found in Hitler's podium looked nothing like this."

"The Devil's crown is carved from onyx," Gareth said.

"So we do know what it looks like."

Gareth handed her back the paper and stared at the book on the floor. When he picked it up, some of the old pages fluttered into his lap. "Why did you take this, again?"

She shrugged. "I don't know. I just put it in my pocket and forgot it was in there. Remember? I don't believe in coincidences. I figure if I kept it there must be some reason." Sighing heavily, Leah leaned back in the comfortable seat and closed her eyes. She had never felt so exhausted in her whole life. She prayed with all her heart that Hansen was just as tired, because she really needed a time out—a short break before beginning the hunt for a shiny black crown.

"Jesus!"

Leah opened her eyes and squinted at the screen. Her mind was confused, as she watched the commercial for the latest and greatest diet bar that helped shed pounds in minutes.

Turning to Gareth, her question stuck in her throat. The skin of the man she loved had turned as green as his beautiful eyes. His hands visibly shook, like a man about to kneel under the sharpened blade of a guillotine.

She stared down at the familiar picture that'd been taped inside the research journal. In the photo, the poor man still stared at the camera with a look of sheer defeat. The ruins of the unknown monument were still scattered around him. The large steps of the amphitheater still circled like a racetrack in the background, and the shade tree still drooped over his exhausted figure.

Leah's gaze moved back and forth between the love of her life and the picture of the unknown man. Reaching out, she placed her hand on Gareth's shaking shoulder. "What's the matter? You look like you've seen a ghost!"

The terror-stricken eyes focused on her face. His white lips parted, making him resemble a corpse that was about to issue his very own eulogy.

"*What?* Speak!"

Turning the picture over, Gareth lifted it up for her to see.

Leah squinted at the small black print. "Pergamos, 2009. So?"

He turned the photo back over and pointed at the desolate man. "Leah…that's my father."

EPILOGUE

Gareth flew from his seat, screaming at the pilot to change course immediately.

Leah sat perfectly still. Staring at the face of a man who supposedly died over twenty-years ago made the blood turn to ice in her veins. She breathed in and out slowly. Her mother had warned her that they were in the fight of a lifetime, but the participants of this truly strange battle were changing rapidly.

Anxiety and panic filled the interior of the metal cabin. Leah stared down at the runes that'd been cast from the pocket of her leather coat.

ᛗᛋ᛬

The rune of victory rested between Leah and her now mysterious enemy. Gareth's father…a dead man…was rising from his grave. A mother she didn't really trust was back on the scene, and a man with yellow eyes was out there somewhere who knew far more than she did about what was coming.

Leah swallowed hard. She remembered the words from the one and only book she'd ever read in the Bible, and her heart felt as if it was going to break in two. After all this…after all they'd been through…Leah found herself wondering just how many precious hours she and Gareth had left together before *their* day of judgment arrived.

"13"

TALLENT & LOWERY: BOOK 1

"Snappy dialogue, fast pacing and attention to detail complete the formula for this successful novel!!"
—Romantic Times (4 ½ Stars)

In 1902, in a dark room on the fifth floor of Carnegie Hall, thirteen people came together to continue a tradition that had been set in stone thousands of years before.

In 2012, Leah Tallent is Head of Research at the New York Public Library. Stoic and stable, brilliant and cynical, she has forever enjoyed her existence among the book stacks. But even with her unparalleled intellect, there was no way to know that on the historic steps between America's famous lions, she would become involved with a crazy man on a fanatical quest.

Gareth Lowery has spent his life searching for the ultimate artifact that he is certain exists. His life's pursuit has been to retrieve twelve keys hidden by men whose job it was to protect the single biggest secret ever kept. To find the keys he must enlist the help of an unwilling guide who, unfortunately, knows much more than he bargained for.

From the first page to the last word, this fantastic duo become immersed in a whirlwind treasure hunt with historical and passionate repercussions. From the strange and eerie Winchester House to the blustery darkness of Loch Ness, Gareth and Leah will quickly learn that the theory of duality is correct: For every bad there is a good and, for Heaven, there most assuredly exists...Hell.

"THE SAPPHIRE STORM"

TALLENT & LOWERY: BOOK 2

"A flat-out, slam-dunk, no-questions-asked-terrific-adventure. Try not to turn the pages too fast because the wonderfully complex characters deserve your time! This is truly a magical story that had me in its thrall from the very first page. It's so exciting to discover a new talent like Lignor and have more books to look forward to."
—International bestseller, M.J. Rose

After going up against a man who believed he was the Devil, himself, Leah Tallent and Gareth Lowery are exhausted. Now they are about to embark on the most terrifying journey imaginable . . . a trip to meet Leah's parents.

When Leah arrives where the 'home fires burn,' her sarcasm burns even brighter, while Gareth Lowery—the handsome adventurer—uses his charm to sway the 'odd' Tallent clan. But when a frightening call from Gareth's sister arrives telling him that her love has disappeared, the daring duo is soon running away from one horrific situation directly into another.

A new puzzle from the past has come to life. Following clues left behind, the courageous couple become embedded in a world filled with liars, killers and greed. And when the riddle of a famous 'Bard' is solved, a strange woman appears who has far more in common with Leah than she can possibly imagine.

The heart-stopping suspense of this new quest takes them from Coptic Cairo to the magical world of Petra, in search of a cave deep underground that once housed a true 'Illuminator.' Yet again, they must find the answers and stay one step ahead of true villains who are determined to make sure that—*this* time—*Tallent & Lowery* do not survive.

"THE HERO'S COMPANION"

TALLENT & LOWERY: BOOK 3

"Right from the start, my heart was pounding in my chest from all the intrigue and adventure that awaited me."
—Tammie King, Night Owl Reviews

With their second battle behind them, Leah Tallent and Gareth Lowery find themselves still knee-deep in hell. What should've ended with a celebration becomes a nightmare once more, as a mysterious man demands Leah to return home, or else her beloved father will be found at the bottom of the sea.

Scrambling to figure out what's happened, *Tallent & Lowery* walk in on a family that has literally gone insane: A mother filled with accusations, three sisters who wish them nothing but certain death, and a frightening story of a blood-red eye that leads to a puzzle with immense repercussions. The woman named Anippe who readers questioned in "The Sapphire Storm" is back, with an item in her possession that will have *Tallent & Lowery* heading out on an adventure based on pure emotion and ultimate fear—where victory may just depend on their willingness to sacrifice each other.

They have only seven days to travel to Athens where the original 'Hero's Companion' awaits. From the stage atop the Acropolis where the most brilliant minds once performed to the discovery of a location that was never even proven to exist, 'Great Mysteries' come to life as Leah and Gareth work against time in order to stop a man from attaining the power he so desperately wants.

But as she stands by the side of her own courageous warrior, Leah will soon find out that she's in the crossfire of her own father's secrets; a life of lies that's far more frightening than anything she and Gareth have faced in the past.

The time has come for *Tallent & Lowery* to go head-to-head with the mysterious voice from "13," as a villain is unveiled...and a war begins!

ABOUT THE AUTHOR

As the daughter of a career librarian Amy grew up loving books; 'Patience & Fortitude' at the NYPL are still her heroes. Beginning in the genre of historical romance with, "The Heart of a Legend," Amy moved into the YA world where her first team from *The Angel Chronicles* became a beloved hit. Moving into the action/adventure world with *Tallent & Lowery*, Amy has created a new, incredibly suspenseful, team that has once again exploded with readers everywhere. Born in Connecticut, Amy is now living in the bright sunshine of Roswell, NM, delving into her next adventure.

To learn more about Amy Lignor, check out her website at http://tallentandlowery.blogspot.com.